LARRY DUBERSTEIN

THE MT. MONADNOCK BLUES

THE PERMANENT PRESS
Sag Harbor, NY 11963

Library of Congress Cataloging-in-Publication Data

Duberstein, Larry
  The Mt. Monadnock Blues / by Larry Duberstein
  p. cm.
  ISBN 1-57962-093-0
1. Custody of children—Fiction. 2. Brothers and sisters—Fiction. 3. Gay
men—Fiction. 4. Orphans—Fiction. I. Title: Mount Monadnock blues.
II. Title.

PS 3554.U253 M7 2003
813'.54—dc21

           2002038194

           CIP

Printed in The United States of America

THE PERMANENT PRESS
4170 Noyac Road
Sag Harbor, NY 11963

To Jim Hannah and to the memory of George Hall III.

The harvest is past, the summer is ended, and we are not saved.
—Jeremiah 8:20

There ain't no cure for the summertime blues.
—Eddie Cochran

Other titles by Larry Duberstein

Novels
The Marriage Hearse
Carnovsky's Retreat
Postcards from Pinsk
The Alibi Breakfast
The Handsome Sailor

Short Stories
Nobody's Jaw
Eccentric Circles

I

BLIND DATE

Tim Bannon made a fairly typical human error: he answered the phone. What is it that makes us optimistic when the telephone rings, or the mailman arrives? Why do we persist in believing some glad moment is at hand? For of course it was his mother.

"Mom. But I can't talk right now. Actually, I have a date."

Another mistake—and so soon! If he hoped to get away promptly, Tim ought to have known better than to reference his love life, as Anne Bannon liked to call it. Her last deep worry on earth was that her son, still single at forty, would remain single forever.

"Is this anyone special, Timmy?"

"It's a first date, Mom."

"Isn't it always. I never will understand how someone can have as many first dates as you do."

"Maybe I exaggerate sometimes. But if it turns out to be someone special, I promise you'll be the first to know."

"How is Eleanor? Is she still single?"

"She is. She made it through another week."

Ellie Stern, one of Tim's partners in the travel business, would also (in Anne's view) make him a fine wife. Anne was pro-Semitic, as she liked to tell her Carolina neighbors, not all of whom were likewise inclined.

"I'm really late, though. I'll call you tomorrow—promise—in case it's love at first sight."

Even as he labored to round her off, Tim was buttoning (or attempting to button) his shirt. In the best of times he was incapable of doing two things at once; now he saw the buttons were misaligned, the shirt accordingly lopsided, so that he looked caught in an epileptic shrug. And his hair was ridiculous.

He did not waste time over it. Now that it was thinning and had lost its wave, his hair seemed ridiculous to him no matter how he fussed. He rushed out the back door, latched the iron gate, and dropped into his green '83 Honda. Bumped up the narrow rutted mews to Columbus, then turned onto Mass. Ave., where he got lucky. The light at Symphony went green for him right in stride and Del Shannon came on Oldies 103 singing "Runaway."

7

This was momentum

He swept past the Berklee School, hit two more friendly lights at Tower Records and The Eliot Lounge, and bombed onto the bridge at 45, on this lovely summer night, with a run-run-run-run runaway blaring out the window. Not bad.

To Tim, growing up in 50's Carolina, the very best of life was defined by open cars, and booze, and music flowing from the radio (Del Shannon himself, many times, but to be sure Elvis and Jerry Lee, the Coasters and the Drifters and the Shirelles) and never a cop in your rearview mirror. Berline was too small a town to suffer a smalltown sheriff. Crime there was confined to the unenforceables, the sins of fun, chiefly drink and fornication.

Now on the Cambridge side of the Charles River (on Mem Drive and cresting 50) Tim sensed a car drawing alongside and feared his luck had changed. Here they did have cops. But it was only more good karma, a balding babyboomer who had the same station blaring. They glided in lockstep briefly, lane by lane and doing the run-run-run-run together (and then the falsetto) before waving when Tim hooked off toward Kendall Square.

He took a chance parking behind Dolly's and went in, barely five minutes late. (Which to Tim meant early.) And right away he spotted (back to him, seated at the bar) the long blonde ponytail he knew to look for, since this was not only a first date but a blind date as well. How refined to have a "date," Tim had laughed when he agreed to be fixed up.

Dolly's was one of his places and Robby, the bartender, was already pouring his Maker's Mark as he approached. The barstool spun around. Tim saw dark eyes, a closed narrow mouth, silver hoops in both ears.

"Eric," he said. Which Eric acknowledged with a nod. "I'm Tim. I've heard about you forever."

"I guess you're a slow worker, then."

"Slower every day," Tim confessed, blushing. Aware that a sort of inquisitive desperation had driven him to call Eric. He had heard about him, but what he heard was at best mixed. "You look like you're ready for another."

"Why not?"

Tim caught a roughcut edge to the voice (Southie? Dorchester?) that carried faint suggestions of danger, for which Tim did have a weakness. He was no masochist, had never been beaten even in fun and did not wish to be. It was not violence that appealed, only the suggestion of it, the air of danger.

Eric kept a poker face, which naturally nudged Tim's basic insecurity into play. An insecurity which had automatically doubled, a negative bonus, on his fortieth birthday. His self-image was fairly realistic, though. However others saw him, he saw himself as a pleasant-featured man who might pass for thirty-five easily enough, five-ten and weighing a trim 150, with muscled arms and a narrow torso. Brown eyes his best feature, brown hair his worst—by its absence, increasingly noted.

Tim could not have described his own voice, a soft delivery (with the faintest trace of a drawl) set off by exclamations, sudden arias of delight in the absurd. Tell me this is a *joke*, he said, each and every time the visage of President Ronald Reagan appeared on the television screen. His yawp was the sound of innocence perennially surprised, or of innocence long since yielded up yet still surprised it had to go.

"Another of whatever, for Eric," he told Robby, "and I'll have another, too."

"That's not slow," said Eric.

"Nerves. But I'll stop there. Two is what I tend to have."

"For the nerves."

"Right," said Tim, taking a smooth skim of bourbon off the top. He was almost done with blushing.

Tim was glad to get home—and if that wasn't middle-aged, what the hell was? But the days when he would venture out after midnight, to the Fens to seek love in the weeds, were done. If he found himself awake at midnight now, most likely he was watching the end of a rented video, which back then he dismissed as a "warped little midget movie in a plastic box."

Eric Schuyler? Early Clint Eastwood, basically—or gay Clint, with precious few words and the one facial expression. Eric was a little weird, and yet how many times had Tim and his friends laughingly acknowledged their own weirdness and the weirdness of all sentient creatures, gender notwithstanding. It was what it was. They had struggled with the talking, did much better with dancing (through two more rounds of liquor), and ended up in Eric's car. At forty, no less. In the car.

So the drive home was different in tenor from the glorious

9

voyage out, and yet such contrast was perfectly familiar, was the very essence of gay life—perhaps of all life, if that was any consolation. Mood swings? Well *sure*.

In the shower, Tim stood face up and eyes closed to the stream of hot water. He towelled dry and slipped straight into bed. The red message light was blinking, but weariness beat out curiosity (and the reflex of optimism) like scissors/paper/stone. It was the usual suspects, most likely: Anne, Ellie, Karl Trickett, the Peters. Possibly a telemarketer who had failed to hang up in time to void the bips.

Tim's drifting thoughts were mundane. Best he could hope for was four hours of sleep...which used to be enough...so hard being forty...hard to be losing hair...the Mastronardes' cat screeching in the mews....

He used to wake like chickens, on instinct and at the earliest hint of daylight. Today, though, he might have gone on sleeping through dawn and breakfast, through lunch and dinner. It was not mere fatigue, it was a mild depression that had been gaining a purchase on Tim in recent weeks. Which was no big deal. What justification was there, Tim would point out cynically, for *not* being depressed?

He did wake, however, to a loud pounding that registered at first like a reverie of distant drums, and then the fearful dream of fascists coming for him in the night, smashing glass and kicking down doors. The recurring bad dream of a kristallnacht for the homos.

"Hang on," he called, wrenching himself upright, nerves on edge as he fumbled for his robe. " I hear you."

And there they were, fascists for real, two of them in the doorway in Smokey hats, motorcycle jodhpurs, and glossy black boots. A dream after all, until he saw in the interstices, in the shadowy recesses between those jackbooted jodhpurred legs, his niece and nephew. Two New Hampshire state cops, these were—plus Billy and Cindy? What the fuck was this?

As his brain came unclotted, as the taller cop began to speak (and as he saw Billy's look of blank white confusion, Cindy's red-rimmed eyes), Tim felt a long visceral shiver down the back of his neck. Something terrible had happened.

"Hergies!" he found the presence of mind to say, lowering himself into the forest of jodhpurs to extract them.

10

"My Hergies are here."

The children pushed forward into Tim's arms and he locked them there. Looked up past their feathery heads, waiting for the cops to tell him what terrible thing had happened to his sister.

"I'm Moss," said the tall one. "Lieutenant Jeffrey Moss. Maybe the kids would like to watch some TV."

Like the test patterns? (Did they still have test patterns?) But Tim grasped that Moss was simply clearing the decks. He suffered one brief flareup of paranoia (they were going to accuse him of something, of child molestation) but the back of his neck still told him it was Jilly.

"Do your thing, guys. The maps, the drawers, the closet—TV, if you want. We'll be right here."

Shyly, reluctantly, they went.

"They were both killed, Mr. Bannon," said Moss, stepping into the foyer. "Mr. and Mrs. Hergesheimer. It happened early this morning on Route 202. I'm terribly sorry to have to tell you."

"An accident? This morning?"

"Yes, sir, around 12:40 a.m. at the intersection of Routes 202 and 119 in Rindge. They were on their way home from a party, according to the babysitter."

"Judy Heikala?"

"That's correct, sir, Judy. I gather she is the regular sitter. The children seemed very attached to her."

"But this is—" Tim trailed off. What this was he could scarcely begin to calculate. At the moment, the very idea of a world without his older sister, the one member of his family in whom he had ever confided, was far too radical.

And Monty. He could register the accident only as a sentence, not as a reality. Trying to picture the two of them in a tangle of limbs and injuries, trapped inside the crumpled Subaru, all he could see was their lively faces on Memorial Day, a few short weeks ago.

"I'm just stunned by this. Amazed, to see you here."

"It was an emergency detail, sir. Normally we would involve the Massachusetts forces."

"Oh God, I don't mean that."

Which surely he did not. Would Massachusetts state troopers look or act differently? Tim meant that it had never crossed his mind that Jill might die before him. Or that he (not Anne, not

11

Erica, not Jilly's friends in Jaffrey) would pop up first on anyone's screen when the children needed caring for. He could only shrug by way of conveying (or not conveying) that he was a single gay male with a receding hairline and how did that get him onto anyone's screen at a time of crisis?

"At the house," Moss was saying as his gaze travelled the room with waxing discomfort at the decor (a handful of almost tasteful el flamo details, like the Nureyev poster and the Mae West lamp), "we debriefed the sitter, Ms. Heikala, took down phone numbers and so forth. We did attempt to reach your other sister first—"

"Sure," said Tim, because Moss seemed to need a verbalized forgiveness for attempting him second or third.

"—from being located close by, in state."

"Sure."

"But there was no answer, and no sign of life at their place. We did send a man by there."

"They go on the road at this time of year."

"RV enthusiasts, I gather. Which explains the house looking the way it did. We were struck by it at first."

"They go on the road for a couple of months," said Tim, his amazement undiminished as this bizarrely casual chat proceeded.

"Ms. Heikala related to us how close the children were to you, sir, so we next attempted to reach you here. No answer, but it's the night, so we took a shot. Figured it's worth the mileage if we can avoid putting them into the system."

"Thank you for that, Lieutenant. They hardly need to be in any system at this point. It's great they're here, whatever needs to happen next."

"Well yes, sir, there is a fair amount that does need to happen, as I'm sure you understand. Formal I.D., further notifications, insurance claims, funeral arrangements...."

Moss' voice softened in diminuendo, as if someone was turning the volume down one notch with each awful chore he listed. When Tim had no response to the list, Moss went on. "We found no record of an attorney's name. You don't by any chance know—"

"Not really. I mean, they didn't have a lot of legal issues. I suppose someone must have handled their real estate closing."

"We'll learn what we can, sir. In the meantime—"

Moss offered his hand, then he and his silent counterpart had

12

vanished, leaving Tim alone with two orphans. Two children he dearly loved, yet had not the faintest notion what to do with.

Though this was not strictly true. In a larger sense (school, church, home) he hadn't a clue. Why should he? In a more immediate sense, though, what to do at a given moment, his guess had to be better than most. Tim liked kids; he loved these two kids, and while he believed there was nothing in the world he was particularly "good at," the truth was he had always been a good uncle.

But that was just fluff and fun, this was all too real, and the image of Jill, smiling, suddenly disabled him. He could barely breathe, could not swallow. Tim never could swallow when emotional (indeed, with all his clever defenses, it was the best way he could know he *was* emotional) and for a moment going to Billy and Cindy, walking ten steps to the living room, seemed literally impossible.

As usual, it was Calvin Coolidge who saved him. Coolidge, the Thirtieth President, had not done much, but he was Tim's inspiration on the basis of a single pronouncement, a soft fortune-cookie thunderclap of wisdom that Tim had blown up, framed, and hung on the wall above his desk. YOU CAN'T DO EVERYTHING AT ONCE, BUT YOU CAN DO SOMETHING AT ONCE.

Here was nothing less than the key to unlocking all human action. Faced with a list of fifteen calls (faced, therefore, with paralysis), Tim would think of Silent Cal, reach for the phone, and make one call. Not fifteen. Which always worked; things started getting done after that.

Blinking Jill away, he went to the kitchen, dug out the buckwheat flour, found the whisk. What he could do was make pancakes. "No one's hungry?" he called down the hallway, just as though life was ongoing. "Can we have unhungry Hergies?" And there they were, red-eyed yet clambering onto stools with a look of clear relief. Maybe they felt, on some kid level of credulity, that once the messengers left the message was erased. Or that their Uncle Tim would know the cure for dead parents.

What had they been told? Tim should have asked—or no, Moss should have said. Instead, Moss had behaved like the United Parcel man: sign here and have a nice day.

"Eat first or talk first?" said Tim.

"Eat," said Cindy. First word from her.

13

"Where do they have our parents, Unk?" said Billy.

"I'm not sure. What did they tell you, those men?"

"That something really awful happened. A car crash."

"Anything else?"

"The lady said they were hurt. And they might die."

"Oh boy. Hang on, Cindy, I'll get some kleenex."

"I'm not Cindy," the little girl sniffed.

"You *were* Cindy," Tim smiled gently, prepared to be astonished if this was a joke of some sort.

"I'm Cynthia."

"Well, that's true. I can do that, sweetheart."

"Do you think they'll die, Unk?" said Billy.

There had to be a correct way of doing this, the one approach that experts on child psychology would take. All Tim had was his own conviction that it was generally best to treat kids as intelligent humans from our own galaxy and tell them a version of the truth. "This lady, was she the police too? Or some kind of expert on children?"

"She was a shrink. You can call her. She said her name is Olivia, and she gave us these cards."

"I will call her. But first, maybe we'd better have a three-way. Come."

They jumbled together in front of the stove, shoulders and arms and heads in a great confusion, the "three-way hug" cemented as always by irregular comic tremors. But Tim noticed he again could not swallow. Should he tell Billy, who was past eleven, and not Cindy at eight-and-a-half? Why would Olivia Goldsmith (with her impressive cards, raised blue lettering on deckled cream) leave this delicate task to someone like him? It seemed so unlikely.

It seemed so much more likely that she had told them already.

He thought about introducing the dogs. Their dog had died last October, his own dog had died when he was Cindy's age.... Probably the dogs were a mistake. Bathos, indignity, something. Dogs were dogs, after all.

"Your grandfather, my dad, died when you were little."

"We know that," said Billy.

"He died in the middle of the night and I was thirty-four years old when I got that phone call but I felt just like a little kid. It was the strangest thing to realize you would never see him again. It was like getting hit in the head with a log."

"Did you ever see him again?"

Cindy had begun to cry and Tim drew her closer, squeezing her ribcage, kissing the top of her head.

"I never did, sweetheart. Except in pictures, and memories. I never *forget* him, I mean." The girl's tears were catapulting from her now.

"Are they buried?" said Billy, standing straight and manly even though he had begun to quiver. Then they were all sobbing. Tim wanted to stop, for their sake, but his face just kept doing what *it* wanted. He needed to wipe Cindy's face, too—it *sounded* necessary—but her head was locked in the down position. Billy's as well. Tim saw the two crowns of hair, hers curly and not so blond as it would be in a month, his a thick dark thatch.

When he finally managed to lift Cindy's chin, he saw that wiping was inadequate. Tears and snot and maple syrup had blended together horribly. Through the blur of his own tears, past the two clouds of hair, Tim noticed the clock. It was seven a.m. The day had not even begun.

II

IN LOCO PARENTIS

So he was back to having no idea what to do; back therefore to Coolidge. He had them brush their teeth. Wash their faces. He told them it was time to go to the office.

"I want to go home," said Cindy.

"Sure, everyone does. But first they have to go to work."

"Paid work?" said Billy.

"Absolutely. The usual rate plus lunch at Betty's. Are we set to hit the pavement?"

You pretended everything was going forward according to form and then it could; that was the trick. And getting out of the apartment, starting along the southwest corridor to Copley, was a help, an immediate distraction. Billy and Cindy loved this sinuous path behind the dead-end blocks, where there were exotic dogs (not to mention the comedy of equally exotic owners with their poop-pickup gloves) and green haired punks on skateboards. There were tennis matches on the sunken court where Greenwich ended, and there were all the graces—balconies and gardens—of a Victorian row-house enclave.

And there was Harriet. A stout, absurdly rouged woman who dressed in winter layers regardless of the season, Harriet had been a finalist for Miss Maine in 1958, or so she testified. To those who gave her money, she would display an old snapshot of a young bathing beauty. Tim more or less believed it was Harriet in the picture; Billy always said no way.

"Can I give her the money?" said Cindy.

"You sure can," said Tim, handing Cindy a dollar, which she placed in Harriet's frayed mitten.

"A whole dollar?" said Billy.

Lately he had begun to worry about money. Ever since he overheard his parents discussing the roof (they could not afford to replace it this year) he had taken steps on his own. Stopped asking for magazines, stopped asking for his allowance. No one seemed to notice this initiative, but Billy figured it had its impact. He was not so sure the old lady was poor—at times suspecting a con—and he was absolutely sure it wasn't her in the silly picture, yet it always did feel good when Harriet said Bless your hearts and winked at them.

Ellie Stern was on the line when they trooped past her desk at Trips, Inc. She raised her eyebrows in a smile and brushed fingertips with Cindy, gave a little wave to Billy.

"Air conditioner or air?" said Tim, as they took over his cubicle. Billy, who knew the right answer, was already opening the side windows.

"Will we be here all day, Unk?"

"I'm not sure. You used to like it here, back when you were Cindy."

"I do like it, Unk, but I don't have any of my stuff."

"We're here to work, Simp," said Billy.

Before Tim could get them started sorting and filing the new brochures, Ellie appeared. "You brought the Hergies," she said. "I'm delighted, even if it is a transparent coverup for being late."

"Not as late as Charles," Tim pointed out. The third partner, Charles Tashian, was nowhere in sight.

"Charming Billy," she curtsied, as if receiving royalty. "Lovely Cindy."

"*Cyn*thia."

"If you say so, Miss Mouse."

"Ell?" said Tim. "We need to go over the Venice package—at your desk?"

"No problem," said Ellie, hardly missing the shift in tone: the Venice package and whatever he *really* needed to say. "Why don't you take charge here, Bill. If the phone rings, just tell them we're all at a seminar on the Congo."

"It's not Congo anymore. It's Zaire."

"Of course it is. And you see why we put you in charge."

Ellie's "office," like Tim's and Charles', was simply one-fourth of the floor space they rented. They had it divided like a square pie, the fourth fourth serving as a combination coffee room and waiting area or minimalist buffer zone. Partitions rose just high enough to trim the tops of the connecting doors.

So they whispered. Tim whispered the terrible news, and Ellie had to whisper her exclamations of disbelief. A soft explosion somewhere inside her flooded her eyes and puffed her face, after which again she whispered: "Why did you come in? You didn't have to come here, Tim."

"I had to go somewhere."

"But you seemed so normal, the three of you. You seemed to be having a good time."

"We're in shock, I guess."

"What will happen? Where will they go, Tim?"

"No idea. I do have a sort of plan, though—for the next few days."

"You? Have a *plan*?" Ellie was literally smiling through tears.

"Yes. Charlie runs the office—"

"Assuming he can find it."

"He can hire a temp if he wants, at my expense. And you come with me. Just for a couple of days—"

"My favorite role."

"No, it's not my mom. I have to go to New Hampshire to sort out the official part of this. And it would be so great if you could come along to help me with the kids."

"Your mom must be devastated."

"She doesn't know yet," he said, as Ellie turned her head away in distress. "I mean this just happened."

Tim pictured his mother, alone in Berline, seventy-four and without the slightest notion of the coming blow, the grief that was about to swallow her whole. There was her son (a *bachelor,* at forty) and there was a hornworm attacking her tomatoes: such were Anne Bannon's chief concerns, insofar as she communicated them.

"What about your other sister? She's in New Hampshire."

"She isn't, actually. They are on the road, impossible to contact. That's Big Earl's great self-deception. He goes off in his fifty-thousand-dollar Chinook and thinks because he doesn't carry his cell phone he's morphed into Henry David Thoreau."

"I need to think."

"It's just a couple of days, Ell, and I promise I'll make it up to you. And I'll make it up to Charlie when the ski season comes. I'll stake him to a weekend with The Beast."

Charles' fiancée Lynda McMullen was gorgeous. Just as Tim had nicknamed Joanne Bettworthy "The Beast," he christened Lynda "cindycrawford" for her strong resemblance to the super-model. ("Everything but the mole," he said—"And the money," added Charlie with his patented serpent's leer.) Lynda was gorgeous and Joanne, to put it politely, was not. So Charlie's winter sneakaways to Okemo and Gunstock had always baffled Tim, even before he discovered one day The Beast did not even ski.

"No she doesn't," explained Charles, at last, "and yes she dresses badly. But then she *un*dresses, capiche? And she can après-ski like the Devil's youngest daughter."

"I'm not concerned about Charles," said Ellie. "I have to be back here by Saturday afternoon at the latest."

"I promise. You'll be back." Something was informing Tim he ought not inquire the reason for this, and he repressed the urge. Ellie could not refuse, Ellie was not refusing, so leave it at that. But now that it was settled, reality began seeping in. He did have to make the call to Anne. Cindy was either laughing or crying at his desk, and the smart money said crying. Plus all three phones were ringing.

"It's too awful, " Ellie said. "Jill was just the loveliest human being."

Tim heard the jarring disharmony of the three phones, and the single jarring lyric 'was.' Jill *was*. And then he thought he heard himself crying, from far off somehow, as though inside another dream.

The town of Jaffrey, New Hampshire, where Jill and Monty had settled eight years ago, wore many faces, the most famous of which appeared dramatically as the road curved and dropped just before Trumball Farms, the roadside restaurant. Between curtains of green on either side of the roadway lay an avenue of sky straight to the rocky pointed peak of Mt. Monadnock.

There were old Yankees in town and there were rural poor. Around the ponds and lakes, stately old mansions stood alongside ranch houses and summer shacks. And though the arts were quite prominent here, so too were shotguns mounted inside pickup trucks—the restraining order crowd, as Karl Trickett labeled them. "We've got diversity, too," Jill liked to tease her brother, who was a fairly hardcore urbanite.

Turning into the Trumball Farms lot, Tim braced for difficulty. Billy and Cindy were at home now, and he guessed they would finally break down. They did not, at all, possibly because it was simply too peaceful for emotional turmoil. (Across the road, Jersey cows grazed a tilting green hillside; above them, a two-seater from the local airfield floated and banked like a giant hawk.) In any event, they ate their way through a couple of clam plates, then took on ice cream cones as big as their heads, and showed no hesitation.

Then at the house—where Tim flinched, mentally and physically—they sprinted inside blithely, happy to be home, which was both a relief and a worry to Tim. How could they not crash here? What could it mean?

They did stay very close together, a tiny nation of two. Tim had seen them grow apart this past year, start becoming male and female, older and younger. For the first time, Billy had his friends and Cindy had hers. But today they huddled close, and frequently huddled with Tim and Ellie, checking in.

"They're afraid we'll vanish, too," said Ellie.

"They aren't showing any *pain*."

"Or we just aren't seeing it."

Nor did they see it that night, although Tim watched them as closely as a research chemist watches his test tubes. He and Ell might be mere parental dummies, propped up at the kitchen table, but the comfort level never wavered, the pain never emerged. Eventually, both children lapsed into television comas and Tim carried them upstairs, one at a time.

"Tim, they have been so easy, so sweet, but I do see why parents always say 'It's been a long day.'"

"Hey, it's going to be a long week," said Tim, pouring two very large glasses of wine.

"What about Provincetown? Isn't that next week?"

"The week after," he said, and Ellie understood that to Tim 'the week after' signified a time far into the future. Ellie was guessing his Provincetown vacation was gone, shot, and wondered if his fall trip—what was it, Ireland this year?—would not prove threatened.

"September? Are you serious?" he all but shouted when she mentioned the possibility. "That *can't* be a problem."

Meaning Tim could not contemplate an autumn that included no new verse of "The Blues." For every year he travelled, and every trip was beset by bad luck, by what his dear friend Karl called (collectively, as though they would be bound and sold) The Blues of Tim Bannon. Last November he had seen the magnificent Sognafjord against a broad spectral sunset, yet had spent three days biking through endless freezing bogs to get there. The Sognafjord Blues.

"The Donegal Blues?" said Ellie.

"Probably. Though I'm still considering Senegal, " he grinned.

"Donegal or Senegal. That's it?"

Ellie raised her eyebrows and let it go. She was ready for sleep and only sleep right now. And she knew it would take Tim a while before he fully grasped that Jill would not be coming back from the dead.

Next morning after breakfast, Tim drove to Keene for a meeting with the shrink, Olivia Goldsmith. She began by reciting how sorry she was for his loss (a rote, industry-prescribed line which nonetheless gave a brief frisson of comfort) and then sat waiting to hear from him, her virginal yellow pad at the ready. One might have called her ambient expression a very faint smile, though it was not exactly that.

"What should I be doing?" he said. "What am I supposed to be looking for? What are they really feeling? *Help.*"

Now he saw the difference, as she did smile. Goldsmith was an attractive woman in her late forties, with short dark hair tinged gray and punctuated by jade earrings that seemed like tiny fragments of the green in her eyes. Tim placed her as a trim, no-frills edition of middle Liz Taylor.

"I like someone who can get to the point, Mr. Bannon, but honestly, just stick with common sense. Feeling? Shock, confusion, sadness—great great sadness. And they will feel anger."

"They don't show any of it. I understand there are no cures, but there must be strategies. Some tips you could give me."

"Common sense is all you'll need. And love, of course. I take it you have no children of your own."

"No," Tim answered, though it was not phrased as a question.

"Children are less apt than we are to disguise feelings, but they are also less apt to know them. And at a time like this, they can disguise those feelings from themselves, if you follow me."

"Not really."

"You want to pay close attention without hovering. Do they seek time alone? Fine, see that they get it. Do they want too *much* time alone? Then you break in on the pattern."

"Try this," said Tim, who was not getting the kind of responses he had hoped for. "What would you do, if you were me. Today,

I mean. Right when I walk in the door."

"Hug them. Feed them. You can't go wrong there."

"Anything special?" he said, with a trace of sourness.

"Oh come on. You mean Mcfrenchfries versus a garden salad? Here's what matters: kids express their need through hunger. The rituals of coming by food and eating it—whatever it is— serve to fulfill them. It's a normalcy thing."

"I suppose it is," said Tim, still starved for behavioral clues, yet pretty sure Goldsmith had said yes to junk food.

At the state police barracks later in the morning, Tim learned details of the accident. A drunk driver, of course. Uninsured, of course. A man named Alfred Chute would face charges of vehicular homicide—jail time—and charges of driving without proper insurance.

"He rents a room on Oak Street in Jaffrey," said Lieutenant Moss. "Hasn't had work since March. I'm afraid it looks like the blood-from-a-stone problem, Chute being your stone. Will you excuse me for a minute?"

"Sure," said Tim, though Moss was already gone. Tim felt useless, passive, just as he had at Goldsmith's office. He didn't care about the criminal charges and he didn't care (though he knew he ought to, for the children's sake) that the unemployed, uninsured Mr. Chute had no money. Selfishly, he wished only to be done with bureaucracies and red tape.

He marvelled at the barren expanse of Moss' desk, a slab of speckled brown laminate with chipped edges that revealed the pressboard core. There was not a single object on the surface: no lists, no files, not even a paper clip or a day-planner. Tim sighed. He gazed out the window at a wide brick chimney, pink against a pale blue sky, and sighed again. He could see himself sighing a lot in the days to come.

His duty, however, was clear. He must hold himself together, somehow restore order to Billy and Cindy's lives, and then return to his own life. Not that he had the slightest talent for an orderly life. On the contrary, he found chaos—or freedom—more interesting. "The curse of being queer," he said, perhaps out loud, perhaps not.

Possibly audible to Moss, who had reentered the room, or possibly not. What the hell, Moss had likely surmised it on his own;

25

even a country cop could know one when he saw one.

Jeff Moss had not heard. And though he had spotted an evening grosbeak at the birdfeeder, his real motive in stepping outside was to give Tim a moment to collect himself. In a town where half their calls were cat-in-the-tree or car-strikes-deer, this was a tough one. Toughest for the kids, but clearly tough for the gay uncle. This poor guy was really stuck.

"Coffee?" offered Moss. "It's fresh. Sort of."

Another long day; accordingly, more TV on Cedar Street that night. Tim gave the children milk and cookies (and how cozy was *that*) when *The League of One* came on. Grateful for the one-hour ease-ment, he and Ellie took their coffee mugs out to the deck and lit a citronella candle to discourage the last battalion of black flies. Drained and weary, Tim had dissolved—pooled down—into the wicker chair when Billy poked his face outside.

"Unk?"

"What, Bill?"

"It's *starting*, is what."

Just as it had not crossed Tim's mind that he would watch the show, it had not crossed Billy's mind his uncle would miss it. The show was a point of connection. The three of them had seen it together a few times, but they always hashed over the latest episode the following day, on the phone. And now it was *starting*.

Dutifully, Tim reported. Cheerfully, he participated. He pooled down into the couch and relaxed around the cast's familiar gestures. Maybe the rap-port among these actors was contrived, but it felt genuine. Tim imagined the whole troupe having a blast at the day's filming, then heading off together for beers after work and high jinks on Sunset Boulevard.

He was gonzo, though, and the first raft of ads broke the spell. He had one sharp pang of envy for Ellie, under the burgeoning stars with her coffee and strudel. After that he was staring in the direction of the glowing tube with-out seeing much. Now and then he placed a cookie in his mouth.

When the cookies were gone, they crowded together, Tim in the middle, Billy and Cindy pressing in from either side. The three of them sat there—paralyzed, really—as their favorite show ended and the next one, whatever it was, began.

*

26

Monty was obsessive—or compulsive. Tim was never sure of the difference. Montgomery Hergesheimer was *organized*, that's the way he would have described himself. Whatever he read, whatever he ate (or intended to eat), whatever he had gleaned of his genealogy or for that matter his dog's genealogy (along with dates of vaccinations) went into his computer and stayed there. Monty had a pension plan in his twenties and a portfolio of dummy stocks long before he had a dollar to invest. So Tim should not have been surprised that Monty did indeed have a lawyer. It wasn't that they needed a lawyer, it was that Monty was Monty.

It was from Attorney Phil Jellinghaus that Tim learned just how far he was from resuming his own life. He had arrived at the lawyer's door without premonition. There were matters to discuss, Jellinghaus had said, which made sense. There must be. Then, right off the bat (as though awarding a prize) he hit Tim with this business about a Will and Tim's being designated guardian of the children. What exactly did that mean?

"That Billy and Cindy are yours, in effect. Yours to raise now. You are *in loco parentis.*"

"Like, forever?"

"Well, yes," said Jellinghaus with some amusement. "In the sense that any parent has them forever. Hopefully it starts tailing off by the time they turn eighteen."

"But that's ten years." The lawyer nodded; his round friendly face wore a look of perpetual amusement, reinforced by the jug ears. "I'll be fifty years old in ten years!"

"Hey, so will I. Though this fifty-in-ten idea is just math to me. I'm still getting used to being forty."

"I'm not," said Tim. And rethinking the postulate, he was tempted to point out he would not likely be fifty in ten years, he would likely be dead. So here was a mistake that required correction.

"Of course," said Jellinghaus, squeezing a rubber ball, "our youngest is fourteen. He should be launched into the world a lot sooner than either of yours."

"You look awful," said Ellie, when Tim came downstairs after calling his mother that night.

"Not an easy conversation." Which it wasn't, to be sure. But if Tim looked awful (and he did not doubt it a bit), it probably had more to do with his conversation with Jellinghaus earlier. He had yet to report on his disturbing new title, and he did not do so now. Instead he said, "And I'm worried about Cindy."

"Well, of course."

"The change, I mean. You didn't notice the change in her?"

"I guess not," said Ellie, taken aback. Tim had been gone all day and the only change she had noticed was in him.

"She didn't say a single word at dinner."

"She ate a ton, though. And really, dinner lasted all of six minutes."

"She's like a little zombie, she's *inert* or something. I picked her up and it was like lifting a bag of sand."

"To me, she seemed lively all day. We went to the river to walk. She took my hand; she talked a lot, actually."

"About what? Do you remember?"

"Of course I remember. A lot of it was what we saw—you know, the mountain laurel, nature stuff. And camp. She's concerned that only half her camp labels are sewn on."

"You see? That's so crazy. Jill was getting her clothes ready—socks, underwear—and now Jill's *dead* and Cindy says her *labels* need sewing?"

"Maybe there is a slight disconnect. But it's not necessarily such a bad thing. She does have to cope."

"But how am I supposed to respond to it? Here I'm paying attention, so I can give her what she needs—"

"So give her the labels. Start sewing. Camp opens on Tuesday, you know."

"Under the circumstances, I think they'll give Jilly back her money."

"You're saying they shouldn't go?"

"To *camp*? I never dreamed they would go."

"It might be worth considering. Especially if your Mom seems okay..."

Okay? Not exactly, though Anne had subsided in the last day or so. At first she had alternated between getting on "the next plane north" and Tim getting them all on the next plane south. Tim convinced her he needed time—Lord did he!—to handle the layers of official business. But he would have to convince her anew every day.

Anne's inertia helped. In the years since Rex had died, she had hunkered down completely, had not spent a single night away from Berline. And she hadn't told a soul about Jill. Hadn't gone to town, or anywhere, in days. Any impulse to act was quickly vitiated by the utter uselessness of action—and by the sheer distance. New Hampshire, which Anne had never seen, seemed strange and very far away.

"Maybe I should ask the shrink," Tim said, a little bitterly. "Maybe she'll say camp is 'the *normalcy* thing.'"

"Well it is that. The kids both think it's …The Plan. And you know how Billy is."

"I do. The world ends in nuclear holocaust, but he goes off to summer camp the next day, because it's The *Plan*."

"You could ask them."

"Ask the Hergies?"

"Yes. Ask what they want to do. At the very least, it might get them to open up in general."

"Sure, Ell, fine. We'll ask them."

"You will ask them," she corrected him. Ellie was tired of his carping tone and tired of playing Pseudomom; tired of being taken for granted in the role. She did not expect Tim to notice her difficulties in the midst of all this, but he surprised her, snapping out of his funk.

"You want to hear my idea for a new sitcom? A truly clueless gay guy raises two perfectly normal children. Uncle Knows Best, maybe—or no, Unk Knows Nothing. That's it."

"Sounds promising, Tim. But please don't save out a part for me."

"Look, Ell, I guess I've been clueless about you, too. I know this isn't exactly the way you expected your week to be."

"Not exactly. But it's fine."

He tried to take her hands, but Ellie put up her stop sign: both hands chest high, palms out. To keep Tim from mounting a phony apology, also to keep herself from sliding any deeper into self-pity. They were switching roles, and she was becoming the bitchy one now.

"This is probably the worst time to mention South Carolina…"

Ellie looked at him with milder disgust than she felt.

"I know, you're worried about Saturday. This would be later."

Up came the hands again, the stop sign. "Tim, I'm sorry, but I am not going to South Carolina with you. I can't."

"We'll talk about it," he said, before she could foreclose the option entirely. But she closed it anyway.

"No, Tim. We won't talk about it—or we already did. But I will cover for you at the office, however long it takes."

Friday started and ended with J.J. Mulhern. J.J. (James Joseph, Tim had asked and been told) was the director of Mulhern's Funeral Home in Keene. White haired, in a crisp black suit, he spoke a language so formal and polite that the subject matter could seem quotidian—as indeed it was, for him. A laminated placard reading "All Major Credit Cards Are Welcome" made it clear to Tim exactly how quotidian.

"You would be surprised, Mr. Bannon, at how reasonably we can ship the remains to anywhere in the world."

The remains, however, would require no shipping. Monty was an only child, whose parents were both dead. His ashes would go with Jill's to Berline, to be scattered or interred there. Such decisions were yet unmade as Tim moved numbly (as numbly as he could manage) through this week of awful chores and he was at his absolute numbest with Mulhern. Luckily, the man was decent, because to streamline these grim arrangements Tim would have signed on any dotted line slid across the table—and slid his major credit card right back the other way, pending what Attorney Jellinghaus termed 'disbursement.'

For Jellinghaus had reassured Tim about money. "My fees will come out of the estate. So you'll see an accounting, but never a bill."

All this painlessness. Mulhern and Jellinghaus both meant well, but it was Lt. Moss who faced up to the reality of pain when he handed over the contents of the car and the decedents' clothing. This was stark, and Tim took a sickening shot to the heart as he held the mundane concrete trivia in his hands. Monty had bought raffle tickets for a 4th of July fundraiser; Jill had made a list of phone numbers for dishwasher repairmen.

Moss grabbed Tim's shoulders to steady him, plumbed him up like a fencepost and looked him in the eye until Tim could work his way back. (That night Moss would tell his wife he felt like a referee checking the eyes of a reeling prizefighter: "Not that I had the option of stopping it on a TKO.")

Goldsmith (four p.m.) was the one functionary who Tim believed might help him. All the others were wedded to past and present, whereas Goldsmith understood there would be a future. "What will your plans be?" she asked, and Tim noted the precision of her phrasing. Not what are your plans, but what will your plans be. Among other things, she was aware that he had not made any yet.

"First I need to figure out where they'll live."

"Yes, Mr. Bannon. That's what I meant by my question."

"Don't misunderstand, or judge me harshly for saying this, Ms. Goldsmith, but everyone assumes Billy and Cindy will be with me. And to me, that doesn't seem possible."

"It's not easy, I appreciate that."

Goldsmith displayed the smile that was not a smile. Her hands were amazingly still, at rest atop her thighs. All of her was still, in fact; she was a painting of herself.

"My life—" Tim started. "Or lifestyle? —"

"You are single. Unattached?"

"Single, unattached, forty...."

Did they have gay people in New Hampshire? Did Olivia Goldsmith know any of them? (Hadn't he heard something teasing in her inquisition, a subliminal invitation to confess all?)

"And Jill never discussed this with you. The guardianship."

"She did, once. But it presupposed this unthinkable situation, so it was hardly a discussion. It was more like a joke. I never dreamed there was anything official, down on paper."

"A *joke*, Mr. Bannon?"

"It's hard to explain."

"Is it?"

Oh she was shrinking him now, wangling it out of him, and Tim chose to let her have it. If he wanted some truth from her, he would have to give some up to her. But how much?

That he was gay, obviously. That therefore he was facing a death sentence, or presumed he was, even if he expended much of his best energy pretending he wasn't. That he suffered from The Blues! For how could he be the loco parentis of anyone when he had to travel great distances on a regular basis? Yes, his life was on hold. And the Summertime Blues, which he knew from Oldies

103 to be incurable, were so far manageable. But late September in Ireland—the Donegal Blues—that was non-negotiable.

Meanwhile they were locked in a staredown. "You know, don't you," said Tim, finally.

"I might," said Goldsmith, extending one hand as though to accept his confession in a neat package.

"That I'm gay."

"All right."

"All right? Meaning—?"

"If you have concerns about privacy, Mr. Bannon, you can be sure this conversation is confidential."

"Sometimes I do and sometimes I don't. It's mostly about my mother when I do. Which seems awfully stupid when you consider that I'm forty years old."

"So you keep telling me," she smiled.

"You'd be obsessed, too, if you were a forty-year-old gay man."

Tim could feel himself going abrasive, but Goldsmith continued to make such riveted and empathetic eye contact he wondered if she might be coming out herself. Not only knew some, *was* one. He dared to ask.

"Myself, no. Many good friends are. Mostly women—though not all."

"That's, I don't know...heartening, in a way."

"We aren't cave-dwellers here. It's really quite civilized. And a nice area for raising children."

"Well, thanks for the recommendation. In Boston, shrinks don't make recommendations, they just sit and listen."

"If you wish to become a patient, Mr. Bannon, I'll be happy to sit and listen. For now I'd like to get back to the question of guardianship. Would I be right in assuming your sister Erica is the alternative you have in mind?"

"No, you would not be right and no, Erica is not an alternative."

"She and her husband, Mr....Sanderson. Do they have children?"

"Not a one."

"You say that so emphatically, as if the very idea was preposterous. Are they very much older?"

"Erica is thirty-eight. Earl, I'm guessing forty-five, but a very young forty-five. I'd put his mental age at about twelve."

"Ah."

"Believe me, it's not an accident Jill named me guardian. Yes, Ric is married and solvent and lives just over the hill here—your whole damned normalcy thing. Except they aren't normal."

"Neither are you. By our society's harsh standards."

"Point taken. Neither am I."

"So what is it about Erica that gives you such pause? Or perhaps it's hard to say."

"Not hard at all."

She was good, was Goldsmith; no cave-dweller she. She had flushed him from the closet so easily, maybe it was unwise to throw open every door and window. And maybe it was hard to say (in a concise way that fit the little boxes of a questionnaire) precisely what was wrong with Earl Sanderson. Hard to convey how Earl recoiled from touching Billy last Christmas, for fear the boy might carry a poisonous mote from having hugged Tim first.

"Let me put it this way. Every year Earl gets himself a new hunting dog. And every summer, when they get set to go on the road for two months, he shoots the dog."

"Rather than bring it along."

"Bring it, board it at a kennel, give it to a lonely kid. Rather than any of the above, yeah."

"The poor pooch must feel betrayed," said Goldsmith, with obvious irony. Meaning to ally herself with Tim, and grant him a gentle mockery of her own tricky profession. But Tim was too worked up to catch any irony.

"Betrayed," he howled, with that slight and sarcastic drawl. "Psychology-wise, I'm sure you're right. But I'm guessing what the poor pooch mostly feels is *dead*."

Tim drove back to the funeral home in what passed for rush hour traffic, a dozen vehicles in motion simultaneously. Sitting on a dumbwaiter, the two urns were more substantial than Tim expected. When Mulhern had brought up the Commingling Option ("a single container for both decedents") Tim had assumed the issue was economic. Now he could see it in terms of portability, though the director laid that to rest with a typically gracious stroke: "I'll walk out with you when we're ready."

His next line ("Though I will need to ask for the minimum before they leave") was uncharacteristically jarring and Tim's

33

doubletake was genuine. *They? Leave?* But that would be the decedents, of course, Jill and Monty. The director had confused Tim by granting them an active verb.

"We understand the balance may take some time," added Mulhern, attributing Tim's hesitation to the financial aspect. "But policy does state we must ask for the minimum."

Ask? And who exactly set this policy when J.J. had his name up there on the marquee and when he was the only visible representative? Yet it was easy to make nervous fun of the grisly business Mulhern conducted; the man provided a necessary service, and presumably he had mouths to feed. Tim slid him a major credit card and then together they placed the decedents in the trunk of the Honda.

He fully intended to hightail it straight back to Cedar Street like a good parentis, but he could not get out of the blocks. As Mulhern's back receded, Tim just sat there with the engine babbling. He paused. (The word itself occurred to him: I think I'll *pause*.) Not to reflect, which seemed a terrible idea, simply to breathe: to be alone and doing absolutely nothing for one minute seemed a little brilliant.

But the peace, the *space* he was desperate to create, crumbled quickly. For one thing (he reflected after all) he was not alone—his sister, his best friend on earth, was in the trunk—and for another he was perhaps more alone than he wished to be, in a larger sense. Before he could stop himself from reflecting further, he had tallied no less than eleven close friends who had died of AIDS in the last three years, and none of them even middle-aged. Even J.J. Mulhern might consider that a lot.

It struck him that alcohol sometimes helped. Not a brilliant insight, but useful. He recalled a handsome inn, a welcoming collage of clapboards and glass, not far from the house in Jaffrey. What if he bought himself a drink or two there, took time out to breathe and even swallow. Tim voted yes, if only to get himself going from the funeral home.

Immediately he felt lighter, disburdened; the mere *prospect* of alcohol helped. And it was a pleasure to drive on roads so airy and empty, flowing past summer greenery as lush as Carolina. It might be worth living here just for such easy passage, and for the parking. Everywhere you went, you pulled up to the door and parked. A person gained much more than time by means of this bounty.

He parked at the door of the Monadnock Inn and went from the afternoon sunlight to the dark wood bar inside, where a bearded gentleman poured him a generous glass—three fingers—and disappeared into the cellar. The cozy bar (eight stools) sat at the end of a vast foyer and dining room, but Tim was the only inhabitant and gentle hornflavored jazz, music so soft it might be sifting from a room upstairs, was the only sound. Finding his smiling face among the bottles arrayed before the mirror, Tim felt a definite attachment to this place. He would never have to worry about bumping into Earl Sanderson *here*.

Sane. That was the word. To sail over smooth uncluttered roads and make easeful pitstops at charming country taverns that had no attraction for Earl would make a wonderfully *sane* existence. No problem swallowing this bourbon. Right now his glottis (or whatever it was) was working fine.

Sex was the kicker, of course, but Tim might be approaching the time of sexual retirement. Forty years old! Already the unruly hormones could lie quiescent for days at a stretch. Why couldn't he do this? Come up to New Hampshire and raise Jill's kids, if he had a whole driveway all to himself for parking? At the moment, the proposition seemed less impossible.

And at the moment, stepping back out into the pre-crepuscular light, the sky of faded blue, he did not even register the presence of ashes in the trunk. The urns clattered slightly as he drove, just a distant insignificant tinkle to Tim. Then Cindy came to him, yelling pick me up pick me up, and all he saw was Jill. When she laughed, Cindy looked exactly as her mother had looked in the third grade. The formulation came first (Jill Bannon Hergesheimer, 1948-1990), then a crushing at his throat.

"I'm so weak I can barely lift you," he said, staggering under the impost, covering his grief with grunts.

"Try me," said Billy now.

"Worse and worse," said Tim, 'failing' to levitate the boy more than an inch off the floor.

"Weaker and weaker!" shouted Cindy.

Then he powered them aloft, one on each arm, and roared like the king of the jungle. Not so weak after all!—and not so very sober, he discovered, setting them safely down. As they ate (and this time Cindy did have things to tell him), Tim's mind stayed fixed on the phone numbers in Jill's pocketbook, for dishwasher repairmen. That and the dates, 1948 to 1990.

At bedtime he read them poetry they had loved two years ago, from Stevenson's *Garden of Verses*. They were old for these poems now, particularly Billy, except they insisted on them, and then they looked so dreamy listening. Whatever works, Tim allowed, verse or bourbon or "other."

Above the sequence of yards, the hills folded together and the North Star dangled. It was dark now and the moon, a flat disc of orange fire, soon shouldered its way to the treetops. Tim and Ellie patrolled the curve of Cedar Street, back and forth to stay in sight of the house, with its warmlit rooms revealed by rows of half-curtained windows.

"Today was the longest day of the year," said Ellie, letting the sweet air sweep her mind clear.

"I will make it up to you, Ell. I absolutely will."

"Daylight, I mean—the summer solstice. Billy is the one who mentioned it, of course."

"They seem better, no?"

"They're great. Though they did refuse to call friends. In a *while,* they keep saying. To any suggestion you make."

"So they hung together."

"Tim, you would not believe the hours they can log with maps."

"I would, though, and it's all my fault."

"The highest elevations! The principal rivers! There was a postcard from your sister and all they cared about was the postmark. So they could locate the spot on a map."

Mail from the dead? No, it was his sister Erica; it was mail *to* the dead. How bizarre that mail would keep coming to Jill and Monty. Bills. Invitations. They would be invited to dinner. And then there was Monty's raffle ticket for the 4th of July. Monty might be the lucky winner!

"Erica doesn't know," he said. "That's the most bizarre of all. Your sister is dead and you're too busy fishing to know it."

"Come on, Tim. You could have been away just as easily. Talk about incommunicado. What's it, the Sognafjord Blues?"

"Still."

"Still nothing. And they can't be as bad as you say."

"Can't they? Earl doesn't even pretend he's not awful. He's got one of those little Sambo men on his lawn, for starters."

"He's anti-black?"

"Earl? He's proud out loud—as he might put it—to be anti-black, anti-gay, anti-Semitic, anti-woman—"

"He must be pro-*some*thing," she grinned.

"Well, guns. And money. He made Salesman of the Year two years running. They gave him golden cufflinks both times."

"This twisted misfit is successful, you're saying?"

"Probably *because* he's twisted. Earl sold the Gardiner house the day it came on the market. You remember that?"

"Should I?"

"An entire family was murdered in the house, and Earl washed the blood off the walls and listed it two weeks later. Got market value for it too, he's quick to assure you."

"He must be convincing, or charming, in his way."

"If you are asking me the secret of his success, the answer is I have no idea."

"Is your sister happy with him?"

"I've always believed she's scared of him."

"He hits her?"

"Let's say I'd be pleasantly surprised if he doesn't."

Now as they went by the house for the eighth or ninth time, Tim shut the flap door of the mailbox, then heard it fall open again behind them. As the darkness filled and deepened, the moon had floated up, impossibly large and bright. It was silver now, an enormous circle of silver above the eastern hills.

"It's so nice here," he said, and he was including the inn (which he had elected not to mention to the long suffering Pseudomom) and the splendors of parking, as well as the night air and the risen moon.

"It's beautiful. I'd pay for the *smell* of it all."

"Do you think you could live here, Ell?"

"No," she said, trying to examine his eyes for a sign, a plot that could include her. "Though I'm not sure why."

On Saturday morning, a neighbor materialized. "Alice McManus," she announced, "mother of the twins"—her claim to fame. That plus her status as Jill's best friend, though Tim's clearest memory of Alice was the orchard of tiny white lights, a wretched excess girdling her house and grounds every Christmas. At *least* a thousand points of light.

37

Her husband was taking the twins to Canobie Lake on Sunday and they wondered if Bill and Cynthia might like to join them. Then, before Tim could respond (that he had no idea what they might like), the woman handed him a casserole. "It's just a macaroni and beef thing, but I know they'll both eat it."

The casserole was in no way inconsistent with the nutty Christmas lighting; Tim simply filed it under Suburbia. Yet it did work. It did help. Right away the kids were racing next door to watch a video with the twins (their first foray back into the World) and they would indeed choose the amusement park on Sunday. They would slide and swim as though grief did not exist, only videos did, and casseroles, and lakes.

Which was fine. Tim was grateful for the simplicity of it and grateful to have another resource in Casserole Alice. A parent needed "coverage." Tim knew that from the travel business. Clients wanted to know what activities, what facilities were available at the Hamilton Princess. Were there tennis lessons, swimming lessons, horseback riding? Translation: would they have some time alone.

With *coverage,* he could take Ellie to the train without dragging the children along. The drive to Fitchburg, to the Boston train, loomed as almost a vacation, a respite at least, and at first they both enjoyed the silence. They went past weedy lakes, past the Rindge House of Pizza (which *was* a house), past the Cypress Grove Lounge where there were no cypress trees but the roast pork special looked good at $4.95.

By the time they crossed the Massachusetts border, the silence had begun to feel weighty, or feel like two separate silences born of separate crises. In Ashby, the sudden drone of a sitdown mower (circling the bandstand on the steep village green) pierced and exacerbated the hush that had fallen on them.

"The good news," Tim tried, foregoing any guesses as to what might be the bad news, "is that you have a date tonight."

"So?"

"So not everyone has a date tonight. I, for one, do not."

He supposed it was The Usual: dating was futile, nothing worked out, tonight would prove to be no more than the latest defeat. Tim had no doubt Ellie was an attractive woman. Nothing about her was unattractive, from her short lively brown hair and trim figure to her kind, observant nature. Did her lack of confidence lose her boyfriends, or did the loss of boyfriends erode her confidence? This was already a tangle when Tim met her twelve years ago.

"It's the 90's," he tried. "People just aren't into commitment these days."

"Then how come my two best friends are married?"

"You could have married Foxley. Maybe that's who your friends married. Did they? Marry Foxley?"

Ellie wished to shrug off Tim's benign silliness, his blatant effort to cheer her up. She didn't even need cheering up, she just needed to focus on Victor and on how best to handle the situation, for she had trusted too much already— had already moved herself into the zone of potential hurt. Of *hope.*

"What makes you say I could have?"

"Well, you were the one who backed out of it."

"My greatest moment, jumping before I was pushed. Keith was just waiting to step up."

"Up? Into the arms of Helena Sitzbath is *up?*"

Her excuse (and Ellie knew it was an excuse) was Victor himself. Why make him answer—Victor, who had yet to put a foot wrong—for the sins of earlier failed contestants?

"I never knew why you called her that," said Ellie, who did know. But she could label Tim catty and still be the beneficiary of his cattiness.

"She was into that stuff, bigtime. Sitz baths, high colonic irrigation. *Worse,* for all I know."

"I hope you never called her that to her face."

"Her face? Hey, with a face like that, who needs enemas?"

They had reached the north end of Fitchburg, a fading Massachusetts factory town. The Main Street movie house had closed. Placard wavers stood protesting at a chain-link gate to the G.E plant. A narrow river that once powered the mills now trickled through the city unnoticed.

At the depot in Moran Square, there wasn't even a platform or trainshed, no shelter at all, just a patch of pavement and the open rails through shallow weeds. Across the tracks stood a moribund 60's mall whose windowless cinderblock façade had attracted graffiti bombers. It was hard to believe the train would actually stop here.

"Don't do anything crazy in the next few days," said Ellie.

"And take the children to that camp."

"We'll see about camp."

Though she was sure he would take them in the end, Ellie understood that Tim was still waiting for some "logic" to emerge, for clarity to shake down from the chaos, even though logic played no part in his own decision-making. That there simply was no solution would not jar him from reverie any more than the AIDS epidemic had discouraged what Ellie called his strange encounters of the third kind. What he called his "evening activities."

"Tell me about the new guy," he said. "The Anti-Foxley."

"He's not brand new. But too new to discuss."

"You make it sound pretty serious."

"Not for discussion?"

Tim hoped the train would appear and transport Ellie into the arms of a true Prince Charming; at the same time, he hoped the train would breeze past them, forcing her to come back to Jaffrey. Ellie had no such ambivalence, despite the maternal reflexes Tim (not to mention Billy and Cindy) had always tapped in her. Her maternal reflexes were other-directed until further notice.

"Cook a nice dinner," she told him as the train, a three-car local, did appear and did stop. "Fatten 'em up for camp."

She leaned forward and kissed him lightly on the lips, as she often did. And as he did just as often, Tim hunched his shoulders, monstered up, and whispered into her ear, "AAAA . . I . . DS."

"Yeah yeah," she laughed, yanking herself up onto the steep metal stair, but her fearlessness was not lost on Tim. For years he had seen people literally cringe, their expressions distorted as if they had bitten a worm, when the deathly contagion of AIDS loomed close. Perfectly intelligent people (not just Earl) were freaked to be in the same room with him. In the same *world*.

"Take this, Ell. Train fare, at least. Please—"

She waved contemptuously at his twenty-dollar bill and vanished inside the cars, behind a row of filthy windows. The train was already moving. It chugged past the graffiti-scarred wall, then rolled out of the black cloud it had just manufactured. It passed beneath a swaying gantry and disappeared around the curve. Tim stood alone on the macadam, his life stretched out before him.

Yes, absolutely, he should cook a nice dinner, save the casserole for a rainy day. But a sinking feeling beset him; anchored him

40

to the pavement; sank him. *Trapped,* was what he was. Come September, Billy and Cindy would go back to school—and he, Tim Bannon, would be assembling Billy's power lunches in the morning? Wrestling with Cindy's braid? *Carpooling* to soccer practice? It was a dirty word to him, suburban death in so many syllables.

But he had let himself slip into long-term thinking, that was the problem. Long-term was never Tim's strength; short-term strategies suited him better, life taken one hour at a time. And Calvin Coolidge suited him perfectly. The car needed gas, so he pulled into the Mini-Mart in Rindge. Then all he had to decide was whether or not to eat a doughnut. One foot after the other.

Instantly, the doughnut conundrum was solved, since he absolutely required a cup of coffee and if you were going to drink coffee in your car (and yes, coffee was bad for you too, but it was understood to be indispensible) then you pretty much had to have a doughnut—especially if it was the weak coffee from a gaspump convenience store.

Coolidgewise, he was good. Gassed up, drinking and driving back, he already knew what came next: the plan was in place, a Camp White Sneaker outing to Lake Nubanusit.

White Sneaker had evolved (or morphed, abruptly) from the earlier "Camp Bannon" joke, the expeditions Tim had always organized—hiking, biking, and canoeing with the kids. Then one day he dragged them to the Boston Public Library to hear a Wampanoag storyteller who was decked out in buckskins, beads, braids...and bright white Reeboks! It was a zeitgeist, all three of them saw at once that they would thenceforth be renamed Camp White Sneaker. All agreed to the single proviso of mandatory white sneakers on future excursions.

Tim loved them so much for this; for having a sense of humor and a craving for the outdoors in what was, for so many kids, a relentlessly technological age. Tim himself had hunted and fished as a kid in South Carolina. ("My life as a straight white male," he referenced it among wide-eyed friends in the gay community.) He knew knots, trees, animal tracks. Not expertly, just with the routine familiarity everyone acquired back then. You did not learn such things with a purpose, they simply came to you, from close at hand.

From uncles, come to think of it. Uncle Jim and Uncle Rollie.

41

And from his father, from Rex. Maybe that's how Billy and Cindy inherited it, via good old trickle-down genetics, trickling down through Jilly. Surely they did not get it from their own father, with his infamous "laptop tan." Monty was literally allergic to the sun. At Crane's Beach the weekend Tim met him, Monty was got up in sleeves, slacks, and a solar topi—and broke out in a rash anyway.

Grateful for genetics, grateful for the Nubanusit plan, Tim nonetheless girded himself as he made the left turn onto Cedar Street. This was his first moment as a single parentis. From the car he watched a lively soccer game flowing back and forth between Jill's yard and Alice's, for they were contiguous and had no fence, no boundary of any kind. There were a dozen kids zigging and zagging madly, yet even from a distance Billy Hergesheimer glowed like a hot coal. When Billy played sports, it always seemed as if he were alive and all the others barely awake.

Including his sister. Floppy and marginally involved, Cindy ditched the game the instant she spotted Tim. She ran to him frowning, or pouting. Doing the thing with her lower lip.

"What is it, sweetheart? What's the matter?"

"I feel sick, Unk. My head hurts, and my tummy."

"I'm sorry, sweetheart."

"I want to stay home, Unk. It's *cold* on Nubie."

Was Cindy sick? Not very, but should it matter? Maybe it was enough that she did not want to go. (Or maybe she did want to go, and needed Tim to persuade or command her.) What would a parent do? What would Jilly have done? *Questions.*

"You know what?" he said, possibly for no better reason than his need to account for the next few hours, "Nubie will cure you. There's definite magic in the Nubanusit air."

"There is not."

"And there's magic in a glass of milk, so let's start there. Then you can make the checklist."

"Do I have to?"

"Yes, my sweet, and this time let's not forget the towels."

Cindy did not forget anything. Nor did she appear sickly, merely engaged, as her list lapped onto a second page. It took half an hour to gather and organize, and another fifteen minutes (ropes, straps, bungee cords) loading the canoe. Allowing for the run up to Hancock plus the time it would take to *unload* all this shit, Tim calculated he was getting them through the afternoon just fine.

Was this good, though? To wish away such glorious hours in the very heart of summer; to muddle through life as though death, at the other end, was the goal? "Paddles!" came a cry from the back seat, where he had them strapped down like prisoners of war. (Because Jill insisted they ride in the back seat that way. But how and when would Tim be liberated from this directive? Would she have wanted them back there at twelve? At fourteen?)

"You didn't load the *paddles*?" he said.

"*You* didn't load the paddles," Billy shot back. Silently, intently, they had been combing down the checklist.

"You messed up, Unk."

"Maybe I was testing you guys."

"Maybe not, Unk. Maybe you messed up."

"Well, then, Cynthia saved the day, with her Nobel Prize-winning checklist."

"Yay, me," said Cindy.

On the skid down to the boat launch, cars and trucks with boat trailers jockeyed for position. Once launched, however, they vanished quickly and only the brightest kayaks comprised the view. A stiff wind shoved and chopped the water.

"Nubie is bigger than I remembered," said Tim. "Looks like tough going for a canoe."

"No worries, Unk, there's three of us. Besides, look at that guy. He's *zooming,* and he's alone."

"He's in a sea kayak, Bill. And he's probably a professional."

"A professional sea kayaker?" This in Billy's tone of particular ridicule, each syllable freighted with heavy irony.

"That guy? I'm pretty sure he was in the Olympics."

"Right, Unk. An *Olympic* sea kayaker."

They were working now, a halting progress as the canoe bucked and turned with the waves. Halfway across, they knew they would make it, so long as they continued to paddle full bore. Billy Hergesheimer was unacquainted with physical doubt (if there was a building to lift, he would fully expect to lift it) yet even he was exhausted when they hit the Spoonwood portage.

There, at the rocky neck of land linking Nubanusit Lake to the tranquil, sheltered Spoonwood Lake beyond, they tied off the canoe and hauled gear up the dirt path to a promontory. They spread a blanket in the sun and Cindy, using one towel for a pillow and another for a cover, was instantly curled into sleep. Tim and Billy stepped onto the broken concrete dam to survey both lakes.

"Wind should be with us going back," said Tim—his way of informing the boy they would not be going on across Spoonwood. For once, Billy was happy to hear it.

"It could shift," he said, playing the grownup, "but no problem for Camp White Sneaker."

"Right. Camp Keokuk might struggle, but White Sneaker can't be stopped."

"Camp starts Tuesday, you know," said Billy, saving Tim the effort; it was to be his next sentence. "Real camp."

"I do know. But I heard you were against going."

"Heard from who?"

"From whom," said Tim, in deference to Jill and her grammatical imperative. "From your Mom is whom."

Tim waited for the sky to fall.

"When?"

"Weeks ago. Maybe three weeks ago?"

"Oh, yeah, that. I didn't want to miss playing in the all-star game."

"You missed a game yesterday," Tim pointed out, but Billy shrugged it off. Not the *all-star* game.

"If we didn't go—to Keokuk?—would we be in Boston?"

"I'm not sure. But wherever we were, that would be Camp White Sneaker. Like a portable camp."

Tim's sidebar reference to Jill still lingered in Billy's eyes, where a glaze of tears had pooled and stayed though the boy pawed at them. And he began to shiver, though it was warm in the sun. Tim's own tears were coming by the time Cindy, suddenly bawling, ran to them on the ledge.

"We won't ever see Mommy again," she said, the words bursting through a mouth bubble after one of those sound delays you get with an injured baby.

Tim dearly wished he could argue the point. To let it be the truth was too stark, too cruel. Enveloping her in his arms felt absurdly inadequate: he had no clue what to tell her, could barely speak at all, most definitely could not swallow. Where was Goldsmith when you needed her? What was the magic bullet for a real and bottomless sadness?

"We can see her on the tapes," said Billy.

He had never meant to let himself cry; had restored himself to

44

poise and bravery. He truly believed it was his assignment, his job, to be brave and to bolster his little sister.

"Is that what the lady told you?"

"She said we're lucky we have tapes of Mom and Dad."

"You are lucky," said Tim, hardly convinced. Grasping, as they were, at straws.

"Her dad died when she was little," Billy explained. "And it was so long ago they didn't have tapes."

"I don't want tapes, Unk, I want Mommy and Daddy."

"I know, sweetheart"—rocking her—"I know." (*More*, Goldsmith, we'll need more than that.)

"Uncle Tim?"

"What is it, Bill?" The boy looked so composed and manly now that the Marine Corps would have taken him on his twelfth birthday. So composed that Tim's swallow went through on the strength of it.

"Camp is good by me."

"Keokuk, you mean?"

"Yeah."

"What about the all-star game?"

Billy shrugged it off.

"Cindy?"

"I want Mommy. And that's not my name. My name is Cynthia."

"Did you like the camp last summer?"

"Don't remember," she said, then started flipping her head back and forth sideways like a rag doll mishandled.

"She liked it a lot," said Billy. "You did, Simp. You remember Tess. And Katy McSweeney?"

"I want to eat the cake now," she said. She was whining softly, but her grief sounded a shade less present.

"Cake?"

Tim, of course, was inclined to stand on the proper sequence: the sandwiches, the carrots, and *then* the cake—with milk. But this was idiotic, not "right" but wrong. Let them eat cake. What the hell, let them eat five hundred doughnuts or a thousand hot-pink Hostess Sno-Balls. Their parents just died, for God's sake, and they are trying to live through it.

"We'll eat the cake, but listen to my idea. This would be a new White Sneaker pact. Whenever we feel like crying, we cry. And then

45

right away we all jump in the water—to rinse the salt off our cheeks."

"And the pepper!" Cindy exclaimed, suddenly light as a balloon. Floating to her feet.

"So here we go!"

"Wait, Unk," said Billy. "Not till we cry."

"We are crying, you goofball. Come on."

A moment later, in water to his waist, Tim confided that this entire lake had been formed in 1616 from the tears of Chief Nubanusit at the time his pet snake Chester vanished. He wagered a nickel that Billy could not spell kayak backwards, then told them about palindromes: they proceeded from kayak to Bob to boob to Madam I'm Adam. And they laughed.

They simply could not help laughing with each dash into the rocky shallows; soon they were laughing before they ran. They would float awhile, splashing and joking until Cindy called for cake again or Billy craved his Gatorade. The cry-and-swim covenant, which they took very seriously, took literally, proved more than a bit useful. They got so much good exercise they would all sleep that night like the glacial erratics surrounding the shore.

And they had cleared some high hurdles. They had faced the subject of Jill and Monty, and they had decided the question of summer camp. Short-term, Tim was all set. He could be in P-Town on Wednesday.

The kids were still sleeping like boulders when Tim kept a telephone appointment with Olivia Goldsmith next morning, to vet the camp decision. "Either way seems wrong to me," he confessed.

"Exactly. So it's also right either way. And since they said yes, go with yes—even if they backtrack into doubt, or one of them does."

"Go with the choice they made, you're saying."

"Yes, but speak with the camp directors, speak frequently with their counsellors, be sure they have access—"

"Slow down, I'm writing."

"No need for that, this is still just common sense. Be sure they have access to one another and access to you. Call, and go to them on the weekend. Be prepared to go sooner, if necessary."

"Got it."

"And, Mr. Bannon, don't neglect yourself in this. You might do well to see someone for a while."

Tim's therapy, so far as he was concerned, was already in place: he had ten days in Provincetown. But he was exhausted when he got there, from all that had gone on and then two days of mostly driving. And though he sat with Karl on a deck overlooking the green waves of Cape Cod Bay, Tim found that Camp Keokuk was still squarely in his sights. On his mind. He had been here only 48 hours and already the future had invaded P-Town.

Not September. That he could keep at arm's length. But tomorrow? Even for Tim, tomorrow was in sight.

"Are you really going up there, Timmy? To Camp Cockatoo?"

"Keokuk. Yes. I have to."

"But on a Saturday? With the *rental*?"

"It can't be helped, Karl. Goldsmith has spoken."

"God has spoken, you mean."

"That's exactly what I'm afraid of, that I'm finally being punished."

"For indiscretions at the bath! Sinners in the hands of an angry homophobic God! But then why just you?"

Once again this year they had taken an obscenely lavish house fifty yards from the water. It was not this ballroom-sized cedar deck or the $400 Möen faucets that compelled Tim and his friends to spring for the steep fortnight, it was—what else?—location. Of course you could pay almost as much for a shanty. P-Town in July was not an economy, but it was a necessity. It was life's reward, at any cost.

Though Tim was not quite so sure about that anymore. Even last July, when he was nobody's *parentis*, he had experienced a new weariness with the whole scene. This might have been sour grapes, for the cast of characters was younger every year—or Tim and his friends were older and being eased out to their own self-contained pasture. As he danced with a handsome young doctor from Providence, it was clear to Tim that the guy barely registered his presence, that he was going through the motions impatiently.

Newly invisible, *devalued*, Tim's impulse was to flee. It had always been a sin to be fat, or dull, or dirty; now it was a sin to be over thirty. Better to be back at the house reading his Dawn

Powell novel—though he had kept this to himself at the time. Imagine it, he confessed to Karl exactly one year later: rather be reading!

"This too shall pass," Karl told him. "We aren't immune to the infamous mid-life crisis, you know."

"We the gay?"

"Yes. And there's nothing wrong with reading, or with sitting here watching this expensive surf, either."

Karl Trickett was the nicest man Tim had ever known. He was the only one who would fetch you from the airport at rush hour. Who would feed your fish. Everyone took advantage of him; it was impossible not to. Even his mother did, saving up crossword puzzles for their Wednesday nights, though she knew he was bored silly by them.

Which made it hard to disagree with Karl—for everyone except Tim. Argument, or a steady stream of lightweight contention between them, served to connect the two men. "Karl, this is serious, I am losing interest in sex."

"Good. Maybe there's hope for us yet."

"Let's not."

"When sex is everything, there's nothing *after* sex. Except *tristesse.*"

"Great. That's the consolation?"

"Well no, there's also friendship. I'm being serious now."

"Oh so am I."

"We'll all help out. That's what I mean. We'll be Tim Bannon's Queer Army of the Republic. Those two children will be raised by a virtual kibbutz."

"A cabal, more like."

"A queer kibbutz. Eight gay men and a baby."

"I just wonder where the other seven gay men will be on parade days, when I need *coverage*."

Leave P-Town on the first Saturday of the rental? Unthinkable, to be sure. Yet Tim had no choice, he was going and so—in a way—he was already gone.

Suddenly Tim shot to his feet, a powerful reflex. It was as though a wasp had stung him, or his chair was burning. "Let's get out of here," he snapped.

"What? What did I say?"

"Nothing, Karl. I just need to get moving is all. I need to walk, right now."

"What hit you, though?" said Karl, hurrying to catch up. "Tell me." But Tim said nothing more as they walked up the lane to Commercial Street. Every now and then he would sigh, and Karl was convinced he had no idea he was sighing.

Karl steered them down the strip (mackerel-crowded with young men binging, blithely sailing their summer days) to the relative quiet of the Zephyr courtyard and ordered a half-carafe of chilled Chardonnay.

"Wine, Karl? Isn't it more like tea time?"

"They have tea, if that's what you want," said Karl, then took a long draught of wine, as though it were cold water answering a desperate desert thirst. It had not been an easy two days. In truth, it had been hopeless: Tim was often a shade outside the mix, but now he was really in the gloaming. "He's no fun," said Jack Sauer bluntly, and both Jack and Arthur (their housemates here) had abdicated. Karl persisted. Not that he disagreed with the assessment; he persisted in the face of it.

So he was refilling his glass while Tim's sat untouched. Faces glided by, and bodies: tan limbs in muscle shirts and short shorts. Pale blue was this year's color. Then someone was veering toward them and they saw it was Eric, Tim's blind date on the night Jill died. Eric grasped the back of an empty chair and loomed over the table without speaking or smiling.

Tim found he was not particularly pleased to see Eric—he recalled that silent smirk—yet he was never comfortable with a social silence and so began jabbering nonsense. "I've been true to you, Eric, since that night."

"Oh really. McTrickett here told me you were a fickle boy."

"Compared to him I am. Compared to you I doubt it."

"Comparisons are invidious," said Karl.

"Hey, I was faithful too, until the next day when I had no choice. I was cruised by a homeless disabled Hispanic trans-gender and I couldn't afford to get sued for discrimination."

"Clearly unavoidable," said Karl. "But don't take Tim for granted."

"Hey, I don't take my next breath for granted," said this newly loquacious version of Eric. Tim was cringing at Karl's earnest intervention. One just never copped to jealousy. Envy could be fun; envy could be spoken. But jealousy only served to complicate matters.

Meanwhile, a fresh half-carafe arrived, along with a third glass, as a shadow made its way down the courtyard. Behind Eric's chinese-red headband, on a high wooden fence, Tim saw where the shadow stopped—saw the precise boundary of the sunlight's cast, highlighting every waver in the row of nails.

"Are you in town alone?" said Karl.

"I came alone. Trusting to fate."

"Never do that," said Tim, refocusing, "or you might find yourself the father of twins tomorrow."

Eric did not get the joke, of course, and at first he looked puzzled; then irritated; finally amused. His smile, heretofore withheld, revealed a chipped front tooth.

"Hey, or triplets," he said, tossing down his wine with a flourish. He still did not get the joke, but he was ready to move on to greener pastures. "Nice to see you girls," he said, and leaned back to give them the James Dean wave.

"Disappointed?" said Karl, when they were alone again.

"Hardly. We can do better than that, if we just—"

"Trust to fate?"

"Keep drinking, I was going to say."

This they did willy-nilly as the sun, whose warmth remained, gave way entirely to shadow. Eventually they were joined by Arthur Justus and by the Peters, Peter Weissberg and Peter Clippinger, with a fine young thing named Leonard in tow.

Tim rallied. The game was not fate, it was more like musical chairs. You had a feeling each time the music started up, a feeling Tim did not get with Eric but did now with Leonard. He and Karl exchanged a glance at this parody of physical perfection: the lank sandy hair, the rich tan, the white bather's leotard, and a faint accent, possibly German?

The glance meant other things as well. There was their shared silent chuckle at how the Peters, who were famously monogamous, liked to shepherd a third wheel, perhaps a wild card for inspiration. And there was the question of fishing rights. For Tim, on the verge of his departure for Vermont, this was a simple equation with an elegant proof: he would get his shot at Leonard tonight, as Karl could take his shot tomorrow.

So there were six of them and soon enough eight, as tables were slid together and afternoon wine segued into supper. Leonard turned out to be Lennart, Swedish not German, and with the speed of light (or wine) Tim was right there with him in Malmo and Trelleborg. Also (Bingo!) on Bornholm Isle, where the lad's dad owned a summer place not far from the cottage colony Tim sometimes booked for clients, even if he had never experienced personally the Bornholm Isle Blues.

"You *slut*," Karl whispered. "And I paid for the wine."

It went well for a while. Then, whether due to age or nationality (or such intangibles as the fact that Lennart was a degree candidate in Hairstyling), Tim and the Swede did not quite mesh. "We are against the promiscuity," Lennart finally confided, at a point in the evening when only the promiscuity held any promise.

"We?"

"My friends. Our little circle at home, you know."

Win some, lose some—as ever. But that chaste goodnight kiss jostled Tim's sleep and colored his waking disposition. Plus it was raining. You could not see the bay a plane-length away. As he made coffee for the still-sleeping household, as he shaved and dressed and hit Route 6 in the foredawn, though, Tim found he was glad to be leaving P-Town. Glad, at any rate, to be zipping away so briskly, motoring alone (on Route 6 in July!), for there was no question he had been spoiled by the Monadnocks.

Driving relaxed him, or this kind of driving did, and he could use the time to get some serious worrying done. There was his mother, for starters. Tim had labored so hard to keep Anne calm and now he was troubled by his success, by the extent to which she *was* calm. She had been concentrating fiercely on the trivial: the ceremony, the burial, the invitations. She fretted about having the right dress. Was this calm, or was it the quiet leading edge of hysteria?

Tim hesitated to trust his ears, of course, allowing that he could *sound* calm too. Probably it was like a moment at war when abruptly your trenchmate's head flew off. Deeply you cared, deeply you were shocked, yet you had to press on before your own head flew off.

He did not worry long about work,or money, because such superficial concerns gave way to more powerful (if unwelcome) anxieties about his health. Tim never *planned* to worry about AIDS (nor was it on the syllabus for today) yet he was always apt to interpret every shift in his pulse as the beginning of the end.

Were his kidneys failing, or was it only back pain from sitting cramped under the steering wheel? He kept no thermometer in the house for fear he might give in some night—sweat was never far from his temples—and take his own temperature. So he had never had a fever in much the same way he was not HIV Positive: there was no documentation of either condition.

He managed to push past to his primary concern, the kids. They needed him, didn't they? He was obliged to go to Vermont, wasn't he? He *was* going to Vermont, leaving P-Town on a Saturday, and yet again last night they both told him not to bother coming. "We're fine, Unk," Billy assured him. "It's way too far to come."

But Goldsmith has spoken, Tim wished to protest, to explain. Might Goldsmith have reconsidered and spoken otherwise had she heard them, or known how far it was? Had she taken into account the obscene cost of the Provincetown house?

Surely she would have reconsidered had she seen them in the flesh. Tim found them both so browned and so sound that he was torn between his delight and his resentment that he really might have wasted his time. Lifting Cindy, weighing her covertly, he did detect a rib or two. The lunch they enjoyed at Badger Hall told the story there, a feast of limp sprouts, soyburgers, and for dessert apples with the taste entirely removed. Surely as many of these delicacies went back to the kitchen intact as had left it a few minutes earlier. Did no one notice?

It was as close as he came to a sense of purpose all day, obtaining permission to take them for a ride, locating a lunchroom in the village that had hamburgers, malteds, and pie, then filling their secret larder with miniature peppermint patties. At least they could not literally starve.

But then he left, just as the Saturday night bonfire began to roar. "You eat my s'mores," he said, kissing them. "I'll call tomorrow night."

It was for the best—surely Goldsmith would support him in his decision, so grounded in common sense. They were tricky to connect with. Something about the bondings (or bondage) of summer camp life in that. Tim was an interruption. The kids were almost sorry to see him, not so sorry to see him leave.

He did not take this personally. They had turned a page, made new friends (and what could be better than that right now?) and

52

Tim's very presence was a grim reminder. Out on stilly pine-ringed Keokuk Pond or sitting around the bonfire watching skits, they were no more orphaned than anyone else. Their condition was hidden, even from themselves, for in this far northern context, in the urgent false family of the group, all summer campers were orphans.

Riding south on 89, Tim felt he had made progress somehow, or gained some relief. He anticipated with disproportionate joy the simple fact that he would sleep tonight in his own bed, completely alone and under the radar. His precise whereabouts unknown to all, he could stop by the office tomorrow, Sunday, without reporting to a soul. Could simply touch base.

Such were the joys afforded him at the moment and, strangely, he was pleased by the prospect. He was alive. It came down to that, remembering that he was alive—and moreover, symptom-free. Tired, yes, downright slaphappy with fatigue after driving nine hours since breakfast, but that was it. That was Tim's final worry of the day: staying awake for another ten miles.

The morning air was cool and pleasant as Tim walked the deserted corridor to Copley Square. He took a muffin and a jumbo Colombian coffee upstairs, opened the windows, and settled into his chair. Touching the button, he unleashed a flood of recorded messages. To work was a gift for once, a freeing instead of the opposite, and he got going in earnest. Chasing information, updating itineraries, Tim was enjoying himself; it was as though he still had a job. Still existed.

As an offer of proof, and of celebration, he got himself onto a dozen answering machines around Greater Boston and two in Salem, New Hampshire. By nine o'clock he had even spoken with a live client, the good gray Eli Pinckney III of Chestnut Street.

Dr. Pinckney was a longtime customer, a man so delightfully helpless he could not arrange his own taxicab to Logan Airport. Tim always joked he should accompany the Pinckneys abroad so as to handle problems as they arose, but this time he almost wished he could do it. Could wriggle out of his own shadow and be off to the Golden Cities of the Baltic, to Lubeck and Riga and the rest. A silly package tour, yet there they were, those ancient northern European seaports, so many hinges of history.

So many new verses he could add to the Blues of Tim Bannon.

For Tim was not at all jaded. He still thrilled to the names of exotic places and despite his past disasters still yearned to disembark anew. Sure it was a shame he had been mugged in Budapest and yet he recalled the night with considerable nostalgia: a sweet sunset cruise on the Danube, the blue houseboat where he drank pastis with a handsome Hungarian motorman....

Abruptly, Tim's reverie gave way to the ratcheting of the doorlatch, and to a familiar aimless whistling. Gone in a flash were the Golden Cities, gone his privacy, his haven. He gazed up at the perfect tan, the inhumanly white teeth and brilliant black hair of his partner Charles Tashian.

"You can't be here to work on a Sunday," was all he could think to say. It struck him that they had not spoken a word since Jill.

"To work? Not strictly, no. I'm meeting a friend. How are you, Tim? I hope you got my card?"

"I did, Charlie. Thank you, it was a lovely card."

"I know how much you loved the poor girl."

Charles consulted his watch, which Tim took as a signal. Half an hour? The time line was unclear, but the need for Tim to vacate the premises would not have been clearer with a neon sign. Why the office, though? Tim felt a small dose of perversity leak into his soul; he might force Charles to beg.

"Everyone who knew Jilly loved her," he said.

"Lynda volunteers to help, by the way. She would be happy to babysit the children."

"That's very nice of her."

"Actually, I'm hoping it will snap her out of it. The panic to breed, that is. Give her a shot of reality, so to speak."

"She wants to have a baby?"

"Now that's putting a fine finger on it. Gosh, we only spend half our life fighting about it. *Discussing* it, I should say."

"You don't want kids at all, Charlie?"

"I don't seem to. This idea that there comes a moment when *you* stop having fun and breed children so *they* can have the fun instead? It's unsettling to me."

"Poor cindycrawford. How old is she now?"

"Now, thirty-four. In October, thirty-*five*...."

The end of the line, clearly. Tim wondered how Charles could be reprehensible and likable at the same time. (No doubt cindycrawford wondered too.) Charles pushed his act just far enough to keep it entertaining, a neat self-parody, like those appealingly reptilian movie villains he resembled—Laurence Harvey came to mind, the white teeth more *bared* than shown.

"You should end it, Charlie. Seriously, for her sake, you should cancel the engagement."

"Seriously, I am stuck. Because it is a misery to end it and a misery to continue. You see the problem."

Tim never really doubted he would cede Charles the office. He was consoled that he still had possession of the day. He would regain and then guard this fragment of time, this opportunity, even if he did nothing more with it than walk the streets clearing his head, clearing the way for a solution. At a café, at a cross light, the eureka moment would come.

It did not come at Tower Records, where CD's had crowded out cassettes just as cassettes had once crowded out vinyl. It did not come at the Avenue Victor Hugo Bookshop, where he loved to browse the musty cluttered aisles and where they persisted in treating him not as the man who had come in sixty times and bought a hundred books but as a thief, about to strike. He did not even expect it to come in the Chinese restaurant across from the B.P.L., where he was certain the potstickers were a mistake before he finished eating them.

He stayed vacant mentally—abstracted, as he continued wandering, awaiting the lightning bolt. On Trinity Church Plaza, he maneuvered through a clump of twitching pigeons (bread crumbs on the bricks), then struggled to navigate past a man eating a hot dog. The man danced with him one step left, one step right—blocking his pathway. But the hot dog turned out to be a microphone, the dancer a TV reporter. Tim was the man in the street!

Or the gay man in the street, because the fellow sought his views on a rash of gay-bashing incidents around Copley. Why here? Why now? (Exactly, thought Tim, his plenum pierced again.) Was our fair city changing for the worse? Was AIDS to blame?

Well, Tim had no idea. Out of the loop, he had been unaware of such incidents. "Just chance, probably," he managed to offer up. "There are bad guys everywhere. There are still Nazis in Germany, you know."

"Keep talking, keep talking," said the reporter, eyes on fire as though he had struck the mother lode.

"Am I quoteworthy?" said Tim, mildly disgusted and sorry he had read the article about the Nazis. "Am I telegenic?" he drawled. But the man motioned him on, whipping the air between them like cream until Tim did continue. "Hey, there are Nazis everywhere. Neo-Nazis. I'm sure there are a few in Boston."

"So in your opinion, this is the work of Neo-Nazis—not the response of Joe Average to this terrible disease?"

"Joe Average may not understand or appreciate gay life," Tim waxed, "but he doesn't go around *attacking* people."

With this, the reporter relented so abruptly and completely he might have been punctured, the air let out of him. From manic to *gone*, in a tick. Tim was slightly stricken, desperately sorry he had said a single word and least of all on the subject of gay bashing. The guy must have seen him coming.

Nearing home, he told himself it could not matter, they would find no use for it, he was anything *but* telegenic. But his haven of mercy had crumbled around him even before he picked up the phone and heard a change in his mother's voice. "I want you here this week," she ordered. "I want you here tomorrow, Tim."

"As soon as camp is over—"

"Come without the children. Just you get on down here."

"What is it, Mom? Are you okay?"

"It's time to bring Jilly home. Let's leave it at that."

He could tell Anne was holding the receiver away to conceal tears of fury. Her voice was hoarse, and breaking word by word.

"What about Ric? What about waiting for Ric to call?"

"She did call, Tim. She will be here tonight. And she is extremely upset."

"Of course she is, Mom. Ric is *human*."

"That is not what I meant, Tim Bannon. Erica is upset about *you*."

III

UNLOVED BY TURTLES

The plane dipped low and skimmed over a plain of red clay unrelieved by houses or even trees. It might have been a strange new planet, but it was Charlotte, North Carolina. The red clay gave way to a cordon of high southern pines and the broad tarmac of the landing field.

Every time he came through here, the city distanced itself further from the Charlotte of Tim's youth. The so-called "New South" was old by now; here was the *new* New South. When he tagged along with Rex on business trips, silent Saturday bonding missions, Charlotte had just begun spilling onto the fringes of the countryside—onto skinny highways with chicken shacks and produce stands. Now it sprawled for sprawl's sake, cloverleafing aimlessly from one superhighway to another, looking no more southern than Bridgeport, Connecticut.

But this was a tired grudge (alterations of his childhood setting, the loss of a whole region's past) and in truth his spirits still rose, especially as he neared the state line, where less had changed. One farm in particular was intact, its hilly fields and rambling barns still straddling the border, begging the absurdity of borders everywhere. Here Rex would always speak, and it was always the same sentence, how this one hog farmer could stand and eat a slice of melon with one foot taxed by North Carolina and the other foot taxed by South.

A week's worth of conversation from Rex.

At the diner in Harlowe, where Tim ate some bacon and eggs done up in the wickedest grease, he still heard the local inflections.

"River's as clear as water in your well, Sam. Usually looks like blood by now, but the clay ain't washin' down."

"It won't, either," said Sam, delivering a jet of tobacco juice onto his saucer. "Not till we get us some rain."

Above them, two tilting shelves held canned goods that might have posed unsold for ten years—or twenty. There was a sunfaded calendar advertising John Deere tractors and a blue xeroxed flyer for the Bingo, Saturday night at the First Baptist in Mead City.

Rex Bannon brought his wife Anne from Charlotte to Berline in 1947, freshly wed and ambitious of nothing more than a decent life. Because of the War and a postgraduate course in engineering, Rex was past thirty. It was his first real job, managing the limestone quarries in Ramey, and it would turn out to be his last. If they respected him, and paid him fairly, Rex would justify their trust with forty years of service.

Rex's was a life that haunted Tim, though not for the obvious reason. They were friendly to the end. (Not close; Rex was not close to anyone.) But his father was a reserved man who preferred work to play. He was comfortable with work. Even at home, Rex was always working on something and these projects provided a stage for their relationship. Around tools, and plans, Rex could communicate.

The haunting went deeper. It was systemic, and insoluble. Lodged in the marrow of Tim Bannon's bones was Rex's sense of what a life was made of, and Tim could neither live that way, nor unload the weight of failing to do so. You did good work, raised a family in the church, paid your taxes, and never complained. Certainly you were heterosexual. The word, not to mention its antonym, did not enter the lexicon.

Tim was not ashamed, or particularly embarrassed. He felt blameless, and free to be who he was, however inconvenient—and he saw it was far more convenient than being black. The crime of Driving While Gay was easily concealed. But he did shield his parents from it, and therefore shielded himself from a disharmony with his father so dramatic as to be unthinkable. Twice he had brought Ellie to Berline; never once had he encouraged his parents to visit him up North, or to meet his friends. He had lived with Karl Trickett for three years, on two coasts, and neither Rex nor Anne had ever heard Karl's name spoken.

He was doomed to failure, or to a sort of incompleteness: he would never inhabit his father's legacy, never reach that core of comfort, and it was in Berline that Tim experienced this failure most vividly. Here, where he had not only failed to become his father, but had failed to become himself. Where no one, not even his mother, really knew him.

First thing he saw was the Chinook, Earl's hulking RV, which stood higher than the green shingled garage roof. Parked alongside it, Tim's rented Geo looked like a bite of provender for the whale-on-wheels, a bit of fish food colored with rental-car-blue No. 6.

60

Then he saw Anne rising from her rocker. She looked thin, but pretty in her loose cotton housedress. Only the wisps of hair at her temples were gray, and he stroked these back as he hugged her.

"Stop burping me," were Anne's first words, and Tim realized he had been patting her back rhythmically. He squeezed and held her, unsure if the tremors were tears or laughter.

"Are they hiding inside that thing?" he asked, releasing her.

"Your sister? No, they took the car. There was no point undertaking a simple errand in that monster."

Tim, who had flown and driven since early morning, had no desire to sit down anytime soon, but Anne made him sit with her in the loveseat. Shoulders touching, faces forward, they swung gently.

"Your sister told me," said Anne, striving for quiet. For a softness. She had rehearsed a lot of this conversation, hoping to guide both of them safely through it. But of course she could not have rehearsed it all.

An alarm sounded in Tim. Which sister? Told her what?

"About you, Timmy."

Now the alarm was bonging like Quasimodo in the belltower. Tim's scalp was alive; he could feel the blood moving.

"I wasn't shocked. I'm pretty sure Jilly told me a while back—or tried to. Left me hints that I chose to overlook. But I couldn't say I was shocked."

"Only horrified?"

Tim was astonished at this, astonished to have batted the ball right back to her, eschewing reflexive false denials. He was kidding around with her about a secret that had lain between them for decades.

"Troubled," said Anne. "And disappointed, in the way you can be disappointed when you turn out to be right about something. Do you know what I mean, honey?"

"I'm not sure, Mom," he said, accepting her hand.

"Well, say you expected it might rain. And the weathergirl tells you rain. But then it really does rain. Like that."

"So Ric told you."

"She had to."

"Did she?"

"It was time. And I will say one thing." She turned to face him now, her eyes blurred with dampness. "It's the first time in all the years he's gone that I saw something benign in your daddy's passing. And God bless your friend Eleanor, too."

"I'm sorry, Mom."

"You didn't kill him."

"Sorry for making you more unhappy. At a time like this."

"Troubled, is what I said."

"You didn't need any more trouble," he said, though it occurred to him that Anne had put it right to work, this revelation of Erica's. Had used it to push Jill's death back toward the shadows.

"I'm not supposed to tell you this," said Anne, and she had rehearsed this too, "but they plan on taking Jilly's girl and boy from that summer camp."

Panic whacked at him like a stick, but Tim labored to stay calm. "And why will they do that exactly?"

"Well, you know."

"I don't. Earl wants to shoot them, maybe? To make sure they aren't corrupted?"

"They want to raise the children. Earl is very amenable."

"Is that right! *Amenable.*"

"That's my word, Timmy. It does make a whole lot of sense, is the point."

All the gongs were bombillating wildly now, as he strived to sort through courses of action. Slash Earl's tires (all fourteen of them) and call in the Law. Get hold of Moss, and Goldsmith, and Jellinghaus (hell, the Law was on his *side*) and get all necessary paperwork to Vermont in a hurry, into the gentle hands of Arn and Eliza Broom at good Camp Keokuk.

These impulses Tim did not express. You want to look calm here, he counselled himself. You want your calmest look of looking calm right out front right now. Sanity sanity, all is sanity.

"Sense?" he said, calmly sanely. "Mom," he said quietly quietly, "Earl is a Nazi."

"Oh stop that, Timmy," said Anne, with a sniff of laughter.

She did not, Tim feared, know Earl. Tim's own deferential silence (meant to sustain Anne's hope of Erica's marital joy) had backfired.

"I'm serious, Mom. It's the whole truth."

"It's ridiculous. And they'll be back here in a minute."

And she laughed again, in a manner that alerted him even

more keenly: her teaparty laugh. Maybe she did know Earl, knew the worst, and simply preferred him to her son the homosexual. She excused herself (to fix her hair!) and Tim was forced to let her go. Their talk was finished. He retreated to the backyard, to process it.

Or to forget it, if he could. On this, the dark side of the house, the bulkhead doors and all the trim boards were in bad need of paint. Up in the magnolia (though not so high up as he expected) he saw the remnants of his old treehouse floating, scraps of pitted cypress planks. He recalled building it with Rex; recalled his father "eye-balling" the spirit-level and announcing this platform would "last the distance."

Eisenhower was the president.

Beyond a grove of pines Rex had planted, in what had been the Stewarts' cotton patch, there were more new houses. Seven or eight, altogether. Grown over was their own patch of corn and the three-tree orchard where they would stand eating peaches right off the limb on hot summer days.

His own mother was set against him. She was okay with his being gay, she could handle that. No interest in it, though. No questions about it, after all the mysterious years. "God bless your friend Eleanor," Anne had said, and her gratitude was very specific. Ellie had come here, once over Christmas and once after Anne had her hip replacement. Tim and Ellie offered no definition of their relationship, yet were so comfortable together, so casually physical, that one was welcome to draw the wrong conclusion.

Or the right one, by Anne's lights, for such was her meaning. Ellie had allowed them, allowed Rex to believe in his son that way. Rex died confident they were lovers. That they chose not to marry he saw as an unfortunate modern fashion, which he could forgive as he forgave Ellie her Jewishness that Christmas Eve.

How stunned Rex was to learn it, no less so than had a large brown river rat stepped from one of the pretty silver boxes under the blinking tree. And Tim cringed. Whatever happened next would be his fault, for having prepared neither of them, his father the mild anti-Semite or his dear friend the secular Jew.

But Rex was brilliant. (His finest moment, in Tim's eyes.) If this girl was Jewish, then Jewish was just fine. Rex did not say it, of course; that would not have been brilliant. He simply absorbed the truth of it as instantaneously as a facial expression can change.

He was already wearing a warm smile, a genuine one, when he said:

"You don't even celebrate Christmas, then. It's—?"

"Chanukah," Ellie supplied. "Though actually, we do celebrate Christmas at our house, in a seasonal sort of way."

Pleasant remarks, disarming byplay—hardly Rex Bannon's calling cards. For Tim, it shone as a moment of greatness, and an occasion of love. Not that he excused anti-Semitism, ever, or was satisfied to see it merely concealed. It was more that he applauded the instinct, understood the effort. And believed in his father so much right then that he was certain the prejudice had been dismissed as abruptly as the face had changed.

He should believe in his mother, too; give her time and the benefit of the doubt. She was not as quick as Rex, but then she did not have as far to go. She would have to see that Earl was unfit. Indeed, Earl was on record. When he shot the last dog, he had put it into words: "If you did this to a kid, you'd probably catch hell for it these days."

This was Earl's brand of smartass charm, understood, but it also told a truth. Definitely, Tim should play it cool. Take a few steps back and let things sort themselves out in the coming days. That made the most sense; that should be the script. Anne would see that Earl was just bluffing.

It was surprising, though, how quickly he lapsed from cool. Cool might not be his thing. For now came the actual Earl Sanderson striding toward him, with inflections far less reminiscent of his native Schenectady than of some dark Arkansas hollow.

"That's all right, Timmy," he said. "That's all right now."

What was all right?

But Earl already had his hand and was busy destroying it. He would get you bone to bone, clamp you across the span where the fingers joined, and begin inflicting pain. Tim fought back the water in his eyes and worked free.

Then Erica. With her habit of trailing behind her husband, in a jumpsuit with vertical stripes, she looked like a prisoner of war. She offered Tim one of her phantom embraces (you saw it approach, never felt it land) and added a sketchy air kiss. Ric was only affectionate to him when their mother was present.

"God, Tim," she said, "how have you managed?"

"Fine. I've managed just fine," he said, and remembered that Ric had outed him.

"That's all right, Timmy," said Earl, precisely as he had said it before. (As though he had *not* said it before.) "That's all right now."

All Tim could think of was Elvis, the gorgeous early Elvis, doing "That's All Right, Mama." Did Earl expect him to sing along?

"Yeah, relax," said Erica. "I wasn't like accusing you. I was praising you. Okay?"

Tim must have missed something. He could recall neither the accusation nor the praise, only that they had outed him and planned to kidnap the children. He concentrated his energy on staying cool in the clear sight of Earl's pith helmet and rose-tinted shades. Then Anne put an end to the impasse.

"What was that dog's name," she said, apropos of nothing, non-sequitors being a privilege of seniority. "I have been trying to remember and I just can't."

"Our dog?" said Erica.

"No, honey, Jilly's dog. That puppy they had. Was she struck by a car? I simply can not remember a thing."

"Yes, Mom," said Tim. "His name was Gus, and he got run over."

It was too unlikely. Something fraudulent in it, as Anne verified with a question for Earl. "What was *your* dog called?" she said, still feigning quizzicality. "I've forgotten that too."

"Hemingway," said Earl.

"That's it. For the writer. Was he run over too?"

"No, Mom," said Erica. "We had to put him down."

"*Did* you now," said Tim. The words escaped him, involuntary leakage. Uncool.

"You know we did. Hemingway had a cancer."

"A cancer? That dog wasn't even full grown."

"Ninety-five pounds," stated Earl, with pride. "He was a good old boy, poor Hem. That dog would hunt."

"Do you know," said Anne, "Mary Simmons has a man giving radiation treatments to her setter. Imagine the expense. For a dog."

"Ventilation is so much cheaper," said Tim. "And think of the *closure* you get that way."

"What are you trying to say? Hemingway was sick. Dogs get

65

sick."

"I know they do, Ric. Yours do—right around the middle of June."

"Not Dreiser," said Earl. "Dreiser got into it with a black bear in Hancock. He was a tough old boy—just not so tough as a black bear."

"A tough old boy about eleven months old."

"Pretty sure he was two. Wasn't Dreiser two when we lost him, hon?"

"I do think it's cute the way you name them after writers," said Anne. This was insincere, yard-talk as she called it, but she was carefully sorting and weighing these canine deaths.

"One or two, Earl. I'm not sure," said Erica.

"Whatever. I never realized Timmy was such an animal lover."

"He did have a pet turtle in the sixth grade."

"No, honey, that was Jilly's turtle," said Anne.

"It was his, Mom. It just liked Jill better."

"Well!" said Tim, temporarily tickled loose of all discipline. "Unloved by turtles! How unworthy can a person be?"

"Timmy, Timmy," said Earl, smelling blood, doubling up on diminutive, ostentatiously draping an arm around Tim's shoulder. Absent the pre-emptive strike by which he would cripple Tim with a handshake, Earl never, ever, touched the tainted homosexualized flesh.

"Earl's right, honey," said Anne.

"He is? What did he say that was right?"

"Come on, little brother, let us set all this cattiness aside. What we want to do is get Mom out of the house tonight, some-place nice for dinner."

"Thank you, Earl, that is thoughtful. But I'm not that hungry, and I was planning to fix some chicken for you all."

"It's not about hunger, Mom," said Earl, pulling Anne to him.

If Tim had a loaded gun and a clear shot, he might have put Earl down where he stood. Earl was goading him, and this "Mom" stuff was new and creepy. When had he ever called her that?

"What about some barbecue?" said Erica.

"Fellows!" said Anne, her appetite restored by the aromatic suggestion of Fellows' pulled pork. But she still didn't want to go out with the lot of them, squabbling as they were.

"Fellows is gone, Mom," said Erica. "That place has been closed for five years."

"Has it? What a shame. Tells you how often I get out since your daddy left me."

"No problemo," said Earl. "We'll find someplace that isn't closed. Won't we, Timmy?"

Earl was a full-fledged son of the South by now, with a big guffaw right out of The Beverly Hillbillies. He liked to stand close to you, emphasizing his height and making you step back. But Tim held his ground, absorbed the sour gust, and smiled. Even managed to pound Earl's arm and return fire: "No problemo." He was regaining his cool.

Sort of. Upstairs a moment later, he marvelled that he had been in Berline an hour. It felt like weeks.

He missed the Hergies; he craved a scoop of pistachio ice cream from Trumball's. He thought of Karl and the others, known and unknown, and yearned to hike out onto the nudie dunes in Truro.

An inadvertent glance in the bathroom mirror confirmed that he had lost another thirty hairs since morning; he was headed for the full Yul Brynner. Vanity was attacking—and then he heard his mother. Her bedroom was a thin partition away, and she was in there sobbing. Dying of sadness a few inches from him, while he fretted over hair loss. He was vain, selfish, and uncool to the max.

But there was nothing he could do. He could not rush in and comfort her, for she had chosen against such comfort. She was on her bed; he could hear the scrunch of the springs as her body convulsed with emotion. On her bed, the door closed. Anne had chosen pride, dignity—and privacy. Tim stopped in the hallway.

The crying stopped too. Ann must have heard him. Tim imagined her wildly dissembling, preparing to act as though her emotions were under control. Which they were, he supposed: under control. She probably spent hours like that every day—sobbing, letting go—before she composed herself (for telephone calls, for visits from her friends) and then went back to grieving in private.

Of course. She had done it exactly that way when Rex died.

*

Berline Package was now Berline Convenience, and the filling station, which had changed from Gulf to Exxon, had changed again, to No-Name Gas. The rest was as he had left it. Dusty sunlight bathed the crossroads; behind the propane tanks, the small scummy pond was humming with mosquitoes.

Tim bought a pound of bread and a pound of butter, as per Anne's instructions. Back at the house, he found her reinstalled in her rocker, hair pinned up, ready to step out. Her eyes were clear and lively. This was at least partly a pose, yet Anne was so good at it she convinced him: something had snapped her into shape. Not versus an hour ago, or a week, but versus the last six years. To hear that her daughter was gone, her grandchildren orphaned (and her son a queer!) had not finished her off. It almost seemed to nourish her.

"Life can be strange. Can't it, Mom?"

"It helps if you keep an open mind. You see how wrong you were about that man."

"That man? Why? Because he isn't wearing his storm trooper boots to dinner? I said he was a Nazi, Ma, not a fool."

"Timmy, I do not understand you. But what a thing to say, of course I don't."

Anne was clinging to good intentions, and her love for Tim had already survived the shock. Yet there was a breach between them that felt solid, a barrier of cold stone she was not eager to touch.

"They don't change back, do they?" she said.

"They?"

"You know. Men who—"

"Queers?"

"Well I don't know the best word, Timmy, but yes. They don't ever tend to reconsider?"

It was impossible for Tim to reconcile the image of his mother wracked by violent tears with this inquisitive, matter-of-fact woman rocking on her porch.

"You mean if they should happen to meet the right gal?"

"You tell me. I don't know, apart from Oprah Winfrey."

"What does Oprah say?"

"Do not make sport of me, Tim Bannon."

"Can I hug you, then?"

"Oh stop."

When they emerged from the hug, Anne pushed and patted her

hair, then did the same to his. "You have gotten almost thin on top," she said.

"Like Daddy."

"Like my daddy, actually. It comes down on the mother's side. And I believe it skips a generation."

"It's not important," said Tim—oddly, he realized, since to him (however insanely) it was of the utmost import. How very peculiar was the human brain.

"Ric appreciates your help, you know. She did try to say that to you."

"My help? I am not helping Erica. Erica has been in Kalamazoo and I am the legally designated guardian of Jill's children. I'm doing what Jill wanted done. Can we keep that part in mind?"

"Legal as in official?"

"Official as in legal, yeah."

"But why you, honey?"

"Best man for the job?"

She had made it possible to talk, to joke; possible for Tim to be himself. He took her hand, mentioned that as recently as the day before yesterday she had actually thought quite highly of him.

"Well sure, honey. But as a single man? And now.... Plus, of course, living in the city?"

"Jill knew all that. Monty knew that."

"Did they? Still, you could know better. Erica is just ten minutes from Jill. I know they both shopped at that same A & P. And they are a family."

"Erica and Earl are a family?"

"Well, with the children they would be. Yes."

"With three heads I'd be a three-headed man, for God's sake."

Anne was laughing as Earl stepped out of the Chinook. The pith helmet was gone, the thick brown hair was brushed up in a wave. In his maroon sport coat and mauve shirt, he looked ready to make the sale. "Don't you look gorgeous!" he said to Anne.

This was a fine thing to say. The right thing, Tim struggled to persuade himself, as Ric followed a few paces behind Earl, moving into the family portrait right on cue.

"Don't *you* look gorgeous," Anne said to her, relieved to have a way to deflect the compliment. Anne disliked compliments, always had, even when they were sincere.

Erica had knobbed her blond hair on top of her head and wore blue earrings and a blue cotton blouse. She really was a pretty woman, thought Tim—though hopefully that was not the issue.

"She does," said Earl, still pushing the repartée. "The girl can't help it. She got it from her mama."

Rolling his eyes, Tim prayed that none of this was real.

It was midnight, with everyone safely consigned to their bunks, when Tim walked back to the village. The darkness intensified the scent of earth and verdure; he could say he was home with his eyes shut. Could specify the season.

"Ellie, you're home," he said. The pay phone was in the same place, though it hung out in the open air now, on a metal post.

"Of course I'm home. I'm in bed, Tim."

"I thought you might be out gallivanting with that heterosexual."

"No such luck. How's your mom doing?"

"Better than I would have guessed—but not really. The big news is that Ric and Earl say they want the kids. No: they say they are *taking* the kids. And Mom thinks it's a good idea. They told her about me."

"They *outed* you?"

"That's why she's on their side."

"Oh my God. What did she say?"

"Not much. It's as weird as can be, really, but the second I was gay, Earl became Jimmy Stewart or something. Suddenly he's this stand-up guy, so good in a crisis."

"But legally...."

"Right, that's what I said. So Mom clucks—you know how she clucks—and says, You and Earl will talk tomorrow. I said, Why Earl? Ric can talk. Ric is Jill's sister."

"And?"

"She clucked again."

"Meaning?"

"Meaning Earl and I are the menfolk, I guess. That's a southern thing, partly. Plus she knows Earl is a bulldog, whereas Ric is—I don't know, *not* a bulldog."

"What are you going to say, Tim?"

"That's why I called. So you can tell me what to say."

"Funny."

"No. I'm perfectly serious."

"Well, you know what you want to happen."

"I know what I don't want to happen. Those two have never said one word to me about who I am. Just their dumb shitty disapproval. Monty and I would talk, Jill and I talked all the time. They wanted to know me. They did know me."

"Isn't all that completely beside the point?"

"Those two probably ran and washed their hands in lye as soon as I left the room. And now they all but feel my pain."

"Tim, it's just not relevant. What matters is what you want for Billy and Cindy. You haven't changed your mind?"

"Oh yeah, like I have a mind. But no, I told you, this is not a solution."

"What if the kids wanted it? Hypothetically. Would that change anything?"

"Chose them? As in, Check either Box A or Box B?"

"Yes. If you asked them directly."

"Maybe they aren't equipped to make that choice. It was the right advice for camp, Ell, but what do they know about storm troopers?"

"That's extreme, surely. But those kids might surprise you. You could trust them enough to ask."

"That's your advice?"

"It would help you get past Earl tomorrow. Which helps your Mom, by keeping the peace."

"Except that Earl plans to just grab them."

"Tell him he can't. Tell him they are expecting you to come get them and how terrible it would be to upset their expectations."

"Ell, you don't know this guy. You have no idea how small an impression that suggestion will make on him."

"All right, then tell him it will constitute kidnapping if he does it, and he will go directly to jail."

"Not pass Go, not collect two hundred dollars! Now that might do it. I'm so glad you were home."

"Remember me? I'm always home."

"Not for long. This new guy...What was his name again?"

"His name was, and is, Victor."

"*Victor*. Wow. There it is: the victor. The winner."

"God, I'm so sorry I told you. It was stupid of me."

"Victor's the one, I can feel it. Haven't I always said what a fine heterosexual Victor is?"

"And he says the same of you, Timmy. Good luck tomorrow."

*

Erica and Earl were sequestered in the Chinook (lovebirds, Anne offered; co-conspirators, Tim rebutted) when they went to breakfast. Slim as a girl, famously "a slip of a thing," Anne did love breakfast out, second only to barbecue. She and Tim had made a tradition of it, after Rex died, of going each time he was home.

For today, he made a rule. To avoid tricky issues, they would play a game, discussing only what they could see. And they would both wear their Gamecocks feedcaps. Down here, folks would smile on a child molester, so long as he wore his Gamecocks cap to breakfast.

"See, Mom?" he said, feeling comfortable with her, feeling she might have regained her comfort with him, as they sat in the Mullins Diner. "I'm just me."

"I know you are, honey."

"It's just sex," he said, amazed at the liberation of speech. In a way the stakes were raised on this long-deferred conversation, in another way the truth had set him free.

"Don't break your own rule now."

"I mean, sex doesn't exist in this family anyway. You never said one word to me about sex."

"Nor will I."

"I don't mean you and Daddy. I mean the birds and the bees. So why should it even be a topic?"

"It shouldn't. And it isn't."

"I just wish you could see it."

"That you are otherwise a nice healthy young man?" Anne leaned toward him and whispered, "Are you? Healthy?"

"I'm fine," he said, and this might be true. Tim wondered if his mother, educated on the epidemic by Oprah Winfrey, would ever in her life pronounce the word gay, or AIDS. "So now let's just sit and move our jaws over the food, like true sons and daughters of the South."

"I didn't start," she reminded him. Nor did she want him to elaborate. Say he was virus-free and she would, as he expected, be happily finished with the discussion forever.

72

Had he said that? Should he? Anne would turn seventy-five late this year and a lie (if it was a lie) might well outlast her. There could be one less tragedy in her life, and, this week in particular, that carried a lot of weight.

"Really, Mom," he reiterated. "I'm fine." And left it at that.

In the car heading back, Anne reached over to turn off the radio. Nothing to say, as it happened, she just wanted it quiet. Tim steered to the roadbed at a rusted, lowslung bridge that took the Seabird rail line over a narrow bend of Little Lynches River. It was more of a creek here, eight feet wide and shallow. Clear water slipped over the sandy bottom like a thick belt of glass.

"Daddy and I always stopped here," he said. "Coming back from the sites."

"I'm sure you did."

"You are?"

"Yes, I am. And I know what you want to tell me."

"You do?"

"Yes I do," she grinned. "So *don't* tell me."

"But now I have to tell, to see if you're right."

"He and I did it too," she said. "And that's enough."

"*You?*"

"Females do such things, yes."

Such things. Bodily functions! But Anne sounded almost flirtatious, or nostalgic, recalling younger days with Rex.

Under the stand of black willows, Tim and Rex would relieve themselves, side by side. It was unique in Tim's iconography, a silent statement from Rex that he was not so predictable, or hidebound: he would piss outdoors.

But Anne would too! How true it was that Tim knew little of his parents' private lives. Perhaps they had been loud and joyous, jumping one another's bones the instant the schoolbus pulled away. Perhaps they peed side by side throughout the old New South, skinny-dipped in back country rivers, rolled together in soft green meadows.

"Your father was always impatient that way."

"When you gotta go, you gotta go," said Tim, marvelling.

"That's enough now."

Anne was smiling, though. Happy memories did not have to make you sad. They had left behind the question of AIDS, it was gone, and now the silent landscape (sandpits, cornfields, persimmons by the highway) lured them along in a parallel silence until they were home.

"I enjoyed my breakfast very much, honey," said Anne, patting Tim's hand. "It was a real treat."

"I can't talk long," said Billy.

"Dinner already?"

"No, we've got a game. Against the creeps from Badgers."

"A soccer game?"

"Softball."

Minimalism was being practiced here. But this was the telephone, there was no way to change it for the better—unless releasing him to play the Badgers constituted improvement.

Tim knew precisely where Billy was sitting, in the knotty pine fastness of Arnold Broom's office, and he had no doubt the boy resented being there. It was embarrassing to be plucked from the company each evening for a call from home. His bunkmates knew nothing of Billy's situation.

"Softball, huh. I guess you can't kick 'em in the shins."

"Not really, Unk."

"Bummer."

"Yeah, so, I gotta go."

"When you gotta go, you gotta go," said Tim.

"You want her?"

"Yes, please, Bill. If she's there."

Cindy did not sound quite so put upon. By contrast with her brother, she sounded lively and willing.

"Tell me what you ate today," he said.

"Everything?"

"Yes, please."

"Cereal. Banana. Carrot. An apple—"

"Mint patties?"

"Gone. But Cara gave me some of her Hershey bar."

"That was nice of Cara."

"Two glasses of milk. Tuna surprise—"

"You? Ate tuna surprise?"

"Bread and butter. Rice pudding—"

74

"Are you just incredibly *fat*, from all this eating?"

"I'm the same as I was," she said, saucily.

"Are you okay, sweetheart?" (She seemed okay.) "Are you having a little fun up there?"

"I want you to come."

"Take you home, you mean? Come get you?"

"Not sure."

"But come visit."

"Yes."

"You know I'm at Grandma's, in South Carolina. Do you know how far away that is?"

"Seven hundred miles?"

"I knew you knew. So I can't really get there right away. Unless it's an emergency?"

"No."

"You're okay."

"Yes."

This one-word stuff was a tough pull. Tim's instinct was to press for answers, which he suspected was wrong, a violation of the Goldsmith Protocols. Probably you should stop at the point they stopped you. Even Anne had constantly stopped him, in gray silent space. Maybe, unlike himself, they knew what they were doing.

"Hang on one second, sweetheart. Grandma wants to say hello."

Anne did want to say hello, but not much more. She needed to confirm they were not being frozen, starved, or tortured. She had a hard time framing these concerns, and Cindy was not helping. When, very soon, Anne could think of nothing to say, she said "We'll have a lot to talk about, when you visit me."

When was the last time she had seen these children? Anne was only guessing, but it was more than a year, possibly closer to two.

Dinner that night was pleasantly chaotic, desultory. Fried chicken, homemade biscuits, and collards, set out on the kitchen counter. You ate whenever, took your plate wherever. Tim followed his mother to the porch.

"That's all you're eating?" he said.

"I nibbled while I was cooking. And I have been eating like there's no tomorrow since you all came."

"Let me get you something to drink, at least."

"You can get me something too," said Erica, joining them.

"Our usual," said Anne, smiling as she patted Tim's arm. She had been patting him a lot, both to reassure him and to reassure herself he was still there. Ordering their "usual" was a clear statement, for this was a 'normalcy thing' between them, like the bacon and eggs in Mullins. Anne took one deep draught from the bottle of beer he brought out, then handed the balance back to Tim.

"I do like that top drop," she said. "The very coldest one."

"It's good for the heart," said Tim, handing a second bottle to his sister.

"So was hearing those two on the telephone. It was nice we all got on."

"Kids actually hate that sort of thing."

"Whoa," said Erica. "The expert on childhood speaks."

Tim spun toward her and she flinched (or he thought she did) as if she expected him to smack her. This softened his response considerably. Ric had come on like a midsummer night's Santa Claus, with a VCR for the two of them, Earl's card collection for Billy. Baldfaced bribery, Tim had nearly screamed, and he might have screamed it now. Instead, he was gentle, conciliatory.

"Don't you know what I mean? Like on birthdays, when we had to wade through all the aunts and cousins?"

Erica granted him a shrug of acknowledgement.

"They know we are all there for them," said Anne. "Whatever the mechanics of conversation, Timmy."

"Just for the record, though, we did not all get on. If Earl is part of all, then Earl did not get on."

"Oh, you needn't be so literal, honey."

"Literal isn't the point. The point—just for the record—is that Earl has never said five words to those two. He wouldn't even be able to fake it."

"Will you hush," said Erica. "It's not true, but let's don't argue about it during supper."

"Hear hear," said Anne, moving a wayward strand of hair from Erica's brow, brushing it back past her temple.

Anne had bought two caskets of dark, lacquered mahogany. The ashes would be placed inside them, a costly compromise between

Jill's choice of cremation and her mother's need to have a gravesite.

"I'll need to visit, and tend her spirit."

"It's fine, Mom, it's good. The kids can visit too. They can know where she is."

So the utilitarian plastic boxes from J.J. Mulhern's were set inside the fancy coffins without ever having been opened. Those boxes might contain the residue of somebody's cookout, Earl joked, in complete bad taste. Tim had regained his cool so thoroughly that Erica was the one who had to silence her husband.

It wasn't really cool, though, it was shock. Certainly at the graveside it was. These ashes were Jill. Jill was these ashes. Tim was barely hanging on.

Forty-odd people were at the church service. In the frontmost pew, flanked by her children and her brother Jim, Anne sat at attention, head perfectly still, hands in her lap, until the organ sounded the opening notes of "How Great Thou Art." At that she spilled open in gasping convulsions. Tim and Erica braced her from either side, but Tim feared her bones might fly apart. "That's when I always go off," she said later, dismissively, though she had "gone off" a number of other times, at random. "That song. Even when I don't particularly care for the deceased."

About half the congregation came on to the cemetery, where a single wide excavation had been cut for the two coffins, not eight feet from where Rex lay buried. Anne made no sound, no movement though all through the Lord's Prayer two streams of tears, sharply defined by the sunlight, runneled down her cheeks.

There were cakes and coffee at the house, provided by friends. Anne had tried to retain the job, arguing that she would welcome such distraction, but this was not the way it was done in Berline. Edna Jackson made the cakes, Mary Reidesel did the rest.

"I thought everyone had a nice enough time," Anne said, to no one in particular, after the mourners had departed. She was being brave, of course, but it seemed to everyone that she had retreated into some benign survivalist mode of temporary insanity. More than once, Tim heard the teaparty laugh leaking out of her.

It was almost comical how they left it to the last possible moment, dusk of the final night, to stage their confrontation. At that hour, beyond the cast of the porch light, they were at the mercy of half a million mosquitoes.

"Explain this to me, Earl. We both know you never wanted anything to do with kids. So what is this?"

"That's all right, Timmy, you never wanted kids, either."

"The truth is I did sort of want kids."

"Couldn't get pregnant?"

A mosquito the size of a sparrow lanced Tim's wrist, while another one was landing in his ear. He sensed a mass of them hovering like a magic carpet, humming like high-tension wires.

"I understood it was part of the price for being single."

"Gay. Say gay. Why deny it?"

"I didn't deny it."

"You didn't say it."

"I'm sorry. This is my fault, but we have lost track of the issue here. Which is why you are arguing for something you don't want in the first place. To be a hero?"

"Let me give it a shot for you. I didn't exactly want my neighbor moving in with me last April. But when his house burned down—which it did—why then, yes, we went and aired out the spare room."

"For how long?"

"All morning."

"Christ. Not how long did you air it out, how long did your neighbor stay there. A week?"

"It was damned close to a week!" Earl laughed. He upended his beer can and rattled it, to emphasize how it had gone empty on him.

"Not, say, eight years, though. Not a lifetime."

"It is an example, Timmy. Of how your circumstances can change and how your response might have to change along with them."

Tim slapped his left forearm with his right hand, then his right forearm with his left hand. A mosquito was invading his nose. The general hum was as dense as the wall of sound by a woodland pool on a spring night.

"You had best get yourself some long sleeves, bro."

"I'm fine," said Tim.

"They don't care for me, the insects. Never have."

Who could blame them, Tim thought. Yet the awful part of this was his awareness that Earl was being quote-unquote reasonable. Agreeable. Far more so than Tim.

"You're lucky."

"Maybe they just love that gay blood of yours. Which could unravel the mystery of AIDS—God's way of controlling the skeeters."

"You believe all gay men have AIDS. Is that right?"

"You tell me, Timmy. Do you, or donchoo?"

"Look, Earl. The *law*—"

"Timmy, Timmy. You don't think that paperwork stands up once they know the *truth*. So why create a whole big mess? Why get a bunch of expensive liars involved, and waste a boatload of money?"

"I'm not the one mentioning lawyers. I'm all for keeping this thing simple."

"Which is not what's going to happen, once the liars get started with us."

Earl always called lawyers liars. He was very doctrinaire about this, and quite certain it was, in every instance, highlarious. While Earl chortled to himself, Tim looked like a baseball coach giving out signs, hands flitting from ear to knee, swiping and slapping.

"Why don't we start by finding out what the children think?" he said, struggling to concentrate, falling back on Ellie's strategy. "Give them a voice in the matter."

"Why don't we. But in the meanwhile—"

"In the meanwhile, if you grab them you go to jail."

"Jail? You have to lighten up, Timmy. Be yourself."

"Jail," said Tim, with a relish for the blunt-instrument simplicity of it.

"Tell you what. We all want what's best for Bill and Cindy—"

"Hey, I'm impressed you remember their names."

"Timmy, you are a wild man."

Earl moved closer, to tower, and possibly to lay hands on the plague-infested shoulders. Had Tim been heterosexual and a potential buyer, the hands were there for sure. Tim drove him back by swatting frenetically at insects real and imagined, laying about him on all sides.

"I'm serious," he said, turning back to the house. "What do you know about those two human beings beyond their names? I'll give you a blank Post-It page two inches square, and you see if you can fill it up."

"Why play games, Timmy? It's not about your little quizzes. A court will surely know that."

"And what is it about, in your mind?"

Tim went up the steps first, but Earl was so close behind him that Tim felt the breath which carried his reply.

"Values. It's about values and morality, bro. Nobody requires a Post-It note to tell the right from the wrong."

Boston was somehow warmer than South Carolina, and twice as humid. Tim got into a taxicab at Logan and sat dripping in the back seat. The driver, who was Haitian, said he loved this heat.

Not a lick of wind, and no cold beer at journey's end. The larder was bare. Tim took a swig of flat ginger ale and stood under the shower (dialled to cold, then gradually lukewarmer) before putting on shorts and a sleeveless tee-shirt. Now what?

The apartment needed rearranging. He would have to give the kids his room, and carve himself a nest somewhere. There was major grocery shopping to do, but that seemed way too grim a proposition. The Star Market on Saturday night? That place could bring you down on a *Thursday.*

Truly, he could use some company. A friend, a decent meal, time off for good behavior. In the morning he would be behaving well again, fetching the kids, and that was fine. Being alone was fine too, for Tim was a loner at heart, dyed-in-the-wool loner by choice; still, he was not immune to bouts of loneliness.

He did not want Dolly's, or Colours, he did not think of Karl, or Joe, or Artie. He thought of Jill. A sister or a brother was what your parents gave you precisely so you would never be lonely. Jill had helped him so many times, could not help him now. Ashes to ashes, the preacher had said, a readymade figure of speech. It was possible to not really hear a phrase that familiar, yet it hit Tim as a naked and shocking reality. Ashes. He was sure he would never get over the distance between the sister he had loved so long and the small mound of ash they interred.

He hated this crippling sadness, desperately craved relief from it. Maybe Ellie. His surrogate sister, no less. Whenever she joked that she and Tim should "do it, just once, for fun, as a weird intriguing experiment," he used the incest excuse. They were sister and brother, and while weirdness and intrigue were good, sure-

80

ly incest was bad.

Plus, he and Ellie had rescued one another from loneliness on many a Saturday. They knew the drill.

"Hey, Ell, I just got in. You have plans?"

"I do. But I have time to hear what happened."

"Time for a wee dram at Culpepper's? Meetcha halfway?"

"Not enough time for that."

"Yeah. I should have guessed you'd be booked. Saturday night."

"Right. Like I always am."

"I'm *glad* you're booked," he rallied; lied. "The victor, I presume?"

"Yes."

"No need to blush."

"I am not blushing."

"Eleanor, you are definitely blushing. Isn't it time you brought this man home to meet the family?"

"Are you ever going to tell me what happened? Come on."

"But I'm psyched. I like Ike, but I pick Vic."

Tim was trying to be psyched, or at least to sound psyched, but mostly he was hanging on to her. In truth he had a twinge—it could not be jealousy?—about Victor. Were his options being foreclosed here? Should he consider tossing his hat in the ring while there was still time?

When Ellie would kid about "doing it" once, for kicks, or playing strip poker with help from Jose Cuervo....Kicks?—or her way of transforming them into a couple through the alchemy of games and potions? Dilute me with enough booze and I become a flaming heterosexual? "Don't knock it till you've tried it," she would gently chide.

Tim hadn't tried it in over twenty years, yet maybe he should try it now. They could get a big place (pay one rent, save a bundle) and fill it with Billy and Cindy, dogs and gerbils. They already knew how to share space. They already had a kind of love.

But Ellie went, and the simple truth returned: Tim was just terribly lonely. The loneliness felt like a lump of raw dough in his belly. Then, happily, the telephone rang back. She would do that sometimes, when she sensed an unfulfilled need in him.

"Trips, Incorporated," he said, joking with her. "What can we do for you today?"

81

"Well!" said a strange voice. "What are the possibilities?"

Not Ellie, no one he knew, and yet Tim rambled ahead with the silly setpiece joke he had begun.

"Whatever you require, sir. Reservations, accomodations—"

"What if I require a good blow job?"

Blam.

Tim had been so eager to connect with someone, anyone, that he completely missed the nasty undertone. This man was not playing a nice game. Earl Sanderson? It could be Earl, or some henchman of Earl's, inaugurating a program of harassment.

"Who is this?" he demanded, shaking with anger and fear.

"Joe Average is my name, you slut. Don't you remember me?"

Tim was trembling when he hung up the phone; his scalp was electrified when it sounded again like a fire drill. He let the machine field it, listening with morbid fascination.

"Average," said the voice, "Joe Average"—in the cadence of the 'Bond, James Bond' routine. That was all.

For now. Because this did not strike Tim as a one-shot deal. It felt too personal to be a random crank call. There was Earl, no question about that, but the phrase sounded familiar. Joe Average. He had come across it somewhere recently. Yes: he had used it, by chance, in that asinine "interview" across from the BPL, when he got himself cornered as the man in the street. He had blurted out something about Joe Average and gay-bashing, some throwaway remark that only the reporter, and the cameraman, would have heard.

Unless they had put it on the air, in which case this could be anyone he knew, a friend pulling his chain…. But no, a friend would have revealed himself in the end. Nor did this man sound friendly.

Next time it rang he fled. Up and out, shoes in hand, before the nasty voice could find him. He was on the move, without the wisp of a plan.

It was still broiling. The sun, lower in the sky, buttered the high brick façades and came flowing down alleyways, spattering the fences and vines. From force of habit, Tim launched himself on the southwest corridor, then found himself—blank and slightly numb—in Copley Square, where the heat had banished humankind. There were so few people in sight that you could count them.

The pigeon man was there. An elderly tourist was posing his wife beneath the Trinity Church arches. A second couple emerged from the foyer of the Ritz and folded themselves into a taxi.

Tim crossed Boylston and went up to the office. He pushed his message button and ploughed through, clicking everything directly to Save until he heard what he was bound to hear. No surprise this time. "Hello there, Timmy Tripster, this is your buddy Joe. Joe Average. Buzz you back later."

There were three more. The guy had been checking in every day since Wednesday and now he was calling both numbers, back and forth, a creepy pingpong game. Tim's life had become a Hitchcock movie, in which he was the Cary Grant while outside his darkening windows the bad one (the Richard Widmark?) was watching. Maniacal, eager, high on the happy prospect of torture. Yes it was early, but his mood was altered; a glass at Colours might be in order after all....

Tim had never been as close to Jill's kids as in the days before Camp Keokuk; never as distant as he was now, heading north to pick them up. Two weeks, and he had lost the thread. He had time to regain it—and that was the plan, to bear down—but he wasted the time rehashing Barry.

Why had there been such humiliation? Barry's was a harmless remark, intended as a compliment. Why had the whole business gone so sour? The Romper Room at Colours, the man named Barry who said he was a stockbroker. Why had Tim disbelieved him? Because Barry did not look like a stockbroker? Who looked like anything but meat in the Romper Room strobes? Nor did Tim care whether he was a stockbroker or a stock clerk at Gem Auto Parts.

"I can't explain it, I just tend to gravitate to older men."

Gravitate, do you, thought Tim. "Oh?" he said, feigning interest. He had not connected himself to Barry's statement. Older men?

"I like that they've been part of the history. The early demonstrations? Stonewall?"

"*Ancient* history."

"Were you there? I mean, were you lucky enough to be a part of all that?"

This was respect, absolutely, but post-coital respect was simply not the right note to strike. What was? There among the garish cushions and plastic shrubs, the dark room suffused with strains of Sophie Tucker; what was the correct response? There was none, of course. In truth, they were finished responding, and now were left to escape a spent moment.

Nor did Barry, puffy and slack about the gills, spongy from deskwork and drink, look so very youthful himself. Twenty-six? Tim had not believed that, either. Surely Barry looked older than Tim—or was he kidding himself? In any case, who cared?

Or why? Why did Tim care so much? Why was he as fucked up about age as a crumbling movie queen turning sixty in her whiteface pancake? To be so vain; that was the true humiliation.

Tim was a teenager when Stonewall happened, nor was he aware that it happened. He wasn't even aware he was gay. His own ancient history, placed on the big continuum, made a fairly short arc through time. Oh there had been a great coming-out, no question, when every day held glorious adventure and all sex seemed a sort of love. Life was out ahead of them all, to be reaped from rich fields extending as far as the mind could see....

Which, as things turned out, was not far. The epidemic had aged them fast, for sure, and yet the process did not take long in any case. At twenty-eight you were a stripling, poised at the starting line—you had barely begun to live—but by thirty-eight you were past your prime, your best years receding with your hairline.

Physically, this was undeniable. No thirty-eight-year-old is winning gold medals at the Olympics; no thirty-four-year-old. Biologically, your body begins to die before that. So the prime of life, when you are free and able and finally aware, is a mere ten-year proposition. Gather your rosebuds while ye may!

Not that you are dead. There is life after life, so to speak. There are new lessons, new goals, like garnering compliments from the Barrys of this world. There is achieving respect.

And regret. Regret never entered the picture in 1980, or 1985. Now it was always with him. There would be Barry and there would be regretting Barry, a sort of sad, inevitable, two-step waltz.

Steering onto the gravel lane, Tim followed the blazed arrowheads TO KEOKUK TERRITORY. All the picking-up parents had left their cars in a hot open field, orderly rows of gleaming Asian station wagons. Tim angled the Honda between a Toyota and a Subaru, then took the grassy path up to the bunks.

Billy, fresh from lifesaving class, was as bronzed as a sturdy little Indian brave. Cindy had a shine to her cheeks and eyes, even though—Monty's child—she had avoided the sun. They were energized and eager to hear the "plan."

"Well, this week we'll have to be in Boston."

"How come?"

"I have to work, sweetheart. Ellie has been sort of doing my job for me."

"Good deal," said Billy, ironic and sophisticated on the burdens of working. He did *seem* the picture of health, and balance.

"Yeah but," said Tim, "I owe her big time. Anyway, I found these day camps in Boston—"

"I'd rather stay here," said Billy. "I mean, if we go to camp, I like this one."

Keokuk had treated Billy well. He had small goldplated trophies for soccer and softball, iron-on cloth patches for running and swimming. Both as symbols and as objects, these were meaningful to him.

"This would be day camp," Tim explained. "There's one that's all sports, and another for arts and crafts. But the idea is we'd be home together every night. Eat dinner, talk, watch TV."

"There's room in the next session. Ronny checked it out for me."

"Ronny's his counselor," said Cindy.

"I know," said Tim, who had thanked Ronny, tipped him twenty bucks, and admired the lad's pretty dimples.

"I don't want to go to art camp if Billy's somewhere else."

"Fine. And no one has to go to any camp. I just hated the idea of you guys getting stuck indoors in the summertime."

Getting them launched, extricating them, took forever. Two dozen goodbyes, too much small talk with the other parents, last-minute duffelstuffing. Back in the flattened hayfield, the Honda had become too hot to touch.

Billy kept pressing for more details about the future. Each night from Berline, Tim assured them he was working on it, yet the only plan in place was treading water. He had already done some serious treading—in Jaffrey, Provincetown, Berline, and Boston—but what else could he do? Tim could be treading for the next ten years, if he lived so long.

In the back seat, duly buckled in, the Hergies ate too much chocolate ("before it melts") and sang the Keokuk song of friendship too many times. Eventually, Cindy slept, with her neck so extremely cocked it looked broken. Billy pushed her upright once or twice before he too slumped lower. He had sung to drown out thought—and to dislodge pictures of his parents that stole too close. He replaced them with the drone of the song and then with images from soccer games, instant replays he framed on TV screens in his mind. And with images of Judy Simon.

She had kissed him at the dance—right on the mouth—and she had stroked his cheek with the back of her hand. Billy had gone bright with embarrassment and he could feel embarrassed by it still. Judy was not the prettiest girl, or even the nicest, yet her soft touch persisted. He could rub his cheek and feel it there now, as he drifted through Cindy and soccer and Judy to sleep.

Enrollment closed back in May. Did Mr. Bannon not believe in planning ahead? Mr. Bannon did not believe in it, no, but he did understand the inadvisability of saying so this morning. Soon enough the truth was out: a few slots remained open for the non-planners.

But there were forms to fill out, waivers to sign, and mug shots, so half the morning was gone by the time he hugged the kids goodbye. Then the desk jockey reminded him about lunch; lunch could not be waived. So he rushed to a 7-11 for pre-fabricated sandwiches they would not eat and cartons of milk they would not drink, plus little bags of corn chips and granola bars laced with chocolate. It was after ten when he got to the office.

Almost sheepishly he confessed he had to leave in an hour to eat lunch. "I'll work late," he swore to Charles and Ellie, explaining that Karl had cancelled a client for him, that it was not pleasure but legal business. "I'll stay till midnight."

"What about the kids?"

"Oh shit, I can't stay late. But I'll come back, after dinner. I'll bring them with me."

"It's not necessary," said Charles. "But Tim? We will be keeping score."

The city air was lighter finally, less oppressive, as they sat on the bricks outside Au Bon Pain. Karl with his soup and salad, Tim a sandwich and coffee.

"Let's start with the worst case scenario," said Karl. "Just to cover all the bases."

"Hit me with your best shot, barrister."

"They can go for a Temporary Guardianship. Get a court order that simply supersedes the terms of the will."

"They can do that? Supersede?"

"This would be a motion brought to the *ex parte* session— meaning with no notice to you. If they persuade a judge to grant it, they come with a sheriff and cart the kids away."

"Nifty, Karl. This is your justice system? Some judge simply fucks me?"

"Up the tunnel of love, old boy. But it's highly unlikely, and Erica's lawyer will advise against it. So relax."

"I'm relaxing. Tell me what Erica's lawyer will advise."

"Petition the court for a Temporary Guardianship, but with proper notice and a hearing three weeks from now."

"And the will? What my sister wanted for her children doesn't count for anything?"

"You're not relaxing, Tim. You haven't eaten a bite."

"It's hard enough to keep my napkin from blowing in your soup."

"The will counts, of course it counts. But as with every matter before the probate court, it is subject to challenge."

"You mean, the way some bitter distant cousin can tie up a rich estate, hoping they hand him a fat check to go away?"

"Not exactly, because they do have a case. They could win, you could win. Are you sure about what you even want?"

"I want control. And time, to figure this thing out."

"Hell, in that case you might still be needing time when your niece and nephew are in law school."

"Keep humoring me, Karl. Say they do what you expect, a hearing in three weeks. What do *I* do?"

"The right question to ask. You hunker down with those children and start making some footprints in the sand. Clear prints, that a judge can follow. You begin to carve a trail of trust through the jungle—"

"Easy now, you're starting to lift off."

"Hey, I'm getting into the case."

"Great. I just haven't heard you lift off like that in a while. But these footprints, and tracks and trails—are what, exactly?"

"Patterns. Daily rituals. What really counts in any custody case is continuity."

"And three weeks makes for continuity?"

"Well, you have the last three and the next three, plus you have the precedent of solid relationships with the children going back to their birth. Then you have the paperwork, naming you. That's your case."

"What's their case?"

"Venue, for starters. As in continuity of friendships, neighbors, schools. And then, sadly, the fact that you are a flaming pervert."

"Perverts have no rights? Jilly knew I was a pervert."

"Actually, that could become an issue. Can you prove she knew? And that Monty knew, which isn't quite the same."

"Sure I can. Why can't I?"

Had they ever expressed it in writing, or before witnesses? Jill had opposed his break with Karl, urged him to stay in the relationship. Had she put it in a letter? If so, could Tim locate that letter? Was there hard evidence of even one of the dozens of "reminders" from Monty that Tim get himself tested?

"You'll also need to hire a lawyer, Tim. The cost could be brutal before this is over."

"I have a lawyer."

"Not me. A specialist. Someone who knows this area of the law."

"You're saying I need an expensive specialist."

"Yes. And I strongly recommend it be a woman. A smart, straight woman. In fact, I have a name for you."

"Karl," said Tim, taking Trickett's hand, "I realize it may not seem so, but I'm grateful. I know you have paying customers—"

"Oh Christ, Timmy," said Karl, ripping his hand loose. "Do you have to be a vulgar idiot?"

Hustling back to Trips, Tim let the downstairs door float closed on an elderly gent and gunned the elevator to three. Rocketing past Charles and Ellie to his desk, he was determined to do ten hours work in the three remaining hours. But he was locked on the legal hassle.

Ric had assured him they were going back on the road to finish their trip, or a truncated version of it, a week. But what if Ric had lied, to set him up? With this cute *ex parte* trick, the kids could be whisked away before they had a chance to disdain their shrink-wrapped sandwiches.

He pictured Earl striding in with righteous fire in his eyes and holy writ in his hand, issued by some bedrock reactionary New Hampshire judge, a ninety-nine-year-old wrinkled prune who hated gays and Jews and had never even seen a black man. Live free or die!

Tim wanted to live free, too. He wanted to get Billy and Cindy home and cook them a nice dinner, watch a stupid TV show with them. Today was Monday. Which stupid shows were on Monday?

Charles' face appeared and Tim realized he had not done a lick of work since lunch. Not ten hours worth, not ten minutes worth. He had not even bothered to play his messages.

"One of your fellow travellers checked in," said Charles, in what seemed a disapproving tone.

"A client?"

"Not that sort of traveller, I'm afraid. You left your voice mail on speaker, Tim. Not good. Mrs. Greenglass was with me, and we heard this charming communication."

"I don't get it."

What was Charles telling, or not telling him? Then he got it. It had to be the latest vulgar message from Joe Average. The nut did not even have a day job.

"I am totally cool with your lifestyle, Tim, you know that. But this was not cool."

"Charlie, it isn't what you think."

"No? You should have seen the look on Minna's face when that little gem came wafting over the partition."

"He's a nut case. It's harassment of some sort—no one I know."

He caught the first three words ("Timbo, you bimbo—") before deleting Joe Average, then listened to two clients wondering politely whether Tim had gotten to their respective issues. They each used the phrase, so he resolved to *get to* these matters straightaway. He did so and called them back to say so, as if efficiency had never run higher at Trips, Incorporated.

Punching up routine data on his screen, Tim had to wonder why anyone bothered to call them anymore. Why not just book Net-Trips or piece a trip together on their own? It was a recession, after all. Surely travel agents would begin disappearing from the economy, as typesetters had begun to disappear, and tax preparers. That's why everyone was desperate to win The Lottery and get rich, before their own professions vanished and they starved.

Lucky dentists, he thought, for no one would be drilling and filling his own molar. Lucky plumbers, too—sort of.... But Tim did not truly envy all the wealthy dentists and plumbers; he simply felt negativity crawling over him like a tight suit. And why not? He had *enemies*, for God's sake. He had always had enemies in a general sense, a whole hostile planetful, but apart from the occasional dartboard target (Anita Bryant, Jesse Helms) they were never personalized. Individuals out to *get Tim Bannon*.

Now Ellie's face appeared, to tell him good night. The work day was over. "Call me if you need to talk."

"I do need to talk. Why don't you come to dinner?"

"Not tonight, Tim."

"But you just said—"

"Absolutely. Call me. After you've put the kids to bed."

Ellie had nothing scheduled—and nothing in her house to cook. She was convinced, however, that Tim could benefit from a dose of reality, a succession of nights without help; without coverage. He would know better what he was up against.

Sprinting to the car, Tim did know some of it. He knew the kids could be gone. He steeled himself, imagined bursting into the Community Center and finding no one there, not a living soul. Fury fired up inside him, rage by spontaneous combustion. If Earl had kidnapped those kids, legally or illegally, then by God the battle was joined. He would get his own fucking court order tomorrow and snatch them right back.

The traffic, oddly enough, calmed him down. Horns blared, road rage was real, the swan boats stayed on his left for more than five minutes—yet the fire banked. A second perspective came tickling at the gates of volition. If the kids were gone, his evening was freed up. Short term, this was not so terrible. He could use some solitude, listen to music or read. He could even venture out, if the solitude proved unwieldy.

So he knew this too: what was worse for Billy and Cindy was not necessarily worse for him.

If it was a test, however (angel on one shoulder, devil on the other), Tim passed. As the traffic lurched along toward Tremont, rage rekindled. He was not ambivalent: he wanted the kids to be there, not just clearly but powerfully. He hammered his own horn at a hopelessly clogged intersection, spewed curses at invisible yet despicable judges. Had he spotted Earl Sanderson jaywalking, he might well have run him over.

*

90

Saffron, the young lady assigned to Cindy, reassured Tim that his "daughter" had crumbled only at the very last. "It's a long day for these kids," said Saffron, who looked young enough to remember this precisely. "They just get tired."

Hair stuck with paste, face pale and blotchy, Cindy looked worse than tired. She looked wrecked. Billy had been playing volleyball during the half hour his sister dripped sundry wet substances onto poor Saffron's lap. Nonetheless, he had the answer. "Mickey D would cheer her up, Unk."

Stuffing her into the back seat, Tim asked if she was hungry and she wailed "Nooooooo" and slap-paddled the air in front of her forehead as though breaking up a cloud of black flies. Fine. McDonald's was not Tim's idea and it was not good ritual, either. Fruit and veggies were in order. *Roughage.* Or had roughage been discredited? It was never easy staying abreast of the musts and must-nots. Was cholesterol still the villain? Tim was more attuned to sore throats and subtle hints of fever; every tiny blemish was potentially a lesion.

Sprouts-versus-saturated fat was deferred for the moment by traffic. You could not prove by their ground speed that any of these cars were being operated by living drivers. City driving was masochistic, rush-hour flat out insane. Tim walked or he biked, when he had a bike. (Sometimes he had it, sometimes The Bicycle Thieves had it.) But how could you efficiently transport two kids, heavy laden with gear, except by car?

Gridlock suited Billy. Happy with cacophany, he skated his fingers over the radio spectrum. Cindy issued risky stalactites of snot, then vacuumed them back just before they broke off. (Would a thick shake and fries solve this?) They got bottlenecked at Park Plaza, motionless through two light changes, and Cindy began to moan. "Unk?" said Billy, meaningfully. Meaning Mickey D.

"Let's play a game. Let's do capitals. Cynthia: England."

Astonishingly, it worked. She had the answer and she had to show she did. A face brightened, and out of that face came the word London.

"Bill, your turn. Ireland."

"Dublin. Belfast." But worldweary. Syllable by syllable. Duh-blinn. Belff-assed.

"France, Cynthia."

"Paris," said Cindy, as they finally inched through the intersection.

"Bill? The capital of the Czech Republic."

"There it is, Unk. You know."

"Are you stalling for time?"

"No way. Prague. They got McDonald's there now, I think. I know they got it in Moscow."

"Prague is correct. And they do have it, not got it, in quite a few European cities."

Suddenly Tim saw his way clear, saw that bad parenting could make good parenting possible. A snack at Mickey D's could make dinner possible. It was one of Monty's own tricks—call it a snack, technically, and swear them to secrecy. "If you don't eat your whole lunch," Monty would tell them, "Mom will figure it out."

"Anyone up for a snack?" he said, accordingly.

"Great idea, Unk! What do you say, Simp?"

"Paris," she blurted out, again. She had fallen asleep.

"Unk's hungry, so we were gonna get a snack at Mickey D."

So dinner got underway on the late side, but Tim did make some footprints in the kitchen by enlisting their help. Participation! It was as though he had read the book on childrearing. Cindy put away the groceries and organized the pantry shelves. Billy chopped onions and green peppers, then set the table. Both went about their assignments intently, conscientious to a fault.

While Tim cooked to the jazz show on WGBH, they shifted furniture around, creating a "guest room" for Tim in the large but windowless walk-in closet. They gave him the foldout bed (and made it up) and found a milk crate on the fire escape for his nightstand. It was quite cozy, he thought; to a homeless man it would be paradise.

The sauce was bubbling and Tim had his wine. They were on the couch watching *Jeopardy* when the telephone rang. It pleased him to see Cindy run for it; pleased him that she felt so at home. By the time the squalid possibility of Joe Average occurred to him, she was chatting away, fortunately (or not) with Erica. Billy, reluctant but polite, also took a brief turn.

"Aunt Erica says to say hello," he reported to Tim.

"She didn't want to talk to me?"

Billy shrugged. "I think she was at a pay phone."

So far as Tim could recollect, Ric had never telephoned his house. As he dropped pasta into the boiling water, he understood that she still hadn't—she was simply carving her own trail of trust through the jungle. They were eating when Tim asked Cindy if she liked Aunt Ric. He convinced himself he had spoken tonelessly, without a hint of suasion.

"Sure," she said.

"You don't have to like her. I'm just curious."

"I think she's pretty."

"And Uncle Earl?"

"He's not pretty."

"He's pretty cool," said Billy. "The time we went there he let me shoot at cans. And he can stick a knife in a tree, from like here to that wall."

"Well, that's a handy skill to have in today's economy."

Wrong. What could appeal to Billy Hergie more than sticking knives in trees? But Billy gave him a pass on it.

"Sometimes he takes us to the lake," said Cindy.

"Like once."

"More than once."

"Once exactly, Simp. Are you gonna dump us there, Unk?"

"Not a chance," said Tim, tickled by the boy's bluntness.

"Then how come you're asking all these questions?"

"Just curious."

"Is it cause you don't?"

"Don't what?"

"Like them."

"I like them if my Hergies like them. And I sure did like their dog. What was that pooch's name again?"

(No harm taking a lesson from one's own mother.)

"I don't know, but he was big."

"He was pretty," said Cindy.

Enough. They were children, not idiots, and he did not wish to fool them in any case. He was merely weak, and stumbling a bit. Best stop trying to poison their minds and poison them benignly with some Ben & Jerry's. Surely Chunky Monkey was good precedent?

"How was the spaghetti?" he said, as they cleared the plates. "That's the real question here."

"It was delicious, Unk."

"Yeah. Really good."

"I thought it had a hint too much oregano," Tim said, raising his nose in the air like a comic gourmand. "Don't you agree, Cynthia?"

"Oregano? Hey Unk, what's the capital of Oregano?"

"I haven't a clue, sweetheart."

"Portland!" she shouted.

"Sorry, Simp," said Billy. "It's Salem."

Morning clipped the heels of night. They had eaten late, gone to bed late, and the kids wanted to sleep late. "It's summer," Billy groaned. Tim's best offer was a promise to pick them up from the camp by four o'clock. This was his concession to Cindy, or to the reality that it was his only hope of getting her to leave the house without duress.

But it meant that work was hopeless again, for he had another unavoidable appointment at lunch time, and this one was with his new lawyer—hence a lunch without any *lunch*, alas. Attorney Dee Barnes ran a low-key one-woman shop on the first floor of her Chandler Street row house, so low-key that the tarnished nameplate was unreadable at arm's length.

The furnishings were alarmingly unpretentious (a yard sale desk of old scratched oak) and there was no secretary anywhere in sight. Watercolors, not diplomas, adorned the off-white walls. And to anyone casting about for a tough-as-nails lawyer, Barnes herself was alarmingly unpretentious. She could be a schoolmarm on the big prairie, in her long black skirt and gray cardigan sweater. She wore her brown hair loose, had no makeup, and minimal jewelry—a silver bracelet and a gold wedding band.

Tim thanked her for squeezing him in on short notice, while privately wondering if she simply had no other clients. But then she smiled ("I tried to say no to you") and her smile was wonderful, radiant. Maybe she *smiled* at judges, instead of displaying her diplomas.

"I must have sounded a little desperate," Tim said. "I am a little desperate."

"You said custody. How many children are there? —what ages? —and who are they with for now?"

This was good. Pleasant, yet right to the point. *Concision*, Karl had counselled Tim. "Say no to coffee. The meter is running while you stir in your sugar." But Attorney Barnes had not offered coffee, and seemed ("You said custody") the very model of concision.

"There is a boy, eleven, and a girl, eight and a half. And they're with me. But this is an unusual situation—"

"Everyone thinks that."

Barnes tipped her chair back so far he feared she might go over, but Tim kept his focus. "I mean they aren't my children. It's not like I have a wife and—"

Barnes allowed her chair to fall forward at this and Tim leaned back, in response. Somehow it seemed the distance between them should remain a constant. "They're my sister's kids. I'm their uncle. Obviously. My sister Jill and her husband Monty were killed in a car crash three weeks ago. That's why the kids are with me."

"I'm so sorry. And you're right. It is unusual."

Tim told her his story and she told him, by means of the radiant smile, that he was doing fine here. That he was not a selfish husband trying to beat out a long-suffering wife. For over the phone she had confided, "I generally get the wife."

"Does Erica have children? Cousins to William and Cynthia?"

"Ric's thirty-eight, never wanted kids, doesn't have any, doesn't work, travels a lot."

"The husband works?" Tim noticed that Barnes and he were speaking the same language: shorthand.

"Sells," he responded. "Houses." Concision absolute!

"And travels a lot? Real estate doesn't seem the ideal product for a traveling salesman."

"They travel in the summer. He stops selling to travel."

"Let's summarize. They wish to contest the will and take on— possibly adopt?—Jill's two children, although—or because?— they have no children of their own."

"Not because. They have none by choice. I said that."

"You did say it of your sister. Not of the spouse."

"Oh, more so the spouse."

"So why contest? Is it because you're single?"

"It's because they hate me. And they hate me because I'm gay."

"Okay."

"Okay as in that's cool? As in the Law shows no preference?"

95

"Okay as in keep talking."

"Oh. Okay. Earl Sanderson—the spouse—is a vicious homophobe who probably favors shooting abortionists, lynching uppity blacks, and castrating gays to halt the spread of AIDS."

"Probably?"

"Well, he can be cagey about it. But he is definitely that sort of good American."

"It's interesting to me that you come from South Carolina, you and your sisters, and you find yourself living in the North in close proximity—but it's not an indication of close family ties?"

"Just chance. Monty came to take a job. I came because of a relationship—with a Boston lawyer, come to think of it."

"And Erica?"

"Also a job. Not hers, his. They met down South, where he was stationed. Then some buddy set him up with a job, which Earl quit like one day later. But they stayed."

"Okay."

Barnes pushed her chair back and stood up. Apparently an hour had slipped away, one hundred dollars worth of law. He had filled out the form in a flash, had not been offered coffee (much less lunch) and had been a paragon of concision throughout. The hundred dollars was fine, until you started multiplying it by weeks and months. They had barely scratched the surface.

Tim waited, expensive seconds ticking away, while she leafed through her book. A hundred an hour was cheap, though; Karl said two hundred was possible, more than that for courtroom time. Tim struggled to maintain this costly silence. "Anything else?" he blurted, getting desperate. It had been twenty seconds, yet it reeled out in his imagination to a time millions of dollars hence in New Hampshire where the ninety-nine-year-old flint-and-vinegar judge delivers the punch line, "You have wasted this court's time, knowing all along you were nothing but a flaming pervert."

"Yes. What makes you think this matter will be challenged? Have you heard from their lawyer?"

"I heard it from them. In person."

"Conversationally."

"Well, yeah. In a conversation."

"I'm just trying to understand your sense of urgency. So far there has been civil discussion, about a difference of opinion—"

"A friend of mine—a lawyer friend—says they can get a court

order and grab the kids."

"But they haven't."

"Not yet, no."

"Very likely they won't. It's been three weeks, they are behaving civilly, and given the terms of the will, it wouldn't be granted. Can you be here at this same time tomorrow?"

"Sure I can," he said. Thinking, I can? How can I? Also thinking, There goes another hundred bucks.

"Good. Bring along a copy of the will, any codicils, any letters or documents pertaining to William and Cynthia or to the situation that you think could be helpful. Even photographs of you with the children, or with Jill and Monty. Can you manage that?"

Right, in my spare time. As if he had no job, as if he had no responsibility to produce breakfast, lunch, and dinner for three. And where the hell were these letters and documents? Would Jellinghaus fax him a copy of the will? And codicils? Karl would have to fill him in on codicils.

"No problem," he heard himself saying, though it dawned on him he had nothing but problems, some self-inflicted. He was launched, it would seem, on a headlong quest to attain the precise status he so recently sought to evade: *parentis.*

"Good, then," said Barnes, showing him out.

Twenty-three hours later he was right back in, with a clutch of papers he presumed were worthless. He simply wanted a passing grade from Barnes. Thus his college transcript—unearthed!—a birthday card from Jill containing a broad hint of his sexual preference, photos Monty took of Camp White Sneaker canoeing the Contoocook, and a copy of the will. No codicils, though now he knew what a codicil was.

"Nice work," said Barnes. "You do understand that one burden we bear is to answer the obvious question, namely What's wrong with this picture? Why name the single man, why not name the married sister who lives practically next door?"

"Yes."

"But the Hergesheimers were perfectly clear about it."

"Yes."

"Tim, are you feeling all right?"

"Yes. Fine, thanks."

"You seem so unnerved—and furtive, really. We can't afford to have you looking so much like a criminal."

Her smile released a sigh that left Tim like ten pounds of air leaving a popped balloon. He blushed, briefly, and then came clean.

"I guess I've been a little concerned about the cost of this, and—"

"And you figure if you sit there with a stick up your arse, it will somehow be cheaper?"

"Something like that," he said, as another ten pounds escaped, this time in the form of laughter.

"Look. It's a terrible imposition on you to defend this guardianship, if it comes to that. But it may not. Your brother-in-law may find he doesn't want to invest in a complicated court action any more than you do."

"Earl doesn't think it's complicated."

"In any case, we'll work out something comfortable regarding the money. You shouldn't worry about strict hourly rates."

Now she looked right at him with those arresting blueblack eyes, and smacked the desk like a drum. "I said don't worry and you went right back to worrying."

"Yeah. I worried how much money we just spent trying to stop me from worrying."

"The answer is none. No charge. There will be no charge for a lot of conversations we have here. I'm not Hale and Dorr."

"I get it." Tim did get it, more or less, and was disgusted at himself for hassling her. "I'm not really cheap, you know."

"I understand. You're just worried."

"Yes, exactly."

"Or you *were* worried."

Even knowing Karl Trickett, Tim found it difficult to trust a lawyer. Lawyer jokes aside, how could you trust someone who saw eight clients a day—or eighty, like a doctor? No one could be sympathetic and engaged that many times a day. Yet Barnes had convinced him. If this took every penny he had or ever dreamed of having, it would still be a *bargain.*

"Okay," said Barnes, "let's get back to work. To begin with, I'll tell you that the law, as such, will not decide this case."

"Of course not, it'll take blazing six-guns," said Tim, perhaps too liberated for his own good. Barnes shot him a one-eyed dart that said, that kind of shit I'll bill you for.

"The law leaves room," she said, "for human beings to decide it. We could prepare a perfect trial memo and still lose those kids."

Sobered, agreeable to the max, Tim nodded. Basically he was amazed to find Barnes on his side. *We* could lose those kids....

"There are three human beings," she went on, "who will play a central role in the decision. A family service officer who investigates the situation. A guardian *ad litem*, who also investigates but who represents only the childrens' interests—"

"But that's what you'll be doing."

"Technically, no. I represent *your* interests—which may differ. The third person is of course the judge. With the judge, a great deal will turn on what your sister can offer with regard to your—"

"Unfitness?"

"'Unconventional household' is the term we'll use."

"I like it."

"Meanwhile, you should do some thinking—maybe even some digging. If they do come after you, we would like to be in a position to return the favor."

"Yeah. They don't have such a conventional household themselves."

"Everyone has a few holes in the armor. Drink? Drugs?"

"Oh, without question."

"Abuse, a restraining order, dishonorable discharge—anything. Maybe there's a letter from Jill expressing concern about the children being left alone in Earl's care?"

"Well, they never have been. That's a sort of letter, isn't it?"

"Another consideration: you have a college education and they don't. Is that the case?"

"It is, but do judges take children away from moms with low board scores? They can't."

"Of course not, but education does tend to factor in big. I'll tell you another biggie: to be gay is one thing, to be militantly or promiscuously gay is another. In the eyes of the court," she hastened to amend.

"In the eyes of everyone, Attorney Barnes. Trust me on this."

"As to that, the AIDS virus would obviously be relevant. As you haven't mentioned it, can I assume you don't have it?"

"Have AIDS? I don't. Have it. Thank God."

"Tim, if you gave that response in court, a judge would wonder why you were so hesitant."

"Maybe I find the question offensive."

"Do you?"

"I'm not sure," said Tim, gaining temporary footing in this accidental tack. "Let me try again. I have never tested positive for the HIV virus, much less had an episode of actual fullblown AIDS."

"That's much better. And I'm sorry I had to ask."

"It's fine. I'm fine with it."

What would a judge ask him? What was he permitted to ask? There were rules of privacy that protected AIDS patients and gays in general; protected everyone. According to Peter Weissberg, your landlord was not allowed to ask either question, were you gay or were you sick. And no one could make you get tested.

Almost everyone had been tested, of course. In San Francisco, one hundred percent of them spun the chamber and played Russian Roulette. What a relief for the few who got good news! In Boston, where there were still cowards and holdouts, you went with that in mind: you might be granted a fresh lease on life. For Tim, the alternative was too depressing—and too likely.

He already knew he could not tolerate AZT. (He took it to find out and was violently nauseous until he stopped.) Despite the rumors and the experiments, there was no other defense except health itself. Carrots and peas, vitamins, exercise and fresh air. Prayer! So how was getting tested a help?

His friends said he was in denial and Tim said fine, he wanted to stay in denial. He had been mixed up, going back and forth on the question, until Phil Ryerson's death. Tim was there, taking his turn, reading poems at the hospice. Phil looked at him blankly, lay back, and died. His mouth fell slack and his eyes rolled up glossy and totally white. *Zombies*, was all Tim could think as he sat shivering in that overheated room: we are the living dead.

That night he said to Karl, "Thank God I don't have this grotesque disease." And Karl (who was HIV Positive and guessed Tim was too) stared at him for a minute and then said, very softly, "You have to get tested, Timmy. *Please*."

Well, no. They could test him on his deathbed.

"Can I also assume," said Barnes, "that you have never been arrested? Just to get all the unpleasantness out of the way."

"Never. I patronize only the cleanest rest stops."

"Please don't be offended, Tim. We will need to be able to discuss this in a pragmatic way. The law is at best a horribly pragmatic mechanism."

At the moment, Tim could hardly decry pragmatism. He felt unclean lying to Dee Barnes, or misleading her, but it was simply impractical to tell the precise truth. And fair enough. By refusing the test, he had kept the precise truth from himself for years. Why should he owe Barnes more than he owed himself?

Or so he reasoned, spuriously, while walking home, feeling unclean.

Once, at a Thanksgiving dinner, speaking "off the record," Earl Sanderson let down his hair. It was not a confession, it was braggadocio, for Earl always valued a good con job over mere accomplishments. Twice decorated with the Purple Heart in "Nam" (as he invariably called it, having spent a total of five weeks there in the fall of 1971), he revealed he had never seen battle.

The first Heart came when his company killed some civilians in a village called Binh. Just a stupid mistake, yet it had to be rectified—whitewashed, that is—so an attack was postulated, mothers and children were transmogrified into a Vietcong stealth unit, and a few buck privates were cited for bravery. Earl was among the lucky.

No casualties on the second Heart. Earl and two other soldiers (in fairness to Earl, one was a black man) were holed up in a Saigon whorehouse. They stayed too long, raged on far too drunk, and Earl caught a bullet in his backside from Madame Butterfly. It was worth it, however, as the WW II issue .38 calibre slug had to be accounted for. Wounded in action!

Earl could deny the story in court and his denial might even be the truth. Tim never took such tall tales at face value. Earl Sanderson could deny anything, true or false, as he denied shooting the dogs, and Ric would confirm whatever he told her to confirm.

But what if he had done some time? He could not deny official records. Earl left the service at age twenty-one and re-enlisted at twenty-nine. Hard to believe that the intervening years had been a time of clean living and steady upward mobility. Bad checks would be a nice fit. Petty theft, battery? It might take a private eye to find it out.

Tim could ask. Ask Ric, directly. Her husband could lie with the very best, the Nixons and Ollie Norths of this world, but you always knew when Ric was lying. If she phoned tonight, Tim would corner her and ask point blank about Earl's police blotter. Not only that, he would refuse to put the children on. This rash of systematic *caring* calls was ugly stuff, blatant manipulation.

When she did phone, however, he failed to ask, or refuse. The script left no room for it. "I'd like to say hi to Cindy" provided no segue to "When was your husband last in stir?"

"Sure," he heard himself saying instead. "Hang on, I'll get her."

Before it was over, Earl had jumped in, to sell Billy a house.

"Uncle Earl says we can turn his barn into a year-round basketball court. Heat it in the winter."

"Earl says a lot of things."

"Really. He says there's nothing in there but a lawnmower."

"Fine. If he does it, we'll go over there sometime and shoot some hoops."

Billy looked at him askance. He knew his uncle had stamina and strength. Tim could compete in a triathlon—he could run, bike, and swim all day—but he had no taste for the ball sports. Since putting in two years (for Rex' sake) on the bench in Little League, he had rarely stepped onto anyone's field of dreams to throw or catch a ball.

"I'm better than you think," said Tim, catching his nephew's ironic glance. "Much better than old Earl." As though they were going one-on-one for custody rights.

"Sure, Unk. Slam dunk," was Billy's sly reply. He and Tim were both grinning now, both in on the joke, "but I bet Uncle Earl can talk some serious trash."

By the next night, Tim had smoothed out the details, taken control. If peanut butter crackers and Juicy-Juice stood for routine, they had routine. If the establishment of a reading hour constituted ritual, they had that too. Tim even added something not on Karl's list: rules. The first was bath and pajamas right after dinner, which gave him a real tactical advantage on the hard transitions.

The second was that "for complicated reasons" (which mercifully they chose not to pursue) only Tim was permitted to answer the telephone. They were both asleep anyway by the time Erica called—and how dumb was that? She didn't wish to talk to Tim (refused, in truth) yet she called at eleven o'clock. By the time Joe

Average called, midnight on the dot, Tim was in bed himself.

"I know you're there, hotshot," he seethed, as Tim listened in the freshly poisoned dark. Was Average following general principles of terrorism, or could he actually see into the apartment?

Meanwhile the mornings too had become a lot smoother. Drawing on White Sneaker discipline, Tim had them mustering out so briskly by Friday that he beat Ellie to the office. By ten o'clock he had done enough work to merit a coffee break—forgotten pleasure—and sitting with his jumbo French roast and a lemon-ginger scone he was blessedly back into the rhythm of his own normalcy thing.

By noon, when Ellie brought in his mail (including a FedEx), he was cruising, he was carefree, the world was benign. Had that FedEx contained explosives from the Unabomber (or Joe Average) they would have blown him up for sure.

"You must be expecting something good," said Ellie, seeing his eagerness, watching him strip open the red-white-and-blue envelope like a kid attacking a crackerjack box for the prize inside.

"Just blind optimism," said Tim. "It's probably from the I.R.S."

No such luck. It was from the District Court, Cheshire County, State of New Hampshire.

Though really it was from Earl.

103

IV

DISSOLUTION & PROMISCUITY

....inasmuch as for twenty years the Defendant has led an irregular, dissolute life of promiscuous homosexuality. Moreover, as he is infected with the AIDS virus, he presents a significant health risk to the minor children, as well as a clear risk of further emotional loss to them....

The Complaint, as Dee Barnes was calling it (Motion, Petition, Complaint, it was all the same to Tim, a loud wailing siren calling him before the tribunal bare-butt-naked), went on to provide an alternative to all this dissolution. For as surely as Tim was Caligula, Earl and Ric were Ozzie and Harriet.

"Okay," said Barnes, "there's nothing we can do with the basic fact that you are single and they are double."

"Gay. Straight."

"If the judge is an out and out bigot, yes, that could do it. Assuming we have a shot, it becomes almost a matter of spin."

"I noticed a little spin in the Complaint."

"Oh, plenty. These are subjective words, not clinical terms. Irregular? Dissolute? I am sure we'll bounce a few nasty adjectives off Ozzie there, before we're done."

"I can't quite believe you're on my side in this."

"I'm your lawyer, Tim. And I'm not a bigot myself, if that's what you mean."

"Yes, actually. At the very least, people like me have to be ready for that. Not just gays. Blacks—"

"That's good, Tim, you stay ready on that front. And we'll see if we can't get you ready on the jurisprudential front as well."

"Yes, ma'am."

"This can seem like a crazy game sometimes—my father is stronger than your father. But it is our task to make you look as good as we can and make them look as bad as we can."

"Let's do it."

"We'll start by taking a run at these descriptive adjectives in the Complaint. See if we can reduce them to a careless exercise in semantics. I'm hoping the facts will help us."

"You want the facts."

"One doesn't always. But here the judge can place you under oath right at the hearing and have at you. So I do need to know where it could lead."

It was Friday night, and Tim had left the kids alone, to bloom by the light of the television. It gave him the willies to do this, especially with an hour of light in the sky. Barnes would understand (wouldn't she?) if he wrapped things up here and ran to safeguard Billy and Cindy. The facts, sure, but was there not metaphysical risk in daylight glancing directly off a TV screen?

"Earl will put me with a thousand partners a month for twenty years," he said, facing up to it, mindful that he could run but he could not hide for long. "Every one of them sick unto death with the virus."

"Okay, let's start there. You say you are not infected."

"I'm fine. In fine health."

"Not infected."

Barnes waited for confirmation, but Tim could summon nothing better than a shrug. He thought of the kids again, and of running away; quite naturally he thought about lying to her. All he could do however, was blush and shrug again when she asked it: "When was the last time you were tested?"

"What?" she said, after half a minute more had passed in silence. "Don't tell me you have *never* been tested?"

"Hey, I'll bet Earl hasn't been tested, either."

"You haven't been *tested?*"

"No. So we can truthfully say I've never tested Positive."

"Sure, and pray the other side has an idiot for a lawyer."

"And argue that it's better than if I did test Positive. Or had AIDS, for that matter," said Tim, rallying. These were distinctions he had rehearsed for years.

"Let's move on from here," said Barnes, more curtly, "and have a go at some of these charming adjectives. Irregular, dissolute, and so forth. Homosexual, even. Any chance there's been a lady or two in the mix?"

"Close friends. Dear friends. But I'd have to give them homosexual. I would argue against it being proof of evil."

"It is a statutory crime."

"Oh come on, the judge has been poking his clerk for years."

"I take that for gay humor," said Barnes, with the new sharpness. Thus far, the facts had not helped them a lot.

"Sorry. I can suppress it better when I'm not nervous."

"You have been gay since—when, Tim?"

"Always, I suppose. Outwardly, actively? Since college. Since the time you could be. 1969?"

"You were eighteen, nineteen. And then came the 70's...."

"Oh Lord, yes."

"The infamous baths?"

"All of it. Bath-houses and bars, mostly. The infamous warehouses in New York. The weeds."

"Rest stops, you mean?"

"No. For me at least, that was always a joke. But what we call the bushes wasn't. The weeds along the Fenway, summer nights. That became a very promiscuous scene."

"Are we a good deal more selective now?"

"We are."

"Any chance we could argue constant? Monogamous?"

"Not under oath, no."

"But we could argue selective, and with safe-sex precautions."

"We could. Much more selective, and mostly safe."

"Since?"

"1987. Following a very specific occasion you do not want to know about. Don't hate me, I'm just trying to be honest."

"Since 1987."

"Yes, ma'am."

"Perfect record since then."

"Ninety percent? A-minus?"

"Which leaves unprotected—what? One contact? Two?"

"A dozen?"

"Oh."

"Nine? I'm only guessing."

"Nine in three years, unprotected."

To consult his memory too closely would surely inflate the figure, so Tim let it stand. "I try to eat lots of cruciferous vegetables. And get a good night's sleep."

"And say your prayers, I'm sure. But this sounds more like promiscuous than not, to me."

"Earl doesn't know any of it, though. Whatever he says is just an invention."

"There may be Interrogatories, questions you have to answer

in writing—under oath—even if you never take the stand."

"One thing? Very few of my partners will be going on record. I mean, if I want to look like the average secretary, with an affair here and an affair there, I can look that way. There is a lot of anonymity that comes with the irregularity and promiscuity."

Her mouth went straight and her whole face flattened, as she scratched a note. Tim had taken the spin thing too far, but it was more than that. "You disapprove," he said.

"I suppose I do. I can't help disapproving a little."

"But you're disgusted."

"Only when I imagine the anonymity of it. Tall weeds, Tim? In the dark? You don't see a face, or exchange names?"

"It happens that way. It happens a lot of different ways, to avoid, you know, complications. Are you such a complete straightshooter yourself? Or shouldn't I ask?"

"You shouldn't ask, though I suppose it does seem unfair. The difference is I need to know your secrets, and you don't need to know mine."

"I can tell you are happily married."

"That's not a secret, actually."

Both of them were making an effort to restore good feeling. For Barnes, it never worked to mistrust or dislike a client. For Tim, being disliked was just one of the reasons he hated explaining himself.

"I'll need to process this conversation," said Barnes, gathering notes, gathering herself, "and so better had you. In the meanwhile, keep digging on Earl. At the very least, he must cheat on his wife, no?"

"It's a safe bet. He gets around, and he does have this superficial saleman's charm. But what do I do, get a list of his open-houses and go debrief all the women who showed up?"

"If you have the time. He cheats on his wife, he cheats on his taxes—anything he would rather not be made public. One advantage we have is that Earl lives in a small town, where gossip matters. And you live in Boston...."

"Where God is dead?"

"We'll talk on Monday, Tim. Have a nice weekend."

"Attorney Barnes? I am sorry."

"Sorry for?"

"Being dissolute and promiscuous. For making you hate me,

and making your job harder."

"Worry about yourself, Tim. It's my job, but it's your life."

Barnes withheld the smile, wearing the shopworn desk between them like armor. She still seemed a schoolmarm, but now she was the one who would bat your wrists with a hazel stick.

"You have a nice weekend too, Attorney Barnes."

Chastened in spite of himself and saddened by her visceral recoil, Tim struggled to let go of their conversation. He picked at it, recast it with new improved answers, for surely he was stupid not to have lied. There was something about Dee Barnes, however; lying to her had not been an option. Given this X-Factor, perhaps he should trust her. Barnes would "process" the meeting and she would come through the tough parts.

Maybe.

In the mews behind Tim's building, a man in a frayed work shirt was pacing nervously. With gray fly-up hair, rattling a huge ring of keys, the man paced and muttered to himself. But the mews caught them like flypaper, the whole range from the bizarre overdressed dogwalkers to the crackheads and homeless drinkers. Not infrequently one would be pissing against the fence. Welcome Home, was the traditional significance. Lately, with Tim on red alert for any sign of Joe Average, they had all become suspects.

Just last night a beggar had jumped them, barreling out of shadows toward them with his request for forty cents. (Why not a quarter, why not a dollar? He would *accept* a dollar, he allowed.) Cindy wanted to pay up. "You have quarters, Unk. You always have quarters."

True enough, he did. Quarters *worked*, they were the last coin in America that did, and it was Tim's policy to carry a few at all times. But it wasn't the milk of human kindness that made Cindy so eager to pay. She was scared. Stinking of liquor, the man was right in her face.

Was he a random street cadge, though, or was he Average? Would forty cents purchase the man's absence, or would it assure his ongoing extortionist presence? Tim was no stranger to paranoia, yet the fact remained that someone was Average. Someone who phoned them boldly, incessantly. If he was bold, why wouldn't he press his case in person? What was paranoid about expecting that?

Now Tim stood at a distance—watching the watcher?—as the

disheveled man kept fidgeting with his keys. Dozens of keys. Then a white Bronco came bumping down the mews and erased him: he was there, he was gone. This one had simply been waiting for a ride.

Billy and Cindy were safe upstairs. They were oddly civil, though, eerily quiescent. And so tractable. It was nice of them to lie down at bedtime and from the darkness recite the names of new friends they had made. (And what an education their uncle was providing, for these were black friends, Korean friends, an *Albanian* friend for goodness' sake.) Listening to Tim read, Cindy seemed as peaceful as he was in turmoil.

Cindy's story was the Little House—and the big loving family, all their days washed by clear pioneer streams. As Tim covered her shoulders with a flannel sheet, his heart was aching for her literally, unless he was having an anxiety attack. He stretched his arms over his head and exhaled; drank a glass of water. He got in bed and waited for the pain to subside.

It did, finally, as he lay on his back breathing evenly, but soon his throat was dry and he began to feel warm. Tim was ready for this, however, he had been through this plenty of times. In a way, it was the price one paid for staying in denial. Denial provided fertile ground for the imagination, left room for hourly manifestations and symptoms. Given the tricks of pneumocystis, any sneeze could be the beginning of The End and in any room he entered, every pretty landscape, Tim could ferret out a cause for sneezing. His whole life had been an anxiety attack for years.

Nonetheless his brow was damp, his throat was sore, so that when the phone pierced the air at midnight, it came as a relief. A distraction. It was Average, almost undoubtedly, yet Tim was ready to take the call. "Greetings, fellow sufferer," he said, almost cheerfully.

"It's you, in person. What a pleasant surprise."

"Who are you, you sicko?" said Tim.

"Me? You know. I'm Joe Average."

"It's not funny, and it's not scary, so why don't you just stop wasting your time."

It had become a conversation, between Tim and his tormentor. The conventional wisdom ran contrary: ignore them and they will go away. To date, however, the conventional wisdom had failed, and had left him feeling cramped and useless. Right now he felt upgraded to a better diagnosis. Chest pains, negative.

"It's nice of you to worry about my time. And I'm so glad that *you* have time to chat."

"I'm not worried about you, I'm worried about my kids, who may overhear your demented voice."

"Kids! I don't think so. Is that why we're having this chat? Because you worked out a new strategy? *Talk* to poor Joe Average, be kind to him. Don't talk down, don't say crazy—say kids. Well you aren't kidding me."

"I did say crazy, and I do have two children living with me."

"God help the little suckers! You should turn yourself in to Social Services before there's trouble."

"Two young children who do not need this weirdness in their lives right now."

"When will they need it? You need it, don't you? A little weirdness in your life? Speaking of which, I was disappointed you changed your message. I liked the sexy one. Was that one of your weird boyfriends doing his Mae West impression, or was it you? Do you do Mae West?"

"Where are you calling from, Joe?"

"Me? Maybe I'm not calling at all. Maybe I'm just your conscience, calling you from within."

Suddenly it hit Tim how perfectly pointless this was. It was like arguing with a clever teenager who played by different rules, turning everything upside down and tossing it back at you sarcastically. He was feeding the nut straight lines! But he did want the last word. He wanted to come up with a real zinger, a walk-off shot, then hang up fast. He drew a blank, unfortunately—no zingers—and muttered something lame about sending regards to Earl.

"I'll bite. Who's Earl?"

"You don't know?"

"Well, there's my cousin Earl. Earl Average."

"Right. And my regards to your entire team of psychiatrists," said Tim, lowering himself to the level of smartass teen repartée. Hanging up, he was humming to himself (insanely) "Goodbye Joe/ Me gotta go/ Me-o My-o...." Watching the play of a streetlamp on his ceiling, he resolved to sign up for Caller ID on Monday.

"Jambalay and a crawfish pie and a filet gumbo"—and then

Tim realized he had learned a couple of things by humoring Average. The first was that Earl was not the nut. And whoever the nut was, he suspected a put-on when Tim mentioned the children. No sale, said Average, and this was great news; it meant they were not being watched after all. The next time Tim claimed not to be frightened he would almost be telling the truth.

Billy and Cindy bounced out of bed as though they had just completed prison sentences. They had packed the night before. Rolling out of Boston before the long slack chains of traffic could form, they highballed into Jaffrey so early that Trumball's hadn't opened. As they studied the rich profusion of flavors on the signboard (purely for research purposes), theirs was the only automobile in a sunny two-acre lot.

"Chocolate-chocolate chip, I guess," said Cindy. "With extra sprinkles."

"Banana," said Billy. "Or maybe pistachio."

"Toffee burberry grinch," said Tim, and awaited Billy's in-the-know smirk, Cindy's facial protest of his disinformation.

At the house, the kids sprinted ahead of him, without a trace of ambivalence. Today Tim was not surprised, for he had shared their eagerness to be here. Coming past the brick mill on the river, past the stone churches and the Monadnock Inn, he too had experienced a homecoming. Haunted, perhaps, but Jill's house was also what they had left of Jill.

Tim uncoiled slowly, stretching in the sunlit yard. He pulled off his shoes and socks to free his toes in the warm grass. If all you asked of life was a pretty garden and a peaceful spot to sip your favorite whiskey, Cedar Street was unquestionably a fine choice. What about the world, however? That was the question they liked to hash over: could you achieve a life of ease without surrendering the quest for something better?

Such as? That was Pete Weissberg's ready reply. He and Peter Clippinger would retire to Truro in a minute, if they had the money. A garden, good restaurants, friends and the beach nearby? To the Peters, there was no something-better. But they had love; they had one another. And apart from their happy "perversion" they were terribly normal. The joke was that when they moved to Truro they would instantly find themselves with a golden retriever, 2.3 children, and that stuff that makes your toilet water blue.

What if one did not have love? What, asked Tim, if one did not even wish to have it? Pete argued that all you surrendered was the freedom to suffer, always inviting Tim to *name* the something-better. Tim could neither name it nor defend it. There was good to be done, of course, but the Peters did their share of that, they were activists on any number of fronts. Tim could hardly claim he was making the world safe for Democracy by making reservations for the bourgeoisie in Cancun and Acapulco.

"The house smells bad, Unk."

"It *stinks*," said Cindy, smushing her features together by way of corroborating her brother. The smell was real, though—not symbolic of anything—as Tim discovered upon investigating.

"We closed up too tight," he said. "We just need to air it out. Open the windows."

"There's a can of spray in the bathroom," Billy suggested.

"Throw it away. That junk just makes it worse."

But this was nothing less than the new regime proclaimed, for the can of spray had to be Monty's. Monty's tendency to fight odor with odor. As he saw Billy hesitate, Tim started to retract his rash command. Rehabilitate the noxious spray-can.

To Billy, though, the can had nothing to do with his father, it simply stood for *action,* which he was always reluctant to forego. Quickly he worked his way to a solution, an alternate action, namely slam-dunking the can into the wastebasket. Then, taking the stairs three at a time, he raced to throw open the attic windows.

Tim was racing nowhere. He dragged the lawnmower from the garage, inhaling the perfume of grass and oil. He felt a burgher's ease spread through him. It never crossed his mind that here was Monty's mower, only that the grass needed cutting.

Yesterday, when Ellie asked him when the house would be listed, Tim had balked. Nothing was decided, he said; he and the children might even live there. Yet until she asked, Tim had assumed the house would be sold. Why had he argued the contrary? Now as he scraped clumps of packed grass from the deck of the mower, he realized that he was not ready to sell this house. Whatever *that* meant.

Braving mildew, the kids settled into their rooms. Someone from the church called to solicit them all for a chicken supper that evening. "We miss them," said the voice, "and we worry, of course." With wild expressive sign language, the children said no to the chicken supper and Tim earned their gratitude by politely declining. They rushed back upstairs, and he returned to the lawn-mower.

He freed up the blade, topped up the gas and oil, then yanked twenty times on the cord without a ripple or cough from the engine. Mechanically challenged, Tim was crouching over the machine in puzzlement when a neighbor materialized at his side. "It's going to be the spark plug."

Tim looked up at a face narrow at the temples, but with Howdy Doody smile-lines bracketing the lower half like parentheses. "Monty always fouled the plug on that mower."

"So how do I unfoul it?" asked Tim, standing.

"Let me," said the man, actually pulling a wrench from his back pocket. "If this doesn't work, you can always use mine."

"I'm Jill's brother. Tim Bannon."

"Al McManus. Father of the twins."

"Hi. I need to thank you—both you and your wife."

They shook hands, each with a facial apology for the sundry besmearments. Tim's fingers were grass-stained green and smudged black. "You know," said McManus, "she's taking the twins over to the skateboard park in an hour. If your two have any interest in going."

Al and Alice! He would have to remember their names. And the twins were...Ted and Fred? It emerged that Al McManus edited a software magazine with half a million circulation. You could do a job like that anywhere, he testified; could do it from your own bathroom. Al had not surrendered anything, he had jumped at the chance to move here. Al's word: jumped.

Tim cut pale swaths in the emerald green, going back and forth with lazy pleasure. The twins—Heathcliffe and Horridge?—had gone in the house to roust out the Hergies. Clearly they were great pals, and Tim wondered how many good times the Hergies had missed out on just because he showed up, with his Camp White Sneaker plans. "Good intentions, bad planning," Monty had to tell him once; they were driving away as he arrived.

A red Chevy pick-up came fishtailing into the driveway, like a stray Duke of Hazzard: racing stripes, mag wheels, thrumming dual exhaust. The Earlmobile, no less.

"Came by to say hi," Earl rhymed, singsong.

"Where's Ric?"

"I didn't eat her, if that's what you are suggesting. We are not joined at the hip, she and I."

"I'm just surprised you would come here without her. Or at all, after what you pulled."

"Big Bad Bill!" exclaimed Earl, stepping past Tim to snare the approaching boy and swing him high. Cindy was there in a tick to gain her share of the attention and Earl aired her out, spinning her like a baton before he set her down shouting. After a decade of behaving as though these children resided in Missoula, Montana, he was suddenly their loving Uncle Earl.

Yet so convincing was this act, they seemed won over. In thirty seconds, Earl had rewritten family history. "I thought Bill might wish to fish," he grinned.

"Wish to fish," said Cindy, liking the music.

"Nothing fancy, mind you. Just a line and a pole—and the Schooner, of course. Check out the bass in Powder Mill Pond?"

Hugh and Henry, that was it. He should scribble it on his wrist before he forgot. Hugh and Henry were the twins, and they were the reason Billy, though sorely tempted by Earl's line-and-a-pole, had to pass on his fishing expedition.

"Raincheck on it, little amigo," said Earl. "Another day, we'll go and play."

Tim marvelled at the chutzpah; at the lack of any vestige of a conscience; at the pathetic rhymed couplets.

"You are quite the poet," he snapped, when they were alone again in the yard.

"I was addressing a child," Earl confided. "You may not have mastered the knack."

"Poetry, did I say? More like doggerel."

"Maybe. But youngsters do tend to enjoy old Earl. And that boy will want to learn his fishing gear and lore."

"Guns and knives too, don't forget."

"And ropes!" Earl exploded with glee. "Hey, I know some knots you couldn't untie on your most memorable bondage date."

Tim wheeled away, with Earl in close pursuit.

"I'm sorry, Timmy, I apologize. Couldn't resist the opening. But this is a business deal, that's all it is, where everyone has a point of view. Like the ballplayer who says he's worth four million and the owner wants to pay him two. They don't have to hate each other."

"I'm guessing they do, though."

"Well I sure don't. Hell, I respect you trying to do your best by Bill. Why not respect the same in us?"

Softened by this gambit, and by the sugared tone, Tim wavered. Dear God, he gasped, don't let me buy a house from this man when I know for a fact there is water in the basement. This man who has always ridiculed and despised me. But he did waver.

Arms spread wide to welcome Tim's reply, Earl's gaze and posture were almost Christlike. Over the top? Maybe. But you needed to believe in yourself to make the sale, and Earl did. Moreover, he had registered Tim's confusion the way a boxer senses that a tough body punch has discouraged his opponent.

"Friends?" he said, extending a hand. "We do want to stay friends."

"Stay? Friends?"

"For the sake of the family. For young Bill, and for your Mom. Don't forget your mother now, Timmy."

"I won't forget my mother. I also haven't forgotten the adjectives in your friendly note to the Probate Court."

That saved him. Thank goodness he remembered The Complaint, in all its saturnine verbosity.

"Come on now, Timmy, you have to ignore all that bullpiss. That's not us talking, that's the damned liars. That's how they do. You can't say I didn't warn you against letting them in."

"Quite an imagination those liars have. To dream up all that nasty stuff on their own."

"It's a sales job," said Earl, in a moment of jarring sincerity, where his interests and the truth coincided precisely. "The liars are just selling something to His Honor."

Earl winked. This was all a game. Indeed, it was a fine collaboration, with Tim and Earl on the side of the angels and the corrupt lawyers and judges in Satan's pay. Earl could be seduced by the sound of his own voice; the meaning did not necessarily matter. It might be Holy Ghost Power or a raised-ranch starter home out on Route 31, all the same once he got rolling. And he had sold himself on Tim as well, on this idea of staying friends. Earl was genuine (that is, he meant it while he was saying it), inviting Tim to ride with him to Keene. "We can hash this thing out," said Earl.

"That's all right," said Tim. "I've got a lot to do."

He didn't have a bloody thing to do, in fact. The grass was cut and Alice McManus had whisked the kids off to the skateboard park. Then, with Earl's dust still swirling in the air, he was seized by inspiration. Something to do.

It had been years—decades?—since the last time he had spoken with Erica. Alone, that is. She was like a Russian ice-dancer, with no identity outside the arc of her partner. Her partner, however, would be gone for the next two hours.

Pit stop at Mrs. Murphy's, where the coffee was just good enough to let Tim forego one of Mrs. Murphy's doughnuts, then north on 202 almost to the Peterborough line. He was pretty sure he could find the house; pretty sure she would be home. He sipped past steep farmlands and sand hills on the left, the Contoocook snaking its way north on the right. He would seek Ric out, yes, but what would he say to her? The question was still unanswered when he arrived at her house.

He could see her shock from twenty yards away. As he approached on foot, such panic was in her eyes that he wondered if he had forgotten his pants—at the very least spilled a bad splotch of coffee in a bad spot. Hers was an expression to greet a madman or a rapist, not a brother, however estranged.

"I was so close by it would have been rude not to stop."

"Earl never found you?"

"He did. He came by Jill's house."

"So then—?"

"So I don't know, there's just the two of us now, Ric, and it seems too sad and stupid for us to be enemies."

"I'm not set against you—not the way you suppose. But Earl and I are together on this. Don't go thinking we aren't."

"Meaning you assume I came here to trick you somehow?"

"Beats me why you came here."

"I told you, I came because you're my sister. And you ought to know how honest I am. Don't you remember when we backed into Mr. Lindsay's carry-all?"

"Tim, that was like twenty-five years ago."

"Almost. But do you remember what you said we should do?"

Tim had owned a driver's license for two days and the whole time Erica, who was fourteen, had pestered him for a joyride. Then they smacked into Jack Lindsay's immaculately restored lemon-yellow '48 Apache in the Monty Ward parking lot.

"Well," said Erica, coyly, "it didn't show. No damage

showed."

"Maybe not, but it cost a hundred bucks to fix. Jack got every penny of my summer profits that year."

"You should have listened to me."

Erica had softened. She had braced in the doorway like George Wallace on the schoolhouse steps and now she was offering coffee. Tim said yes, to be agreeable, though he saw that the coffee was instant—undrinkable even had he not just polished off a cup of Mrs. Murphy's. He drank some anyway, to mark acceptance of this newly humane treatment.

Naked of Earl, naked of attitude, his little sister was still a stranger to Tim. An attractive stranger, he acknowledged, with her long brown hair in a silver clip and her signature close-fitting jeans. It was tight jeans, Anne Bannon said long ago, that kept Ric from caring about her high school grades. She still wore them well, even if Earl Sanderson was all they had fetched her in lieu of education.

"Remember Sibby Hopkins?" said Tim.

"Sure I do. What makes you think I can't remember my own life? But why Sibby?"

"He just came back to me. A blast from the past."

Sibby was the first fetch of Erica's snug-in-the-seat jeans, that was why. Sibby had occupied her every waking moment junior year; his senior year. He was a clever suitor, too, always cutting deals on the side with Anne. "We're going to study. I want her to study as much as you do, Mrs. Bannon— so she can come up to the college with me next year."

Anne was flattered, and charmed, for Sibby was a well-spoken fine-looking boy. But neither he nor Ric studied very much, and neither ever went up to the college. Sibby became a Seabee.

"He's divorced," said Erica. "I heard it when we were home."

"I thought they had four kids."

"Five, actually."

"Children having children, as they say."

"Hardly, Tim. Sibby's thirty-nine. And what's-her-face is a year *older*."

"I know, but they had numero uno real early on. He definitely has a twenty-year-old living in Charleston."

"I am well aware of that, thank you."

"Whoops, sorry. I kind of forgot that what's-her-face stepped into your picture frame there. Hey, you can be thankful you aren't down South raising those five kids—on factory wages."

"Not everybody breeds like cattle."

"A good thing, too. Imagine five kids, day in and day out. Man, it's hard enough with two."

Erica changed, like litmus paper. Uneducated, maybe, but not slow. "So: we finally get the propaganda."

"Sorry if it seemed that way. But I wonder if you know how much work is involved."

"Does anyone know? Before they have a kid ?"

"Good point. But at least they get to ease into it. They get the one kid, and he's really small. Can't talk, just eats milk. So there's a period of adjustment."

"We'll manage. People do."

"Hey, tell me about it."

They stepped through a sliding door onto the deck, which looked over a flat, barren yard, with nothing growing. Firewood, stacked tight and square, sat on the sparse grass. It looked as if a boxcar had been packed full of logs and then the boxcar walls had dissolved away.

"At least there's two of us," said Erica. "Plus, kids are in school all day."

To Tim, this smacked of Earl offering her comfort. His retort was gentle, merely factual. "They do come home at three o'clock."

"There's always boarding school, in a pinch."

Parent to parent, across the picket fence, this would be a harmless, cynical jest. But Tim heard Earl again, buttressing Ric with a fallback plan.

"Sure. Boarding school would cut way down on your obligations."

"I imagine it would."

"Expensive, though. From what I hear, private school is as much as college."

"I know that."

Had Tim read her mind a minute earlier, it would have been Sibby Hopkins and summer nights at the tank in Mullins. When he read her now, it was Come home Earl and be quick about it.

"Imagine the cost of two kids over ten years—before they even get to college. Sixty bucks for sneakers? Three bucks for an ice cream cone? It's gotta be a million dollars."

"You're the math whiz."

"I'm the parentis, too, Ric. And I don't want to send them away to school."

"Who said we do?"

You did, said Tim, though only to himself. He saw her steeliness and regretted the way the visit had drifted; knew that he had blown it.

"No one," he said. "And this is my fault. We shouldn't have gotten into any of this stuff."

"It's bound to be on our minds," she said, regaining equanimity, choosing civility, though she had a powerful impulse to kick her brother in the shins.

The children seemed way too calm. They had gone back into society, so to speak, and they moved back into their lives so comfortably. Billy organized his baseball cards, Cindy endlessly rearranged a collection of rubber dolls with comically hideous faces. Now and then, they came to him with harmless questions.

Where was the trauma?

Hoping to find out, Tim placed a call to Olivia Goldsmith—several calls, as the day progressed. He tried her office, home, pager, cell: no Goldsmith today.

Before dinner he assigned some yard work, raking, on general trail-through-the-jungle principles, and they pitched in enthusiastically. When he fired up the gas grill, they practically salivated, and eagerly wolfed down the hot dogs and hamburgers.

There was a basketball hoop mounted on the neighbors' garage, and Billy bounced his ball that way after dinner. Tim went along, to hang out. He retrieved Billy's hits and misses, took very few shots of his own, and avoided altogether the nefarious practice of "dribbling." Billy seemed untroubled. Businesslike, really; basketball was his business.

When Hugh and Henry came out, Tim stood with Al McManus, side by side, arms folded. "It's really Bill's court," said Al. "He uses it more than we do."

"He's good," said Tim.

Al gave him a look, as though Tim had just told him it can get cold in December. "*Very* good," he smiled.

"I didn't want to brag."

Later, Tim suggested an evening cruise on Gilmore Pond—load the canoe and be there for the sunset over Mt. Monadnock.

"Sunset, Unk? No *thanks*," said Cindy, and Billy shot him the high sign. BATS, he mouthed silently.

This would have to pass for the trauma. The one time they had canoed through the Gilmore twilight, they noticed a bat skimming across the water toward them and soon a second bat. (Mr. and Mrs Bat, they joked.) Before long it became a bit alarming—dozens, possibly hundreds of bats, black against the blackening sky, and the creatures were strafing them absolutely, as though the mosquitos were only for dessert.

"You've got bats in your belfry," Tim said to Cindy. "And don't you ask me what a belfry is."

"What's a belfry?" she fired back on cue, with childlike joy he would have to say, still baffled by it.

"Can we stay this week?" said Billy.

"I wish. Next week, though. Promise."

"For real?"

"For real, Cynthia."

That would be the week of the hearing in Keene. Dissolution and Promiscuity, starring Timothy Bannon.

He took Cindy along to pick up milk and bread. (Quality time, he could not help thinking, parentally, though they had run out of milk.) She slid close to him coming home, almost like a teenage girlfriend. Reluctant to dislodge her from any source of comfort, Tim only belatedly registered the departure from form. Cindy had disdained the back seat, disdained her seatbelt, disdained rules altogether.

Jill's rules. As if, on a subterranean level, she too was moving them into an experimental new regime. "I'll be your seatbelt for this trip," he laughed once he had caught on, and comically extended his right arm like a guard rail the rest of the way.

"What's up?" said Olivia Goldsmith.

"Nothing in a way. That's the problem: life just goes on."

"Life does go on."

"It's crazy, it's like nothing happened. They never talk about it."

"Do you? Have you brought it up?"

"I have kind of left it to them—so no, I guess. I didn't want to force it on them."

"That's fine. But what exactly do you see as the problem?"

"Reality? I'll give you an example. Since we were last here, some of my sister's flowers came up. Nasturtiums. Cindy helped Jill plant them, which I know because I know, not because Cindy said so. She noticed the flowers, I noticed her noticing them, and then she sort of skipped away."

"Nervously."

"Maybe. She looked calm to me."

"What did you do?"

"A test! I did do something, I asked her what they were, the flowers that she and her mom had planted. She said 'Nasturtiums —Mom's favorite.' Just like that."

"That's some kid you've got there."

"She was closer to Monty, you know. And not once has she mentioned him. Not one word."

"She will. It sounds as though you are all doing fine."

"You don't know the rest of it," said Tim, and made her listen to a brief synopsis of the legal tangle. "So now I'm supposed to fight off the competition with one hand while I boil oatmeal with the other."

"Try some of that one-minute stuff. My kids actually preferred it."

"Apart from the homemaking tips, I don't suppose you would know who the guardian *ad litem* is up here."

"There's no such office. Different people get appointed to do it. I've done it."

"I'd love for it to be you."

"It can't be me. I've been involved."

Tim was hoping she would ask him to bring the kids in for a tuneup. Instead Goldsmith closed with another tip from her country kitchen: "Honey wheat germ and thin slices of banana. Add them to the instant oatmeal and kids will eat it like a hot fudge sundae."

That night Tim sat in the kitchen with a glass of wine, reading magazines. Monty subscribed to half a dozen and sometimes, on a rainy day, Tim would leaf through them the way one does at a dentist's office. Absently. Because they were there.

But tonight he read them intensively, as though cramming for a final exam on makeovers or celebrity dating. He was digesting every sentence, storing every shard of gossip, though none of it held the slightest interest for him. On the contrary, he hated Michael Jackson's music, hated Woody Allen's movies, didn't care a fig for Alan Greenspan's fiscal pieties. Yet he absorbed it all, *Time* and *Life* and *Newsweek* after *Newsweek*.

Then suddenly he was weeping.

It began with a crooked smile, when he found three unrelated Jacksons in a single issue of *Newsweek*. There was Michael with some plastic surgery, and Glenda the British actress, and then Alan, a hot new country-and-western singer. The Jackson Three! As tears leached through, as he felt them coming faster, Tim allowed he must be seriously overtired. Then the tears were flowing through his arms and legs, through his chest, as if tears had replaced his blood.

A loud animal sound he was hearing turned out to be himself, sobbing. He rushed outside for the sake of the children, got inside the car for the sake of the neighbors; then he rolled up the windows and let himself go. Not that he had much choice.

It hurt to cry this hard. It strained the muscles of his face and kept exploding in his chest and throat as he sat shivering in the airtight Honda. At times the tears reverted back to laughter, or got caught halfway between, in a sort of hiccup. Slowly the laughter prevailed, and Tim giggled at the possibility that someone could mistake him for a pack of hyenas and come out shooting.

Not hyenas, coyotes. There were coyotes in these hills, hyenas were in Africa, their laughter making tracks and trails through the jungle. No shots rang out, no lights came on. He was alone and the street stayed quiet; the emotion was tapering off. Giddiness still threatened. He recalled the Jackson Three and then the three Alans, in that same magazine—Alan Jackson, Alan Greenspan, and Woody Allen, whose real name was Alan Something. Tim sat tight, ticking like a clock, holding the line against giddiness.

But he knew this was a nervous breakdown. He had cracked.

Tim could cry. He cried in movies and he cried at funerals. Still, he handled emotion well—too well for Karl Trickett's taste. He never lost control. He had somehow arranged his interior furniture so as to preclude the possibility, though maybe (given what he had witnessed in his mother and in Jilly's kids) such self-control was genetic.

125

So this was new; way beyond control. And now, as he stood outside, the lone inhabitant of a world of moonlight on lawns, of moonlight on a million white clapboards, he saw Jill and Monty waving from the front door. Saw them distinctly, in sharp focus, precisely where he had seen them last, a month ago.

Tim stared at the doorway until they were gone. Panned back across the yard to the garage to make certain they had not simply moved around on him. He circled the cedar tree, rustled the clump of quince, until he was satisfied.

He was better. It was going to be okay. The ticking within him had spread into a soft general noiseless hum, like a painless toothache, a dose of Novocaine, by the time he got into bed.

And there was life after nervous breakdowns. Next morning, with Billy and Cindy still upstairs, Tim received his first field report from Bannon's Queer Army of the Republic.

"Get ready for this," said Peter Clippinger, sounding as excited as a kid at the county fair. "Your sister was married. Six days ago. In Maryland."

"I don't get it, Peter. Who did she marry?"

"Earl Sanderson. The point is they were never married before, either of them, ever. To each other, or to anyone else."

"That's impossible."

"Their witnesses—you'll like this—were a Mr. and Mrs. Garth Gaylord of Gideon Township, Maryland."

"They lied?"

"Indeed. They have been living a lie for lo these many years. But you've got them now."

This revelation served to bolster Tim throughout the day. It would slide from his consciousness, then slip back in with a delicate flavor. But the day had a flavor of its own. Tim's breakdown seemed to be complete (or completed) and it left him feeling almost buoyant, as shock therapy was said to do.

The children took good care of him. Maybe they knew he had a few screws loose and maybe they were campaigning to stay here in Jaffrey, but they were good company all day. Tim had shaped a firm little speech on the subject of seatbelts and backseats, which he never had to give, because they were way ahead of him, in full compliance. Billy had such unselfish instincts—he noticed whatever needed noticing—and he set the tone.

Out on Gilmore Pond, Tim recalled their earliest excursions (Camp Bannon, back then), voyages that always began with Jill's many admonitions and concluded with her relief upon seeing them alive at the close of day. To assuage her fears, they plied only the tamest bodies of water that summer. It was possible to drown on Norway Pond but you had to be trying awfully hard.

The following year they graduated to larger lakes (none resembling Lake Huron, to be sure) and evolved into a crackerjack crew. While Jill could never relax entirely ("I'm their *mother*," was her excuse) her worries were increasingly *pro forma*. There had been the incident with the bats at twilight, and a time or two when they got caught in the rain, but even Jill could not call that danger.

No sign of danger today, and no stress, as they swam and paddled and gathered blueberries. Twice they voted to stay out "another half-hour" simply because there was nothing better in their world. And later, when they had to pack for Boston, Tim was as sorry to leave as Billy and Cindy. Summer in the Monadnocks felt like unfinished business.

Just before they left, Tim called Erica with a question—and with the hope of tightening their connection. Of course he had to go through Earl, due to the natural perversity of things. "It's Tim. Looking for my sister."

"Wellsir, you are looking in the right place. But how's my buddy Bill doing?"

"He doesn't wish to fish, if that's what you mean."

"Sure he does."

"Oh, hey. Congratulations—" Tim arrested himself like Dr. Strangelove, one hand clutching his own voicebox. It would be unwise (idiotic?) to give away Peter's find before checking with Dee Barnes.

"Congratulations? On?"

"Well. I just assumed you landed a ten-pound bass yesterday."

"Oh my yes, the fish were jumping."

"And the cotton was high?"

Tim burned to smack him with it (Mr. and Mrs. Garth Fucking Gaylord!) and yet how much sweeter to smack him before the hardass judge. He could see Earl fancydancing around it—"True, your Honor, we did get hitched up ten days ago *technically,* but...." It would be more like sixteen days by then. Still, if sixteen days made behavior good as gold, Tim could grab a piece of the action too. (Shucks, your Honor, sixteen days ago in Gideon Fucking Township I went straight, completely eradicating my flamingly perverted past.)

Now, while Earl fetched him Erica, Tim labored to regain the spirit behind this overture. Yesterday (before he blew it) they had managed to bypass two decades of bad history and vault back to high school, or childhood. To a pre-sexual time when he and Ric were pals. There was a year or two (Jilly suddenly older and Ric still a kid, no tight Levi's on her yet) when they had been closest.

"What?" said Erica now, warily. Not close.

"I'll tell you what, very specifically. I have got to know what Sibby is short for."

"Why?"

"I know, and I have always known, but I'm having this mental block, remembering, and it's driving me crazy."

"Maybe you just are crazy," she laughed. "What does it even matter?"

"It doesn't *matter* matter, it's just frustrating."

"Sebastian. Sebastian Hall Hopkins the Third."

"Yes! Thank you! And he would say it exactly that way, when he picked up the telephone."

"He would for a fact. But when did you ever call him?"

"Only every time Mom made me call. Looking for her bad girl."

"Looking for me at Sibby's house? Fat chance."

"You were there, plenty of times."

"Only when they weren't. Sebastian Hall Hopkins the Second, and Katy Mae. That's what I called his mom—she was so damned *southern,* in her gingham dresses."

Erica felt a connection to the past, too, partly from the recent visit home and partly to do with seeing Tim. It was a different past, however, and had little to do with her brother. Erica was fixed on the memory of Sibby and herself undressing one another at the tank that first time, the moon full and shockingly clear as they alternated swigs of pilfered wine with a piece-by-piece unveiling of the gifts they had brought one another. A memory of their flesh coming together on the old cotton quilt....

Tim's mental snapshot showed Erica alone. She was sweet sixteen, her hair in curlers as she stood over the ironing board in her motheaten colordrained nightgown, ironing the beejesus out of those equally paperthin jeans.

"Sebastian," he said. "I can't believe I forgot that."

Tim had not been half an hour at his desk on Monday when Peter Clippinger checked in with a fresh report. Weeks ago, Tim had indeed appeared on four separate broadcasts of a cable station's news loop, pontificating about Neo-Nazis. Peter, who had seen the tape, did not believe Tim came on obnoxious (or particularly el flamo), but roughly fifty thousand Bostonians had watched the interview. One of them, no doubt, was his Joe Average.

At the moment it was academic, since Average had not called in over a week. This was July and (as an average Joe from Boston) he might be vacationing on the Cape, too cheap to make his harassing calls long distance. It was also faintly possible that Tim had done him in, had taken the fun out of it, with his phony bravado. Time would tell.

Karl Trickett had found something too, though his opening salvo was deflationary. "It's not a huge deal," he said. "And, by the way, the Maryland wedding is not a huge deal either."

"Come on. We've got them committing a crime."

"What crime? You can see it's not exactly assault with a deadly weapon. They come in and testify they have been good-as-wed for ten years and now, given good reason, they go ahead and make it official."

"They did it to get Billy and Cindy."

"It seems so, yes. But having a child on the way probably accounts for half the weddings since the time of Christ."

"On the way, huh? It's a big old lie."

"True, and as such it may help offset their potshots at you. Unless they have been filing taxes jointly, though, it's not a crime."

"Fine. So I was happy and now I am discouraged."

"We all have mood swings. Let me tell you what I came up with. Vietnam. Earl was there and damned if he wasn't twice decorated, for whatever reasons. That's unknowable. He was also twice discharged with honor from the Army."

"Karl, I was already discouraged."

"But. He was jailed at Fort Jackson for cheating at cards. Spent forty-eight hours in the stockade."

"The calaboose!"

"It's good, and yet the guy is forty-six and he has this one slap on the wrist—"

"The hoosegow! The jug!"

"Talk about mood swings. Will you settle down?"

"He lies about his marriage, he cheats at cards? We have uncovered a pattern of dishonesty. Who would believe he doesn't lie about water in the basement of an old farmhouse?"

"Two instances, twenty years apart. I'm not sure that makes a very impressive pattern."

"I'm impressed."

"The judge won't be. Who among us is without sin? What this says is that Earl, among us, comes pretty damned close."

"What's the point of all this digging if everything we find is so useless?"

"Well, we are turning things up, we may turn up something better. You are right that his business reputation is worth checking. Scamming the elderly? There could be a few complaints on file."

"Water in the basements of the elderly! I feel his guilt."

"It may really be a pattern before we're done. Anyway, I'm going to poke around up there. Scout out the courthouse, do some homework on the judge."

"Are you serious? Dig up dirt on the judge?"

"Not dirt, Tim. How he reacts; how he likes material presented. Lawyers do this. Right down to researching a judge's taste in neckties and wearing one in that style."

"Again I say, justice is a beautiful thing to behold."

"Judges are human. And a lot of them are just old hack lawyers who happen to play golf with the old hack who ends up being Governor."

"Listen, Karl, this is beyond the call of friendship. I'll have it on my conscience, if you go waste your time in New Hampshire."

"Don't get me started, Tim."

This, of course, was an old dead horse. Tim's proud self-sufficiency (ask nothing, give nothing) versus Karl's lament at the distance it created between the two of them.

"All right, Karl, but at least stay at the house. Eat the English muffins in the freezer. Don't waste your money too."

"The house would be fine, except I've decided to treat

myself. There's a B&B with private hot tub, nice views. I made reservations."

"You're going with a friend."

"Possibly."

"*Possibly*? Karl, I'm happy to hear it. You don't need to protect my feelings."

"I like to think I do. You know."

"The main order of the day," said Attorney Dee Barnes, motioning Tim into his chair, "is getting a firm handle on the Opposition."

"Handle them firmly, by all means," said Tim, who could be giddy at times in the wake of his crackup. The legal considerations were increasingly abstract to him (what "counted" and what did not count) but he had been curious to see how Barnes would treat him. Neutrally, was his early verdict: no recoil, no warmth.

"The Opposition is just a term for the paperwork we need to prepare. It's our memo—in response to their Petition."

"You said you had a chore for me?"

"Yes, I'd like you to chase down an affidavit of some kind on the Maryland wedding. Proof. It will save me time if you take care of that."

"So we can use it."

"Let's just say that if we do use it, I want to be damned certain it's unimpeachable."

"Can I ask you a hypothetical question?"

"Of course."

"What would happen if I went straight? Today. If from this day forth, I had no gay agenda. Was cured."

"Are you considering such a change? Are you capable of it?"

There had been a dustup last night when Tim tried to defend the contents of his closet, which had turned up as an unpleasant surprise in the "Petition." It was very well to argue that men wearing dresses and pearls violated no statute, Barnes instructed, but at a *custody* hearing it would better serve to identify those items as costumes from amateur theatricals, which had been kept because (as was the case) the children liked playing with them.

Tim was to rid himself immediately of any clothing that could not fit this finely spun, benignly spun description (anything in the way of lingerie, anything even negligibly flavored by sexuality— Barnes could not have been more emphatic, or frosty) and furthermore to *lose* any photographs which might show him decked out in such frippery. "Frippery!" he began to protest her biased word-choice, but Barnes shut him down fiercely: "Just do as I say."

"It's a hypothetical," he said now. "I stay at home making soup and watching lots of television. Would that really make me a fitter custodian in the eyes of the law?"

Barnes disapproved with a look of exasperation: their short hour did not allow for frivolous hypotheticals. She was aware, however, that her sympathy had lapsed. "He's not a murderer, Dee," her husband Leon had felt compelled to remind her, after overhearing the dustup.

"It might," she allowed, agreeing with Leon (in absentia) to cut Tim more slack.

"Would it make me the winner?" he persisted.

"Look, face it, what we *don't* do defines us as much as what we do in this life."

"Then how come old Jimmy Carter got in hot water just for lusting in his heart? Remember that one?"

"I do. But think how much hotter the water had he gone and lusted after a pretty young campaign worker in the flesh."

"So it's not morality we're talking about, it's timidity."

Sympathy lapsed anew, and this time her withering glance went beyond disapproval to outright dismissal. What tripped her was Tim's frivolity, his way of constantly shifting the crisis into games and jokes. And while this could be attributed to nerves, it could also be the case that the salesman and the little sister would make better custodians.

"The subtext of this proceeding," she said, electing to simply ignore his provocations, "is shaping a new life for the boy and the girl. A solid framework: home, school, friendships, activities."

"Absolutely."

"You say absolutely, yet you haven't been able to say where you would raise them. If you can't tell me, how will you tell a judge next week?"

"By deciding."

"Look, Tim, I don't doubt you're laughing because this makes you feel uncomfortable. But you really do have to know the answer."

"I'll know it. Five weeks until school opens? A person ought to know where he'll be living in five weeks."

"The court will certainly concur."

"I've thought of changing jobs," he said, more soberly, and it was true he had. Tim thought a great deal about changing jobs. He tossed it out now, however, in an effort to regain Barnes' approval. It hurt him that she had not yet processed the tough parts, not emerged from the fire, but it hurt even more to have lost her allegiance.

"That may or may not work for you, personally. But as a declaration, all it does is bring you before the court essentially unemployed."

"It's slim pickings up there. Part-time telemarketers. Fork-lift operator at $8.65 an hour. The only one that appealed to me was night custodian at the middle school."

"*Nights*," she reminded him with a subarctic chill, "you are at home with the children."

"What if we just *went* for it? Said hey I'm gay but I really love the kids and I'm putting them into public school in Boston and that Jill and Monty wanted it that way and the kids do too. Is that a case we can make?"

"I hope so, since it may be our entire case."

"What, then? Are you saying I should promise to leave the city? Move to New Hampshire?"

"Look, I can tell you that judges like to keep children wherever they are. But I can't say whether you can survive a winter in New Hampshire without bouts of depression, or suicidal impulses."

"Nervous breakdowns," he added—less frivolously, more pointedly than she knew.

"I'm sure it happens," was all she said.

That night, Tim fulfilled a longstanding promise by taking Billy and Cindy to the top of the Pru. Billy was quiet and Tim (processing Barnes) a little distant, while Cindy jabbered merrily about her new friend Lakeesha (who could touch her nose with her tongue) and dogspotted. She logged a collie with a nose like a sharpened pencil and one of those muscled Jack Russell terriers, dogs that were small enough to fit in your mailbox yet felt fully empowered to rule the world.

Then, as they got to the Rotunda and were paying their way in, Cindy said, "Mom hates really tall buildings."

"She did?" said Tim, changing tenses, present to past. "I

thought you guys went up the Empire State Building last year."

"Not Mom. Mom stayed in the car."

"Elevators is what she hated," said Billy, speaking definitively, as he always did.

"True," said Tim, for Jill did mistrust elevators. She would go on about frayed cables and plummeting in free fall. Somehow he could smile at the memory, and by the time they started moving around the panorama, he was exhilarated.

"Look!" he said, pressing close to the glass.

"What is it?" asked Cindy, bouncing to improve her view.

"It's everything. There's the river, and there's the ocean. That's the airport. Maybe we can see our house—over that way, in that row of brick buildings...."

"Hey, they all have little porches on the roof."

"A lot of them do."

"Whoa," said Billy. "Check it out. There's people naked on that one. See 'em, Simp?"

"You could be right," said Tim, for certainly Billy was right. Sprawled on a roof deck visible only from airplanes and skyscrapers, they were not just naked, they were moving toward consummation. "Who wants a Coke?"

"Not now, Unk, they're going to *do* it."

Tim grabbed Cindy's hand and pulled against a mulish resistance. "Stay, Simp," said Billy, pulling from the other side. "Unk, give a quarter for the telescope."

"Get away from there, you little voyeur."

"No way. They're *doing* it."

"What's a voyeur?" asked Cindy, rhyming it with lawyer.

"They are not doing it, they're just hugging. Now come with me or I'm taking you home."

Tim didn't mind them sneaking back a minute later. A parent's job was to maintain certain pretenses—that life was safe, and bland, and innocent—it was not to put kids in jail. Surely a kid who sought to observe the world's workings was a healthy, normal kid. He and Jill had watched together (through the dusty window of a curing shed, voyeurs most assuredly) as a black couple made grunting love. They found it very strange—and funny, that the lovers kept so much clothing on—but they watched, and Jill, at least, turned out healthy and normal.

Far below, taxicabs dominated Boylston Street, floating

through Copley Square like a school of slow tropical fish. For a while the streetlights went off-on-off-on, right at the margin of their sensors. Then the streets bloomed and the sky darkened, as though light was being siphoned down.

Surveying this peaceful diorama, Tim surged with a general joy. It thrilled him to see the kids so spunky, so confident here in the city, but the thrill went beyond such reasons, spreading through him like a headful of wine on a cold night. First the nervous breakdown, and now this new euphoria!

Or was it part of the breakdown, a second episode? The word epiphany came into his mind: a word he encountered in college, had never used (or encountered) since then. Wasn't this an epiphany?

Tim was political only in the broadest sense. Help the needy, deplore all prejudice, abortion if you wanted it, affirmative action if you needed it. He did not meet in meetings or demonstrate at demonstrations, and he sometimes forgot to vote. Peter Weissberg, who solicited for the Salvadorans, the Nicaraguans, for every oppressed people (running off Xeroxed flyers by the hour) had shamed him many times.

It was not outrage that Tim lacked. He was a famous fulminator, forever up in arms at the inanities of a debased culture. His sputtering diatribes were so common that friends performed perfect impressions of Tim Fulminating: about junk mail, about advertising, about "deodorant as a way of life," in his most familiar shorthand. His barbs could be off-putting, until redeemed by that drawl of amaze in which he delivered them.

The tone of innocence dismayed. Custody's Last Stand, he had labeled the folder stuffed with the advertisements for himself he had gathered for Barnes.

Innocence, and reverence, for Tim was forever charmed by the incredible mundane fact of life itself and by all its most casual manifestations. Those two lithe souls fucking on the roof, the yellow taxis gliding toward the theater district, the South Church newsstand which opened every morning before six with fresh newspapers from dozens of cities.

The wonders of the world were not only abroad in sinking Mediterranean lands, they were contained in the molecules that bound us and gave us "life" inside our skins. Life itself was the miracle, and it was a gift so splendid it made protest feel ill-mannered. Who could complain when it was possible to stand in the sky (for, Prudential Building or not, were they not standing in the middle of the very air?) and possible to breathe and to eat breakfast?

And yes, to have sex. Surely sex was one of the good things. Did anyone disagree? Who, Jerry Falwell?

The epiphany was turning weird, with Falwell in it, but it was compelling nevertheless. Everything glowed; nothing was unbeautiful. Tim watched a well-dressed woman chewing green gum openmouthed and could only smile at her enjoyment. When Billy knelt down to put Cindy on his shoulders ("Look, Simp, the Red Sox are home, they're playing right now"), he brimmed with love for these two children. Love for Jill and for Erica too. Definitely.

"Unk?" said Cindy, as they were strolling home, hand in hand while Billy zigged and zagged ahead of them.

"Cynthia?" He still felt high, yet at the same time very grounded. His epiphany had closed all distances.

"I have a question."

"Yes, Cynthia."

"When school starts? Will you have to drive all the way to Boston every day?"

"You don't need to worry about stuff like that, sweetheart."

"But will you? Billy says it costs eight dollars a day."

"Forty dollars a week without counting oil," said Billy over his shoulder.

"Or depreciation," Tim laughed, but Billy had zigzagged out of earshot.

"And also, Unk?"

"Yes, Cynthia?"

"Can we maybe go back-to-school shopping on Saturday? I know it's early, but there's a *huge* sale at Maurice The Pants Man."

"Maurice is having a sale? What does he sell ?"

"He sells *pants*, and you know it."

"Now I do. Say, that isn't why they call him—"

"*Unk.*"

She had stopped to place hands on hips in mock petulance.

"It is why, isn't it? The *Pants* Man."

*

136

Tim drove past a field so steeply tilted it threatened to spin upside down like a Ferris wheel. For a while the mountain stayed with him. There was marshland—and then Monadnock. There was forest, and then another version of Monadnock, reconfigured.

Finally the mountain was behind him and he came through a more despoiled area, past a trailertown and self-storage bunkers set back on broken macadam. He was close to Keene now, but his nerves held steady until he came rolling down Main Street, a boulevard so wide and ample it seemed to have been designed for a much larger city. Now, suddenly, a vice closed on Tim's head; now his mouth was dry as cotton.

When he saw the rotary and the vest-pocket park (complete with bandshell, monument, and fountain) he knew he had reached his destination. His destiny. The words COURT HOUSE were carved on a frieze above the Gothic stonework entry; below the arch stood Earl and Erica, dressed for success. Earl in a creamcolored suit, Ric in heels and pearls.

Tim had planned on arriving early, but Earl looked as though he had slept inside the COURT HOUSE and stepped outside to greet the day. Deeply at his ease, he might have been the mayor, perched grandly on his portico. Tim slant-parked, and watched a second man, also in a creamcolored suit, come bounding up the granite steps. As they shifted briefcases to shake hands, Tim knew this must be Earl's liar. Or else his twin! Same suit, same height, same hair. Earl and Merle!

Then he saw Dee Barnes. Her no-nonsense navy blue suit cleaved the creamcolored twins and sped down Main Street at a pace that undoubtedly marked her as an invading force, an urbanite. Barnes could motor. When Tim finally caught up to her, he could feel her engine idling high. Her energy. "I'm in battle mode, I guess," she gave as an explanation.

"I hope I'm not still the enemy." Barnes smiled for him, did not reply. Behind her, in the window of a shop called Miranda's Verandah, Tim noticed a shimmering silver gown draped on a bubblegum colored manikin. "Where are you going?"

"There's a diner, I gather. We've got half an hour."

"You can eat? I am a complete nervous wreck."

"I see that."

"But I could keep you company."

"Lucky me."

The diner, called Lindy's, was an aluminum lunchcar set adrift smack in the middle of a parking lot opposite the Greyhound depot. Tim followed his attorney inside to the counter, where he ordered a cup of tea just to hold onto it. Barnes ordered the Trucker's Special, an atomic bomb of cholesterol sufficient to kill every middle-aged man in the county, and rinsed it down with what might have been a gallon of jet black coffee.

"They have us scheduled for the entire morning session," she said, once her plate was empty. "There's literally nothing else on the docket, and nothing scheduled for the afternoon."

"What are you saying? Is that good or bad?"

"It's telling me they plan to wrap this up in one day. Save the state some money."

"You don't mean I could walk in there and just *lose*. Over and out? What about the guardian *ad litem* and all that?"

"Why don't we walk in there and just take a look around, for starters. Get you acclimated. It wouldn't hurt with the winning and losing if you could settle down and start looking custodial."

"Custodial?" he said, buoyed up, mistaking her pique for renewed support. "Hell, I'll start looking Presidential."

But back on the granite steps, Tim looked queasy. A courthouse was intimidating simply because it was a courthouse, it didn't have to do anything else. Yet it did. The metal detector detected Tim and went into air-raid mode, as though he was packing iron on both hips. All he was packing was his zipper. Coins, keys, even his ballpoint pen had gone through in a basket.

"True story," he would swear to Karl that night. "A five-alarm nightmare and it turns out to be my fly." But how could the morose guard, pokerfaced upon his stool, not know this would happen, when it must happen to every soul passing through his supersensitive electronic portal? It seemed that Cheshire County did not want you getting acclimated, it wanted you back on your heels from the get-go.

The second floor was hushed, virtually deserted. Barnes walked him like a condemned prisoner down the long corridor toward a pair of massive doors, beyond which lay the Probate Court. Entering this inner sanctum, Tim fully expected to behold the chopping block and the guillotine.

It was just a big room, and empty apart from Earl, Merle, and Ric, who sat at a table near the front. The space mixed tackiness and grandeur in roughly equal proportions: the majestic fourteen-foot ceiling clad with cardboard tiles, the half-walls panelled with stained veneer and moulded with cheesy clamshell.

Suddenly the scene came to life. A bailiff proclaimed "All rise!" as though hundreds of extras were waiting in the wings. Then, with the command to rise still hanging in the air, the judge came hustling in, almost at a trot, and countermanded it. "Please, please do sit down." So they sat, all five of them, at matching bare wooden tables. But his presence had charged the room with electricity. Everything pulsated; static abounded.

He was a youthful sixty, with gray hair clipped close at the ears and an olive complexion that went well with his black robe. Something of the medieval cleric in his look. Gold wire-rimmed glasses rested halfway down his small beaked nose, and though Tim would feel a constant urge to nudge them higher, the judge never did.

"Good morning, Attorney Barnes. I believe you have not appeared before me."

"No, your Honor."

"She has not had the honor, your Honor," said Merle, apparently a comedian.

"Mr. Giddings here has done so many times. Rest assured he is hardly apt to fool me on account of that circumstance."

"So assured, your Honor."

The judge offered something half nod and half bow, then formed his closest semblance of a smile. This was a faintly etched crease at the corners of his mouth, which he then would erase with the thumb and forefinger of his right hand. When the two digits came away, the creases had gone with them.

"With your permission, I would like to place all parties under oath and simply leave you all right where you are while we chat about this tragic situation. Attorney Barnes, this may strike you as unusual?"

"Unusually sensible, your Honor."

"Mr. Giddings?"

Mr. Giddings—Merle—nodded assent, yet attaching a delicate frown which may have been intended to convey serious ratiocination, or may have represented notice of a differential in titles employed by the judge. He was Mister; she was Attorney. Meanwhile, a stenographer had materialized and sat expression-

139

less at a corner table. The bailiff, with something—egg?—on his blue blazer, sat expressionless in the corner opposite.

"I am Judge Enneguess, should you have need to complain about me to anyone. Two n's and two s'es, anyone's guess why. Mr. Giddings, you can go first. You have brought this Petition before the court. Tell me about it."

"Very good. It is fairly clear cut, and the gist of it is laid out in our memorandum. My clients are extremely happy to be able to offer these youngsters a safe haven in the bosom of their family home. They come before the court with loving hearts."

"I am going to guess that Mr. Bannon does the same?"

Barnes shrugged (not too urbanely, Tim hoped) to indicate as much was obvious and that Merle's initial offering was your basic crock of shit. They waited for Merle to continue with his presentation, but Merle was done. He was sitting down.

"A question or two?" said Enneguess, bringing him back up. "The Petition trumpets the importance of continuity in the school district, whereas the Opposition alleges petitioners intend sending the minor children off to boarding school. What light can you throw on this apparent contradiction, Mr. Giddings?"

"Without prejudice, your Honor, a good boarding school is not necessarily a hardship. And surely it is not against the law."

"I recall the law, and I agree it is not. It does, however, rattle up against this other point. And the question of continuity does interest me."

"If I may?" said Barnes.

"You may, in a moment. Mr. Giddings?"

"I should stress that my clients have made no such plan. That was just me thinking out loud, on my own."

"Oh, don't do that, Mr. Giddings, or we'll soon be onto the Red Sox' bullpen woes."

"This is an early and confusing time for all concerned, your Honor. It seemed only responsible to retain some flexibility—"

"Fine, though again, that position does *differ* from the position taken in your own Petition. Attorney Barnes, you had something?"

"Yes, I was going to suggest we resolve the contradiction by stipulating that the boarding school option be eliminated. But now that I see the need for flexibility—"

"Would you be willing to so stipulate, Mr. Giddings?"

"I would have to ask my clients."

"I can ask them. They are right here."

"I would like to explain the ramifications, your Honor."

"At the first recess, then. Meanwhile, here's one for you, Attorney Barnes. We're just chatting here, you see. Can you tell me the significance of this wedding ceremony in—yes, in Maryland."

"We believe it goes to integrity, your Honor. To honesty. The Sandersons have made a rather serious misrepresentation—sometimes called a lie—and have maintained it over many years. To family, to friends, to the society at large."

"Perhaps."

"With all due respect, I do not see perhaps here. I see a willful misrepresentation of fact and can not help wondering how these same facts have been represented to the Internal Revenue Service, for example."

Judge Enneguess cocked an eye in Merle's direction and Merle brushed the matter away with a curt wave of the hand. "This is just a detail, your Honor, and in fact the tax status is one reason my clients have long intended to see to formal marriage."

"Then why," said Barnes, "the secrecy about their effort to set matters right?"

"No secrecy. Several close friends can testify they received postcards from Gideon Township."

"Did Erica's mother receive a card?"

"I see your point, Attorney Barnes," said the judge, "but it does seem that the ten years' relationship, combined with this renewal of vows, makes a solid enough statement of union. No?"

"Renewal?" said Barnes, straining to repress the urge to nitpick his surprising distortion.

"Surely a solid union by comparison with any similar showing Mr. Bannon can make to this court?"

"Ah," said Barnes. Though it was the business of newal and renewal she had questioned—not the solidity—she was now fully subsided. "And I take your Honor's point."

In a vital organ, Tim Bannon feared. He had been a bystander, auditing this jockeying almost as pure theater, but now he registered that the repartée was aimed at defining the rest of his life. Meanwhile, Enneguess was waving a sheaf of papers in the air.

"Tell me about this," he said to Barnes, for apparently it was The Opposition he waved. *Convince me*, is how Tim heard the invitation and his hopes were somewhat restored. A moment earlier, he was seeing nothing better than homophobia with a human face.

"Do you mind if I wander?" said Barnes, showing Enneguess a fraction of the irresistible smile. "Around the room, that is. Moving helps me think, sometimes."

"The court does not mind if you think," said Enneguess, who had little choice: she had already gained six yards on the ground. "Just so long as you don't get Mr. Giddings thinking again."

"I'll try not to," she said, widening the fraction, but Mr. Giddings was already on his feet with thinking-cap on. Enneguess apologized before he could verbalize his protest, for clearly the badinage had gone too far.

Way too far for Tim's taste. To him, this was looking like another day in court, replete with the hollow gestures of respect and the smirking jargon. Tomorrow they would retake the stage with a fresh batch of clients. But Barnes had begun.

"Montgomery Hergesheimer was the kind of man who spent his Sunday helping Cindy with her science project. A water wheel, quite nifty, you can see it at the house. You can feel the fun they must have had.

"The kind of man who treats his son's soccer team to pizza. Not as a reward for scoring, or winning, but for playing. Not the only such man, but one of them.

"Monty liked to bring his wife flowers and presents on days that were not birthdays, or Valentine's Day. Everyday days. He made a game of fooling her—pretend to be in a bad mood leaving the house, then come home at noon to take her to lunch."

"Where did they eat?" said Merle.

"All right, Mr. Giddings."

"I apologize, your Honor, but I do wonder what all this can be about."

"I am curious as well," said Enneguess, gesturing to Barnes.

"They had scallop rolls at Trumball's," said Barnes, an artful dodge that had Enneguess pursed to whistle. Tim was impressed, too, by her casual insertion of a local detail she had only secondhand, from him.

"Jill Bannon Hergesheimer," Barnes went on, resuming both her travels and her indolent narrative, "was the kind of woman who took in her husband's parents when they were ill. Monty's parents loved Jill, could never quite believe their son's good fortune in marrying her. 'Whatever Jill wants' was their vote on every issue—from what to have for lunch, Mr. Giddings, to where Jill and Monty should go for a rare overnight getaway."

"Tim Bannon stayed with the children on that occasion, by the way. And The Balsams, Mr. Giddings, is where they went."

"You do hold a grudge, Counsellor." Merle was grinning, being a sport, but Barnes ignored him.

"Jill was the kind of mother who never missed Billy's games or Cindy's recitals. Who sang her kids to sleep, taught them music, read them poetry—"

"Your Honor. Please."

"Fair enough, Mr. Giddings. Attorney Barnes, I do not believe a soul here has uttered or even considered one word of criticism of the deceased parents. I fail to see the relevance of this."

"With respect, your Honor, I am sure you will see it shortly, even if Mr. Giddings does not."

This was pushing it, it was wanton, and Tim flinched. The judge took it, however, after a pregnant admonitory pause. The semblant smile formed at the corners of his mouth, the spanned thumb and forefinger came up to erase it. All he had to offer Merle was a philosophic shrug.

"*Motive*," said Barnes.

"Motive," said Merle, "is not at issue here. This is not a criminal proceeding, your Honor."

"Motive," said Barnes, cutting back from the sideline. "Why we do what we do. Let us remember that although the expressed wishes of Jill and Monty Hergesheimer may not bind a court of law, they ought to bring serious force to bear upon it. And perhaps even greater force upon the minds and hearts of family members.

"This court would not be involved, and none of us would be confined here on this beautiful summer morning, were it not for the action taken by the Sandersons. But why did they take such an action, in direct contravention of Jill and Monty's wishes?

"I spoke a bit about Jill and Monty so we might keep a clear sight of them today. Who they were, and how thoroughly involved they were as parents. To name Tim Bannon custodian of their children had to be a clear, conscious, rigorous choice on their parts."

"Am I wrong, your Honor, or is Attorney Barnes stating the

obvious, that we are all well aware of?"

"Not so aware, apparently," said Barnes. "I think we need to understand why Jill and Monty made the clear, rigorous choice they made. A remarkable choice, it seems to me."

"Oh it seems that way to us, too," said Merle, scoring. Enneguess had to wipe one away.

"If it is not the obvious choice, as seen from the outside, the court may agree its unexpectedness only makes it more significant."

"Though not binding," reminded Enneguess.

"Not binding on the court, no. Would it have bound me as a sister? Would it bind your Honor, as a brother? This crystal clear wish of a sibling, on an absolutely vital issue?"

Barnes riveted her gaze on Enneguess as though she expected a response. Which she did: she expected him to *form* one, though he would never state it. But it was here that Tim noticed Enneguess' rare—inhuman?—ability not to blink. Barnes' was a steady gaze, she did not blink much herself, yet by the end of this faceoff she was made to seem a coquette.

"Have you finished?" was the only response forthcoming.

"Almost, your Honor. Since William and Cynthia were born, Tim has been a central figure in their lives. And I must remind the court we are talking about a period of eleven years. Tim often saw them weekly, never less than monthly. They pursued regular activities, shared running jokes, kept track of favorite TV shows.

"Last summer, for example, the three of them set a goal of discovering ten different lakes from which they could see Mt. Monadnock. They succeeded, too, after a world of fun and adventure together. Ask the kids to name those ten bodies of water and you will find out exactly how memorable those outings were.

"They are very close, your Honor. Tim and Cindy and Billy. They love one another. It's the sort of unique bond that can form with an uncle, an aunt, sometimes a grandparent. Jill and Monty saw this bond, they were delighted by it, they nurtured it....

"But now we turn to the flip side of this equation—the negative that proves the positive. Because I could talk all day of Tim and Cindy and Billy, but I couldn't fill a fifteen-second slot on Super Sunday about the Sandersons and these children. There is nothing to say. There is no relationship to describe.

"I don't wish to say terrible things about these people. Does

Mr. Sanderson still cheat at cards? Does he cheat his customers, or cheat on his wife? Does he beat his wife or, to be fair, does his wife beat him?"

"Oh yes," said Merle, popping up. "I can see how fair you aim to be. Objection, your Honor?"

"No need, Mr. Giddings. Don't you worry. You can't fool me, but she can't fool me either."

Tim could not read the judge, unless his extraordinary patience with Barnes meant something. At the moment, he seemed to be play-acting, leaning forward in almost a pantomime listening posture. He all but cocked his ears.

"We don't want anyone fooled," said Barnes. "On the contrary, we very badly want the true state of matters within this family made manifest. Because versus Tim's thirty, forty visits a year with the Hergesheimers, the Plaintiffs might boast one or two. Versus a hundred occasions of which Tim cared for the kids on his own, the Plaintiffs can point to one. One visit in their lifetimes, to the home of an aunt who lived a few miles away!

"And it doesn't matter *why*, at this point. Some people don't relate well to kids, or wisely choose not to have them. No doubt Mr. Giddings would like us to believe that love, or at least a sense of responsibility, is the motive behind the Plaintiffs' effort to contravene the Hergesheimers' wishes. And we would all rejoice to see them exhibit some affection or interest in the future that they have failed to show in the past.

"But as to fitness? It could well be argued that in naming Tim Bannon their children's guardian, the Hergesheimers were declaring quite literally who ought *not* be named. Isn't that a conclusion we would draw, objectively?

"Even setting aside the past, I doubt any guardian *ad litem* could fail to reach this same conclusion. Billy and Cindy will make it unambiguous. They know who they love. They know who was there for them, not just on Thanksgiving or Christmas, but on April 11 and June 17. On the everyday days...

"And they also know who was *not* there."

In finishing, finally, Barnes had finished her peregrinations directly before the judge's rostrum. Enneguess came out from his listening posture, to listen in fact—or so it appeared to Tim. But what had he heard?

He popped his loose black sleeves, then let his arms descend slowly to the table, as though descending through water, not air. He thanked Barnes for her "thoughtful and thought-provoking remarks," then spread the two memoranda side by side in front of him. For an instant, Tim thought he might shut his eyes and pick a winner.

Instead, he called a recess.

"What I did not hear, Attorney Barnes—though I was waiting to hear it—was the motive you attribute to the Sanderson Petition. *Motive*, you said, and you all but typed a full colon after it. I heard the colon, at any rate, and I waited. Motive?"

"That was the negative that proved the positive, your Honor. I can only speculate unkindly on motive, but I can say with some assurance what was *not* the motive."

"With all due respect," said Merle, "this may be too subtle for me. It's just a rehash with some heavy topspin on it."

"Let me hear you spin it back the other way," said Enneguess. "I presume you disagree with the Manichean dichotomy?"

"Translation?" Say this for Merle: he did not embarrass easily, he was happy inside his skin.

"Good and evil, Mr. Giddings. Do you agree that Mr. Bannon has been the ideal Walt Disney uncle and Ms. Sanderson the wicked Disney witch?"

"Uncle, your Honor, or fairy Godmother?" Enneguess' eyes, visible above the half-mast glasses, narrowed meaningfully. "Withdrawn. With apologies."

"Is there anything concrete you would say in mitigation?"

"To begin with, it's wild exaggeration. My clients have taken a great deal more interest in the children than was stated. Mr. Sanderson has a standing offer to take the boy hunting, for example, and my understanding is that the boy is eager to go."

"Please sit, Attorney Barnes. Mr. Giddings is still at the plate. Or at the baseline, I should say, if we are having topspin."

"Here's the thing," said Merle. "The kids had two loving parents, perfect parents. My clients are not meddlesome people, plus of course they have a busy life of their own. While they wished to see more of family—like us all, they had good intentions—they had no pressing need. Hell, Judge, I swear I love my sister Carol, but I haven't even called her in months."

"Fair enough. And that has changed, for the Sandersons?"

"The children need them now. It has become a matter of need, and of responsibility. The time for good intentions is past, if you will, and the time for good actions is at hand."

"Ecclesiastes," said Enneguess.

"And this bit with the ailing parents? Monty's folks, who moved in to a soundtrack of weeping violins? Well, sure. Earl's mom did the same. She died in the Sanderson home. Because when the time came for that level of caring, the Sandersons were surely there to provide it."

"A time to embrace and a time to refrain from embracing," said the judge, sticking with Ecclesiastes.

"Exactly. And all this about positives proving negatives and negatives proving positives is a bunch of refried air."

"Attorney Barnes, I'll take your comment now."

"Thank you, your Honor. Billy Hergesheimer never went hunting with Mr. Sanderson because of two serious obstacles—his mother and his father. They didn't want him shooting animals, even apart from the question of his age."

"It is inappropriate, you think, to hunt at age eleven?"

"Myself? No idea. We don't hunt much in Boston. But I am aware that Jill and Monty had specifically prohibited it."

"Well, you are a most thorough practitioner, Ms. Barnes," said Enneguess, and Barnes heard the edge on his voice (thorough here might not be good?) and the downgrade from Attorney to a mere Mizz. She had been defrocked, made a civilian, like poor Merle. Was this judge a gun nut who thrust artillery and camouflage on his children and grandchildren?

"Thank you, your Honor," she said. "One tries to be as thorough as possible when vital issues are at stake."

"Excellent. Can we take that same thoroughness now and apply it to a consideration of Mr. Bannon's personal qualities? I have been studying The Complaint—"

"The allegations are inspecific and highly prejudicial."

"Are they untrue?"

"They are. Tim Bannon is no more promiscuous than the average single man in today's America. He conducts his life in a dignified manner, and runs a thriving and reputable business. The Plaintiffs can no more say he is dissolute than we can say it of them. I for one do not even know what the word means."

"You do not?"

147

"Not in real terms. Is there a line one crosses? If I take two drinks I am on one side of the line, whereas a third puts me over into dissolution? Three failed love affairs is okay, but a fourth becomes dissolute? What if I'm unpopular and keep losing out in the arena of love? Am I obliged to stop trying?"

"Suppose we take a fairly high hurdle, Attorney Barnes." (Reinstated!) "Suppose we agree that a new sexual partner every month, roughly a dozen each year, constitutes dissolution?"

"Promiscuity, I would have said."

"Fine, we have got that one too. Can you assure me Mr. Bannon does not meet the definition?"

"I haven't cross-examined my client, but I have a strong impression of him as a decent and responsible person."

"Shall I ask him directly?"

"It is your privilege, of course. If you do ask him, though, I hope you will also ask Mr. and Mrs. Sanderson."

"I am surprised at you, Attorney Barnes. You know that no such suggestions have been made concerning the Sandersons' character. Now then, Mr. Bannon?"

"Yes, your Honor," said Tim, standing and bracing himself to lie. Did he need to lie? Twelve a year? Probably he needed to lie. Should he? Only if he could do it well; if he could fool them. He simply had no idea what would happen to his face, his hands.

"Sorry to be so personal with you right off the bat, but one a month? One hundred twenty in ten years? Have you had one hundred twenty sexual partners?"

"Most definitely not," said Tim—stoutheartedly, he felt. This might work. "Nothing like that many."

"One hundred? Seventy-five? How low can we go and still hear a confident denial? I am merely asking."

"A lot lower. I would consider myself lucky to meet someone in a year, or two years, who was important enough to introduce to my family." (Not bad!)

"So you have categories—important, less important, unimportant—within the range of your sexual partners?"

All right, thought Tim, if you have sex in New Hampshire it is supposed to be *important*. Was that the trick in Enneguess' trick question? Uncertainly, he turned to Barnes, a clear admission (of *some*thing) to Enneguess, who pounced:

"Try this one, sir. How many unimportant partners have there

148

been this year. Just the one year, if that helps memory."

"May I object?" said Barnes.

"Of course you may." (But you had better not...)

"Well, I would not wish to say this line of questioning verges on sarcasm, but it does seem grossly unfair to speculate on relationships this way. To be asked to rate human beings—"

"It was not my idea, Attorney Barnes."

"But surely everyone, male or female, who is in the dating game, or whatever it is called—"

"Look, folks. This isn't evidence. None of this is substantiated. We are chatting. And I am attempting to get some rough sense of the man's habits, of how he conducts his life. Give me a plausible answer and I'll be delighted to move on."

"Six," Tim heard himself croak.

He spoke reflexively, to halt the pain and embarrassment. Enneguess was going to have a number and six was a numerical way of crying STOP. Six was the biggest lie Tim could manage. To say anything less was like telling the I.R.S. you earned nine thousand dollars last year: they would only laugh and start toting up your dry cleaning receipts. Still, in the formal quietude of the courtroom, the number six seemed way high.

"Six," repeated the judge, suppressing an exclamation point. To Tim, the judge looked like a man who had taken fewer than six lovers in his lifetime. Possibly fewer than one.

"*About* six."

"You do not know? You have love affairs, even within the past year, that you can not recall?"

"No, your Honor. I meant some years are different than others. Some years there might not be any."

A brilliant recovery. Excitement gathered in Tim's chest as he shot this wild lie out into the room. Or not lie, technicality. Tim had very few love *affairs*, as he understood the term. (Continuity, planning, lots of arguments about commitment....)

He braced himself anew, in case the little devil came after him on one-night stands, or started tabulating orgasms, but the gunfire had ceased. The smoke had cleared. Enneguess had a number, and he turned his attention back to Barnes.

"The AIDS," he said. "What can you tell me of Mr. Bannon's health, with particular respect to the AIDS?"

"Tim's health is excellent. He hasn't lost a sick day at work in four years. His blood pressure is normal, his weight enviably in line with the Surgeon General's guidelines, and you see for yourself he has good color."

"Who is being facetious now, counsellor?"

"Not toward the court, your Honor."

"You are telling me the claim is patently false. Mr. Bannon does not in fact have the AIDS."

"That is my understanding, your Honor."

"Mr. Giddings, I assume you have medical records to back up your assertion?"

"Not at this time, your Honor."

"This is the time of the hearing, is it not? You have your information from what source, counsellor?"

"At this time, your Honor, we would rather not say."

"You did not subpoena the medical records?"

"I didn't expect them to deny a known fact."

"You must not have endured the beneficial exercise of moot court at your law school, Mr. Giddings."

"It was a fishing expedition, like the hunting expeditions aforementioned," said Barnes, on surer footing now. Enneguess had proved an equal opportunity sarcast, but for the moment Giddings was again in his crosshairs. "Here, however, is a fact. Earl Sanderson has smoked two packs of cigarettes a day for twenty-five years."

"Your Honor?" Merle did appear genuinely astonished.

"Oh, I suppose we are informal enough to hear about your client's bad habits, Mr. Giddings. If that is the point?"

"His health more so than his habits, your Honor. He smokes two packs a day and his beer consumption is both fact and legend, apparently. Given that he is seven years Mr. Bannon's senior, the medical experts would place him much closer to glory, statistically. If *that* is the point."

"For the love of God, your Honor."

"Your Petition does invite this line of thought, Mr. Giddings."

"But surely *AIDS*—"

"The medical records would have been helpful," said Enneguess, who then dismissed them for lunch with such mournful, martyred eyes that Tim nearly blurted out a full confession to relieve the man's suffering.

They went back to Lindy's, where this time Tim matched his

attorney cheeseburger for cheeseburger. "I'm glad to see you have your appetite," said Barnes, who apparently always had hers.

"It's strange, but I don't feel nervous anymore."

"Well, the worst is over."

"Is it? What happens next?"

"Judge Anyone's-Guess is a tough read. He seems to get a kick out of keeping everyone off balance."

"The AIDS. Does your client have The AIDS," mimicked Tim, doing a foreigner attempting tricky English.

"He does play little games. But there's something I learned about this court. They'll assign a G.A.L. in ugly divorce cases, but never in a guardianship. Just doesn't happen."

"But then—"

"Guardianships are usually stopgap. A single mom goes into rehab, or a single mom with an abusive boyfriend fights to keep her kid in the house. So they designate the grandmother, on a temporary basis. Unless the father kills the mother, which happened in one of Enneguess' cases a few years ago. He designated the grandmother on a permanent basis for that one."

"You're saying it's always the grandmother."

"I'm saying they don't like assigning a guardian *ad litem*. Which is why I did what I did."

"You were sensational, Attorney Barnes. But what did you do, exactly?" Tim was confused, still sorting out the part about grandmothers. Anne wouldn't throw her hat in the ring, would she?

"I put Jill in front of that man and tried to keep her there, that's all. Because if this case was Bannon versus Sanderson?—he would decide it today, with no G.A.L. and no further expense to Cheshire County."

"But it is Bannon versus Sanderson. He's got those two sets of papers all but balanced on the scales of bloody justice there."

"To me, it's Hergesheimer versus Sanderson. I've felt that very strongly—felt I was representing Jill. I wanted her pounding on that man's door in a hurricane, demanding to be let in."

The waitress, remembering them from breakfast, was ready with the coffeepot and Barnes nodded assent to her fifth cup in this venue. Likely her tenth of the day (dissolute?) as Tim could hardly imagine her leaving Boston with less than a quart in her fuselage.

"I also turned up an article about Enneguess in an old law journal, a profile they ran when he was appointed to the bench. In which he is quoted as saying he walks home for lunch every day—to avoid the cigarette smoke in restaurants."

"You really *are* thorough. So that was Earl and his two packs a day."

"The beer, who knows. But we had to get the cigarettes in. I'm betting it gets us our G.A.L."

"Really? The way that guy was grilling me about my sex life? He looked at me like I was a copulating fruit fly or something."

"No comment."

Well well. Barnes still had not finished processing the tough parts, yet she had advocated for Tim as though there were none. He wished he could hug her.

"If you're right, Attorney Barnes, and I come out of this no worse off than I went in?—you are definitely worth every penny I haven't paid you."

V

THE MT. MONADNOCK BLUES

At four o'clock, Tim called around to report on their victory: case continued for a month, a G.A.L. to investigate. By ten that night he was calling everyone back, crying out for help. "I've never been so depressed in my life," he whined to Karl.

"It's like a post-partum letdown," Karl assured him, though he had no idea if this had any validity. "You want the baby, but there's a chemical kickback."

Highpowered chemicals. The walls had closed in on him now, the trap was fully sprung, and Tim wondered how he would kill the night, much less the month. Or *ten years*.

The night, at least, he killed with Jack Daniels. In the morning Ellie called, concerned and hoping to help by tendering a paid sabbatical. "Charles and I will manage through Labor Day. It's a slow time. And he's fine with the money."

"He must be getting a little," said Tim, incapable of being straightforward in the face of charity, however couched.

"Maybe Charles and I are both getting a little."

"Fair enough."

And it was fair. They had to work, but were happy, while he was liberated from work and miserable. Except that he wasn't; not one bit. Karl was right. After that dark post-partum night, what fell out was a sweet, surprising time of grace. A magic. It would be days before Tim trusted it, even slightly, and a week before he identified it as the breezy expansiveness of summer vacation. Something one had as a child, then lost forever. Something Tim had accidentally regained.

As they slipped across the gin-clear water of Thorndike Pond on Tuesday, he wondered how such a paradise could be so exclusively theirs. Then he remembered, the rest of the world was at *work*. They paddled round the island, stripping blueberries from the overhanging bushes, then sat in the canoe eating. Soft blue sky, soft sun on the water, not a soul in sight. When they swam, their toes were in perfect focus far below the surface.

They stopped at Coll's for a dozen ears of fresh corn, steamed them that night, and ate four apiece. Billy still wanted his money's worth, eating right down to the marrow; Cindy still used corn as a means of drinking butter. Her cobs were scratched and

155

gnawed as though by rodents, while half a pound of butter disappeared. Tim let them taste the wine and they both hated it cheerfully.

By Thursday Tim was so relaxed he took a nap. With a mystery story tented on his chest, senses humming with rural grace notes, he drifted off in the hammock. Twice, briefly, he opened his eyes on a sky so intensely blue it seemed painted. Yet napping, like paragliding, was a trick Tim had never even attempted.

Billy took charge on Friday. His father had read a short story about a man who runs from one end of town to the other, jumping into every swimming pool as he goes. Doesn't say hello or introduce himself, just dives in, swims a length, and heads for the next pool. Joking, Monty suggested Camp White Sneaker should undertake a lake-and-pond version of this bizarre quest, but it was no joke to Billy Hergie. He drew a map, worked out an itinerary; he set goals and he waited, and today was the day.

"It's an awful lot of driving," said Tim , glancing at the paperwork. His true concern was emotional, for what did it say (or not say) that Monty was the unaccredited source of the scheme?

"Forty miles," said Billy with a dismissive shrug. Then came the accreditation: "It's worth it—for Dad."

Worth it, to be sure. This proved to be one of the most joyful days of Tim's life and much of the joy derived from the fact that it was so silly, pure nonsense. What a freeing-up lay there, essentially in becoming young again. (Younger than sex, Tim smiled. Innocent, he would later elaborate—for all his insights came retrospectively.) Tim was a neophyte at the sort of freedom that had no truck with good old promiscuity and dissolution.

Contoocook Lake was sandybottomed, Skatutukee and Frost were squishy and festooned with liquid green shadows. A wind they encountered nowhere else came roaring across Nubanusit, but today they didn't need to fight it. They jumped in at the boat launch, swam the obligatory minute, and sped away to Dublin Lake. Cindy's trail mix (a few peanuts in with the Raisinets and M&M's) was a far cry from the healthy seeds of Camp Keokuk's recipe, but no one could deny their energy level was extraordinary.

The weekend filled with the children's friends. Saturday they played baseball on a real ballfield in the village, with a real scoreboard covered in zeroes, Home and Visitor with nothing to show. Billy blasted home runs (no zeroes for him) and Cindy snagged a "really high fly." On Sunday the same wolfpack reassembled on the lawn for tag and dodgeball, oldfashioned games Tim assumed had vanished from the planet.

These children got along so well. Ranged in age from six to fourteen, they exhibited a complete mastery of inclusion and tolerance. *Lord of the Flies* was made to seem a big lie. Maybe if you put them in uniforms, with parents in the grandstand shouting, they would go tooth and claw. Self-governed, however, they had astonishing reserves of fairness and compassion. They had innocence.

Tim was moved to undertake ice cream all around as a reward. He wrote down orders (two scoops, three scoops, marshmallows, sprinkles) and enlisted Cindy's help. She in turn subcontracted a McManus twin (Hugh?) as her own helper, for there was some serious girdling to be done at the base of so many fastmelting cones in transit.

"You performed a miracle," Alice McManus would tell him later. "My twins were actually apart for half an hour."

Tim and Alice were standing by Jill's perennial bed, the colors quieted in the fading light. "I thought it was a miracle those kids stayed outside all day," Tim said. "No TV, no headsets? No video games?"

"It is relentless sometimes, isn't it?"

A hush fell with the dew. Tim was not bored, not depressed. If sad, then a little sad to see Alice McManus where Jilly should be standing. Jill (arms folded over her breasts, brown hair loosened at the temples by work) proudly surveying her Canterbury bells. Her lemon gems. This moment should be Jill's.

Alice felt it too. It was a truth so palpable that she stayed, and in no accidental way maintained with him the holy silence. It was full dark when childrens' voices called them inside.

"It's partly this incredible weather. And the countryside really is beautiful."

"Sure, but you hate the country, Tim. Remember?"

"No, sirree, I'm *from* the country."

"That's probably why you hate it."

"Karl, I like it. It's beautiful, and very calming."

"Well, you always *said* you hated the country."

"Not hated—only that I couldn't live there."

"But could what? Die there?"

"Be there. Maybe live for a while. All I know is I've been happy. Plus I don't have to worry about Joe Average up here."

"I thought he stopped anyway."

"He started back up. But the messages aren't really hostile. It's like he's an old friend wondering why I don't call him back."

"He leaves his *number*?"

"Of course not. I'm just saying he sounds needy."

"My heart bleeds for the sicko. But getting back to your lovely landscape, I'm coming up this weekend."

"Here?"

"Yes, and I'm coming by myself this time. To follow up on a few ideas I had. So I thought on Saturday—"

"Saturday's pretty full for us. I promised to take the kids shopping in the morning, and the G.A.L. is coming to *observe* us all afternoon."

"I've got a busy day too—because people are harder to find on Sunday."

"The hell. I found twelve of them on my lawn yesterday."

"My lawn? Tim Bannon, country squire? Listen, I won't come to observe you, I'll just show up at six with three pounds of salmon."

"You're saying dinner."

"We'll grill. That's okay, isn't it? You country squires would be *grilling* of a summer evening, no?"

"I'll grill you, you sonofabitch. You and your ideas."

Tim had done no back-to-school shopping since the days of 89¢ black marbled notebooks and four dollar dungarees. Now a glance at the advertised "specials" served notice he could be in over his head at the mall. Perhaps the time was right for inquiring into Jill and Monty's assets....

"Frozen. It's all been frozen," Attorney Phil Jellinghaus told him. "Nothing is lost, you understand—it gathers interest."

"But there's cash flow—"

"No there isn't," said Attorney Phil, unable to pass up the opening. But hale fellow not so hale was Jellinghaus. Not hostile, merely businesslike. Yet the last time through he had been all set to have Tim down to the club for some racquetball. Of course he knew exactly *why* Merle had frozen the assets.

Tim called Erica to propose a deal. Until the court's decision came down, why not have each faction cover half the children's expenses? What could be fairer than that?

"How are you going to pay your Boston lawyer if you can't even pay for sneakers?"

"Good question, sis. I don't suppose you want to pay half the attorney's fees too?"

"Yeah, right." But she was laughing.

"After all, you guys are why I *have* a Boston lawyer."

Erica's laughter was real. Her brother could be a funny guy. He had always been funny and Ric enjoyed his sassy brand of humor—until she stopped letting it in. When was that? And why? It was Earl, she would have to concede (or being such a *couple*) and then there was the whole gay thing. That was pretty bad. Embarrassing, mainly.

"Forget the lawyer's bill, let's talk about sneakers and Trapper Keepers."

"I don't even know what that is, but the answer's no. Earl will say it's a matter of principle."

"I couldn't agree more. But what do you think the principle is?"

"Doesn't make a cat's hair difference what I think. That's what he'll say and he won't even tell me what the principle is."

"You could leave him, you know. Flat in his tracks. You and I could raise the kids; maybe get Mom to move up north."

"One big happy family."

"Why not?"

"Surprise, Tim, I'd rather live with my husband than with my *mother*. And my crazy brother."

"You believe that? I'm crazy?"

"Gay, then," she said, though she did mean crazy in a benign sense. Zany, with a sprinkle of some negative spice.

"So gay is crazy. Different is crazy."

"Whatever," she said, merriment still ringing in her under-voice. "Hell's bells, Timmy, why don't you just borrow some money from the bank? I mean, *sneakers*?"

Things were not that bad. Unless his Boston lawyer smacked him with a sizable bill, Tim was not yet destitute. He called her next, to worry about it, and reliably she advised him not to. "Put it on a credit card," she counselled. It would stand as a clear

159

record of expenditures and he could pay it off later, once the frozen funds were thawed.

Such an approach had its risks for Tim. Where cash was not required, he tended to operate differently—as though no cash would ever be required. So at The Pants Man, where they sold a lot more than pants, he signed for $300. At the sneaker man (who, based on his price schemes, must be right up there with the Kuwaiti oil sheiks) $200 more. And this was only the beginning, for Billy had grown an inch, Cindy had grown two. Their arms were longer and they had new feet.

By age twelve, Tim consoled himself, most girls would reach full growth. But no, full *height*. There would still be the "chest," as Anne Bannon always called it, and the backside. There would be the hips.

They each required four "Trapper Keepers" for their school-work ($30 worth of Trapper Keepers!) so he signed for $100 more at Steele's and they had yet to procure the recommended pencils. Unloading all these purchases shortly before the G.A.L. was scheduled to arrive, Tim was torn between hiding the stuff and flaunting it. Was it proof of his fine upright guardianship, or evidence that he was buying votes?

The same uncertainty carried through Michele Taggart's ugly four-hour visit. Should he 'fess up to fried food at Trumball's or pretend he prepared only the most virtuous of meals, carrot-rich and tofu-centric? What about television? Tim considered TV a blight on the minds of the young. Ten years ago the experts agreed, or at least understood; now it was scarcely a point of view. TV had replaced life itself. TV was the lifeline that kept America breathing, it was the normalcy thing entire.

Taggart herself confused him. Her complete lack of humor made communication impossible; it was as if they were speaking different languages. Her voice was so soft (dead?) and her move-ments so careful they seemed choreographed. When she rose from a chair, she did so in slow motion, a Martha Graham dancer, the pivoting of the shoulders as gesture.

But then a hard fire, a redhot coal, would burn in her eyes, and her blade-thin lips were mortared shut with unexpressed anger. The lips barely parted when she spoke. Tim would not have been surprised had Ms. Taggart stepped out of her skin, leaving the placid false husk standing while a smaller more intense creature, released, began barking like a dog.

It made him feel unclean. He hated himself for trusting what Cindy might say, while doubting Billy. Billy was a wild card. The first hour (with the four of them sitting around the kitchen table) Billy submitted he did not mind change. Already this summer he had been to two camps and two houses and he liked being on the move. "It's good practice for road trips," he said, pounding his baseball mitt with deadly earnest, baffling Taggart who knew nothing of the boy's future in the major leagues.

And Billy was vulnerable to Earl's folderol. Over there he would be offered a new deal, with tin cans to potshot and a tractor he could drive in circles. Perhaps a Michael Jordan poster, signed—by Earl, of course—"To Big Bill, from your good buddy Mike."

Earl could sell it, the same way a DeNiro could. A great actor could give you the Middle American verities or, with equal conviction, the serial killer of those same Middle Americans. So Tim felt obliged to do some acting of his own, selling himself to the impassive Taggart—not that she was buying. Every word he said was "true" yet it was truth in the service of manipulation and by the end he wanted to scream, Get out, go, do what you must but leave us in peace.

Unclean. The whole day had been a splash in the muck. Not just Taggart with her trick questions, but The Pants Man and The Sneaker Man. The Trapper Keeper Girl. At least they smiled while taking his money. Not Michele Taggart; no free mints by *her* cash register.

"Hey, Unk, is it safe? Is she gone?

"She's gone," he laughed, though they had already emerged.

"She's *creepy*. She was *searching* my room, for drugs or something. Isn't that against the law?"

"Ms. Taggart is the law. So you didn't like her?"

"Hated her," said Cindy, a frosty glaze over her rolled-up eyes.

"She was so ignorant," said Billy. "When you were saying all this nice stuff, and making jokes, and she just sat there?"

"Why did she have to be here all day?" asked Cindy.

"I guess she had a lot of questions to ask."

"Dumb questions. Who are my three best friends, who are my three worst enemies. What's *that* about?"

161

"I think she's a lesbian," said Cindy.

This hit Tim like a wild crack of rifle-fire from the blue edge of the forest. His eyes widened. Where was this coming from? (Or going to?)

"No way, Simp. Check out her hair."

"Wait a second, hold on here. What do you two think a lesbian is? What do you know about anything like that?"

"Mom told us that stuff."

"She told Cynthia, too?"

"She told both of us, Unk, and it's not like we're against lesbians. It's just Cindy thinks that lady was one and I don't."

"I'll bet you could tell, Unk."

"I could, sweetheart? Because—?"

"Because of you-know," she answered slyly.

They knew. Tim had just begun to absorb it.

"Or," said Billy, "is it like two separate worlds. Like all the basketball guys know the other basketball guys and the hockey guys know the hockey guys but the hockey guys don't know the basketball guys."

"Is that a question?" Tim was touched by Billy's tangled formulation, by what he heard as eggshell-stepping to avoid giving pain. But they knew! They had taken it upon themselves to make this exchange occur. "You mean do gay men know lesbians, and lesbians know gay men?"

"Right."

"Well sure they do. Everyone knows all sorts of people, hopefully. But it never crossed my mind she might be lesbian. I was pretty sure she was a Martian."

"No way," said Billy, rolling with it. "Check out her hair."

"You don't know what a Martian's hair is like!" shouted Cindy.

"He might," said Tim, beaming a bit on the newly subtle brow of his nephew. But they knew, and they were okay with it; he was gay and he was still Unk. Tim had seriously underrated "the minor children."

"Did she hassle you, Unk?"

"No, Bill. You mean—?"

"Right."

"No. She wasn't exactly nice to me, but that's probably just how she is. At least when she's doing her job."

"She wasn't nice to me, either," said Cindy.

"Which proves she's not a lesbo," said Billy, stretching his sophistication past the snapping point.

Billy was on the muscle now, charged up, freed from Taggart's cold probe. Did he like his friends, she kept asking—with all kinds of ketchup and mustard on 'like' and 'friends.' Was he gay, that's what she wanted to know, but Billy knocked that knuckleball way over the fence. "No ma'am, I *hate* my friends. What do you *think*?"

"Listen up now, Hergies. I forgot to say we're having company tonight. An old friend is coming and we're cooking on the grill."

"Ellie?"

"No, sweetheart, it's someone named Karl. You met him once, a long time ago."

"He's not a friend, he's your boyfriend."

"Slow down, Bill Hergie. What he is, is one of the world's nicest people."

"So are you, Unk," said Cindy.

"So isn't The Alien," said Billy.

"Okay, it's time to forget The Alien. I want you two to go over to the McManuses and invite them to the cookout. It's a late invitation, but round up as many as you can. I'm awarding five points for every McManus you bring."

"But what do we do with the points, Unk? What's a point?"

"Yeah, Unk, what's the point?"

They asked, but giggled and did not stay for an answer. Disburdened both of Ms. Taggart's looming inquisition and of a secret they had carried too long, their feet barely touched the grass as they sailed off in search of points.

When a couple of small planes from Silver Ranch floated over, Tim thought of Monty. Monty would shake his fist at them, dream of launching mortar shells, threaten to call Congressmen. He did research on how high one's property rights extended.

Tim liked the way they punctuated the sky, counterpointing the quiet with their lazy drone. Flipping hamburgers with his right hand, he waved to the pilots with his left, as though he had been standing out there barbecuing for decades. In the strong late sun every color was extreme, luminous—a Fellini concoction.

"By the way," said Karl, as they saw Al McManus approaching, "are we—?"

"We are, though it won't come up.... Al, this is my friend Karl. Karl, my friend Al."

"The father of the twins," said Al. "Something smells almost good enough to eat."

Children, two of whom were the twins and two who were new to Tim, chased a skimming Frisbee. Someone's Irish setter got to it first, but he seemed to know the drill. He would chomp the Frisbee once, almost furtively, and then release it.

Billy was busy, but not so busy he didn't have Tim's back. He identified Karl as one of his uncle's "buddies," nothing more, and when Tim told him not to worry, not to make it a deep dark secret, Billy gave him a solicitous pat. "Sure, Unk, but you don't want to go shouting it out, either." Impressive balance, from a lad so classically heterosexual.

And Billy was a changed man that way. In the wake of his summercamp kisses (and matured in numerous subterranean ways) he perceived Joyce Arsenault in a new light, this one also luminous. Where previously Billy had noted a reasonable throwing arm (for a girl) and decent speed on the basepaths, tonight he noticed freckles and brown curls. Smiling eyes that confessed to fealty.

Joyce was a very cute twelve-year-old, no question. Tim, perhaps ungenerously, saw her future through a glass darkly: saw cigarettes and serial hairdo intervention and a weight problem at thirty. This he kept to himself (you don't want to go shouting it out) while enjoying the hell out of Billy's new lemonade-bearing courtliness.

The kids were fed and the "grownup food"—salmon and grilled vegetables—was just coming off the fire when a gray Tercel steered into the driveway. It was Ellie and Mr. X. Ellie had barely stood before Cindy flew into her arms. "Don't worry," she told Tim, over Cindy's shoulder, "we've already eaten."

"Victor Perry," said Mr. X, shaking hands. "And she's lying, we're starved. Not that we expect to be fed."

"Feed them, Karl, for God's sake *feed* them, these people are starving. Bill, we need two more beers—no, five more. Six, if you're having one yourself."

It became a party, with plenty more beers. And as Al's

Heineken and Victor's Sam Adams went down, the communal spirit eased higher and higher. Tim experienced an enormous rush of trust for Al and for Victor, though he hardly knew the former and had only just met the latter. On the strength of fermentation, goodness hung about them like an aura.

"This one's a keeper," Tim whispered loudly to Ellie. "You're the one," he said, pounding Victor on the chest. They thanked Tim for his offer of lodging, but kept to their plan of heading to the seacoast, where Vic's sister was expecting them.

The night concluded with hugs, everybody hugging everybody. "If this was your ideas," Tim said to Karl, "they were excellent." He was so lit with affection for all concerned that beneath these hill-vaulting stars, Tim might have hugged Joe Average too. Average was back—on both machines in the city—and sadly diminished. Barely audible, he sounded close to tears.

"I want you to hear this, Karl. I want you to tell me I'm not crazy."

Karl listened. "No, you're right, the guy is in serious trouble. But you will be too if you start leaving him friendly memos."

"He's sick, Karl."

"Very. And you have enough problems of your own."

"None. I have no problems. I'm happy happy, and poor Joe is miserable."

"Go to bed, Timmy. When you wake up tomorrow morning, you may remember a problem or two."

"Son, let me say that you may have good ideas, excellent ideas, but you are a fucking pessimist."

Cindy's door lay ajar and her voice came as a clear invitation: "Hi, Uncle Tim." It was too dark to see her, but Tim managed to locate her hand, then brushed back her hair and kissed her on the forehead. Tears were permissible, but he was relieved to feel none on her cheek. If only they could preserve the sweet delirium of this night.

"I love you, Uncle Tim."

Inside the pitch black, with both eyes shut tight, Cindy liked to pretend her parents were still alive. That they would call soon, from the Manchester airport. Or that they were the ones making noise downstairs. There was no evidence to contradict it, even now; she had simply chosen to interrupt the game in favor of an extra goodnight kiss.

"I love you too, sweetheart. Very much."

This was such a perfect ending to their serendipity that Tim was taken by the throat, the old swallowing problem, although this time it was pure sentimentality. "Poor Joe Average," he said, at the mirror with his toothbrush, as he spread wide the net of that sentimentality. He was drunk, he finally grasped. Seven beers could do that to you.

Or *for* you, God bless 'em. Maybe they should be asked to do it more often. Maybe it was precisely what a country squire required: elbow patches and an ocean of alcohol.

Eight hours later, still in bed, Tim labored to reconstruct the previous evening. It had gone fuzzy on him. He recalled Ell's arrival and his approval of her new beau, the Victor. He just could not summon Vic's last name, or his face. Plus there had been an important bit of gossip about Charles....

Finally the fog blew off his brain, and there was Vic: sandy hair slightly receded in front, round brown eyes and a round blunt nose. The shy smile featuring a snaggled bicuspid. Victor *Perry*, he was, in khakis and a blue oxford cloth shirt—and they were off to Kittery or Portsmouth, in an '87 Tercel. Yes.

And Charles had done it, ended his long engagement. Poor cindycrawford had caught him with an exotic younger woman— half Korean and half Swiss?—caught him at any rate and Charles had come clean. Ratted on himself and The Beast, on himself and others, and offered an unanswerable self-critique: I love you but doubt I can ever be faithful to anyone.

What response could cindycrawford conjure to that? It was a formulation that precluded ultimatum. Tim could see the words, THE END, blooming on the screen of her sad beautiful face.

Well, Vic Perry's face said the exact opposite. A kind, intelligent face, it spoke of a clean start on a strong foundation. His was the visage of a solid character actor, one of those old pros who kept Hollywood's feet on the ground. "Martin Balsam," said Tim aloud, just as Karl walked in with a breakfast tray.

"*Twelve Angry Men*," said Karl. "These were fresh—yesterday. They're from the place you hate, on Newbury Street."

"I hope you treat what's-his-name half this well."

"Jay is his name. You'll meet him soon. We want to do another of those weekends."

"Hot tubs, candlelight dinners—plus your excellent ideas."

"Speaking of which—the ideas, not the candles—I never had a chance to tell you what I learned."

"He files a report!"

"A preliminary report. You know the double lot across the street? Looks unbuildable? Skinny saplings, kind of wet and squashy-looking?"

"Geesh, it's a good thing Earl sells the real estate around here and not you."

"Earl owns that lot, my dear. Earl Sanderson, Limited, no less. And he has an offer on another one. He's buying up the block."

"He is a realtor," Tim shrugged.

Karl was astonished. Where was the outrage, where was the paranoia? Where was the real Tim Bannon? This one, sitting up in bed sipping coffee, was relaxed, impervious. "I don't think it's the kids he's after, it's the house."

"The house? What's it worth, one-twenty tops? If you have two kids that age, a hundred twenty thousand isn't break-even. Not over the long haul."

"I haven't made it add up yet. Unless he plans on doing them in, like the dogs."

"Don't even joke about it, Karl."

"He gets the house and the kids, shoots the kids, and pockets the whole one-twenty."

"When you get ideas, you get ideas."

"At least I do more than lounge in bed all day and criticize."

"Get your hands off me, you masher. Stop that or I'll spill the damned coffee."

Camp White Sneaker had sparse company again, on the old Beeline Trail up Mt. Skatutukee. One older couple stooped for mushrooms near the trailhead, and two younger couples, in a foursome, kept gurgling through the forest like some rare uphill-going brook. The music of their progress filtered back from altered courses, fresh angles of referred sound.

Tim sparked a fantasy game. "We're being followed," he said. "Be very still." As the three of them crouched behind a fallen oak, he refrained from adding the suggestion that the little *ad litem* was stationed in these woods, to monitor the quality of their interac-

167

tion. And though he did give them Butch and Sundance on the lam (they had watched the video) he withheld Pete Weissberg's version, in which Butch and Sundance were two gay sombreros fleeing a posse of rabid homophobes.

Billy kept driving them for the peak, in any case. That was the game for him, versus crouching and daydreaming of Bolivia. "We have to hurry," he said, "if we're going up Thumb, too."

"Let's not and say we did," said Cindy. "I'm hungry."

"But it's the plan, Simp. You can eat while we hike."

The *plan*, the day's little engine, was to survey the peak of Mt. Thumb from Skatutukee, then in turn the peak of Skatutukee from Thumb. These were miniature mountains, two-thousand feet high, yet the scheme was undeniably ambitious. Draining. Wrestling his nephew for power, Tim made them rest at times. There were ragged windows through the foliage opening onto views of the Wapack Range and at these infrequent prospects they would stop and sip the sewer-green Gatorade that was Billy's current lifeblood.

"No Thumb," said Cindy, as they sat finally on the rocky top of Mt. Skatutukee. She was trying to surrender: *no mas*.

"You'll feel stronger after lunch," said Billy.

"No Thumb, please no Thumb."

She seemed fine, though. Tim's decision was based on common sense, as prescribed: enough was enough. No Thumb. And it was the right choice, for he ended up carrying Cindy much of the rocky, rooted way down. More than once he was glad to sample the sewer-green ambrosia in Billy's canteen.

Though a week had slipped away (and though autumn, and anxiety, were one week closer), Tim was still relaxed. Still on summer leave, until reality intruded. Not the future, the present. For that night came word that Seth Turley had died.

At first he felt guilty for being alive—as always. Yet he was also petty enough to resent the inconvenience, so much so that he considered not going down. Because he also felt a step closer to his own death—as always. How could you not? This was a war, and they were losing every battle.

Seth had the AIDS variant which disabled first speech and then the brain. It killed you quickly and "painlessly." It had initials, of course, an acronymic name which Tim could never remember; to him, this one was the brainkiller.

"You have to be there," said Peter Weissberg. "No exceptions. If necessary, I'll pay for your babysitter."

"It's not that simple," said Tim.

"It is exactly that simple. You have to be there for Seth."

Tim dreaded the memorial service, dreaded the pathos and the self-pity, the justified depression and the labored uplift. And Peter would hound him about getting tested, as he was hounding him now about attending.

"I'm definitely not coming if anyone sings 'The Rose.' Seth hated that song every bit as much as I do."

"You wait. It'll make you cry like a baby."

"So would 'Danny Boy' but who wants to cry? I don't want to hear that song and I really don't want to hear the speech about Going On, how we are all Going On, and this isn't a funeral it's a celebration of *life*."

"Stop being such a prima donna, Tim, and remember who you are. It's Seth you should be thinking of."

"You're right. These things just wear me out."

"Fine, then don't come," snapped Peter, finished with imploring. But this injured tone of Peter's invariably ended a discussion in his favor. Tim would have to scramble back.

He would also need coverage. He could call Judy Heikala, Billy and Cindy's regular sitter—he should have called her anyway, long since, on general principles. But then Al McManus, appearing at the door as Tim was fishing out Judy's number, made an easier target.

Al was an absurdly good neighbor. He said yes to babysitting, and then handed Tim a fresh peach pie. This was the flip side, the A-side, of those wretchedly excessive strings of Christmas bulbs. "Alice says to let it cool at least half an hour."

"You bring me homemade pies, you solve my childcare problems. When am I going to see your dark side, Al?"

"Winter," said Al.

"Well it's no sense wasting good peaches," said Tim and then, when he saw Al staring at him, "What? What did I say?"

"Nothing, nothing. Jill would say those exact words in the exact same tone, that's all. It hits me, when stuff like that happens."

*

169

Tim drove first to the office, and parked at a meter directly below his window. Had this ever happened? In Copley Square?

But this was the time of year when Nantucket and the Cape sank under the weight of a quarter million souls demanding their fried clams; conversely, when Boston rose up on its toes. With the herd thinned, Boston was still a pretty vision of sunlight on red brick, closely resembling the city Tim twice had chosen to call home. Before and after San Francisco.

He and Karl had come back from the west coast together, and then stayed together through the hideous unraveling. It was worse for Karl, who convinced himself Tim was going through a "phase." (Hell, they all were, it was so insane it had to be temporary...) Karl believed in love. Love was real; it was different, and identifiable.

Tim tried to identify it, most nearly succeeding with Karl Trickett, where he did feel a difference. That was as close as he could come, though, and it still wasn't love. Not if it stood in the way. If it constantly imposed upon you.

The fault was his, he acknowledged. We fall on the leaning side, and to Tim freedom loomed larger than love. Or the illusion of freedom larger than the illusion of love, as he cynically restated the matter upon hearing, upstairs, that Charles was head over heels.

One could discount Charles. Charles was fun, but it would be out of place to take him too seriously, when Charles had never taken himself seriously at all. Except that now, freshly disengaged, he was madly in love with Cassandra. The half-and-half girl was already ancient history.

"Cass has the most beautiful neck I have ever seen," said Charles, not thirty seconds after Tim walked in. Hoping to gain respect by celebrating a non-erogenous zone? No. "The most beautiful breasts as well, mind you—perfect nipple placement— but then this girl even has the most beautiful knees."

Tim waited to see if Charles would pan on down to the toes. "Has she brain, Charlie? Or only these nether parts?"

"As a matter of fact, she's a Harvard M.B.A."

"How did you meet her?"

"At a club. We danced."

Charles' shrug of besmitment told all. Danced! The rest was far too obvious to bear repeating. One touch, no doubt, of the famous neck and *voilà*, true love.

Well, bully for Charles. Bully for Ellie and Karl, too—the lot of them seeking love and finding it, apparently. Why should Tim feel left out when the choice was his? He could be tucking up at that B. & B. with Karl if he were so inclined, if he could believe in love, or feel it. The trouble was he could disbelieve, could fail to feel it, yet still experience a void.

"I have to stop back after the service," he said. "To collect my packet."

"You may be in luck, old man. I've got some photos to pick up. Cassandra in all her glory."

"Dynamite," said Tim, backing towards the door, shaking his head in wonderment.

Through the handsome arch of divided glass, sunlight flooded the room, spilling across the wide mahogany floorboards. Its progress, displacing shadow, distracted Tim as he tried his best to listen. He heard a lot of it, and he spoke, unearthing his anecdote about Seth stranded on the Pike in Framingham yet reluctant to call AAA because his boa constrictor was in the back seat.

And, in spite of himself, he cried at 'The Rose,' beautifully rendered by a balding tenor he had never seen before. Hired talent? But the stories droned on and his attention slipped back to charting the incoming tide of sunlight, now three floorboards from his toes, now two.... This was nothing against Seth, certainly, and nothing against death, either. Death could hold its terror through a hundred of these fucking memorials, for the fact remained that someone sitting in this room would be *next*.

And here once again, among his best friends remaining on earth, Tim felt distinctly apart. This had nothing to do with Jill or the children—his "situation" as they were calling it. Tim remembered who he was. He recognized bits and pieces of himself in everyone present. He was one of them, no question.

But he was also apart from them. Different from the different, a freak among freaks. Tim weighed the possibility that everyone felt this way, gay and straight, black and white. Maybe it was the famous human condition revisited, as in such clichés as the one reminding us we all die alone. It came in forms as trite as the old high school nightmare—everyone desperate to be included, everyone feeling left behind.

Included, warmed, sheltered from the intergalactic coldness. Absolutely. Tim understood that his was the unnatural response, for even in high school he embraced aloneness. Noticed that he preferred it. Could not call it loneliness, as he so rarely felt lonely.

When he tried explaining this to Karl, Karl joked that Tim had missed his calling, that he should have been a poet or a composer. Travel agents were not supposed to be existentialists. So Tim burrowed deeper into solitude, he stopped trying to explain himself, even when he could taste the explanation on his brain. He went abroad twice a year, rarely more and never less, and he always went alone. The Blues of Tim Bannon.

Tim's reputation for soured adventure was so ironclad he could predict the stories they would string together at his own memorial, right here at The Meeting House. Peter Clippinger would kick things off. Tim always gathered his maps (Peter would testify) and researched the history. Even studied the language for a month, then went off brimming with enthusiasm. Soon after, all too soon, he would begin sending what Peter called The Postcards of Doom.

News of the Blues, Karl would chime in, and open with The Budapest Blues. Tim was in Budapest for one night, yet managed to get himself rolled by a gypsy working the Danube River cruise. And in Czechoslovakia (The Moravian Blues, Karl would laugh through tears) his bike had been stolen, but then his bike was always getting stolen....

And Carlos would quote him (they would all quote him, in harmony) dismissing it with a grin and a hint of self-parody in the Carolina drawl. "I'm resigned to the blues, man, it's the least I'm owed."

For this was an old routine, Tim's rendering of a fellow named Ted Copeland, a black porchfront singer back in Berline. Blind Teddy Copeland, the white kids called him, for authenticity— there was nothing wrong with his vision. But Ted would finish a song and shake his head and say it: "I am resigned to the blues, my man. It's the least I am owed."

Tim took his paper cup of wine out to the courtyard, where Karl was chatting up the bald singer. They were bent over a flower (identifying and classifying it, if Tim knew Karl Trickett) and when their two heads simultaneously turned toward him, Tim realized the singer was not hired talent, he was Jay Collingsworth, Karl's new beau.

"Sorry," said Jay—disarmingly, before hello—"Karl warned me you hate that song."

"Generally speaking, I do prefer the blues," said Tim, going along with his own private joke. Wondering briefly what Ted Copeland would make of "The Rose."

"Does he ever," said Karl, always ready. "Timmy went to this tiny fishing village in Scotland? And they told him it was the first sunny day the Firth of Forth had seen since the fourth of Firth, or something? And Tim came down with the flu."

"Pittenweem," Tim acknowledged. "Three days in bed."

"The Pittenweem Blues. Then last year he was off to Ravenglass—"

"All right, Karl, enough."

"Sorry, Timmy. Don't be sore."

"I'm not. Not at all. But the thing is I'd better get going. The Mt. Monadnock Blues, you know. Time to hit the road."

"Well, I'm glad I finally met you," said Jay.

"Likewise. And though it is an awful song, you sang it like the angels."

That was that. Tim wasted no time bolting back through the room, or tomb—that gorgeously appointed portal to death. In that room, inevitably, you made two mental lists (the ones who had died and the ones still breathing) and you left, invariably, with at least a trace of imagined fever, a definite moistness at the temples.

He tried to leave it all behind as he descended (*fled*) down Mt. Vernon to Charles Street, where he was startled to see spaces between the parked cars. *Parking* spaces, on Charles Street! Was Boston trying to lure him back?

There were distinct signs of autumn in the Garden: an outbreak of red leaves, squirrels madly stuffing their cheeks with acorns. Humid as the day remained, he felt September closing in on him. September would come, and Tim would not be in Donegal, as planned. Ideally, he would be in New Hampshire.

Ideally? What it boiled down to was this: the time was fast approaching for Tim to go out and get The Donegal Blues, but Tim would not be free to get them. It was a joke, the Blues, yet the animus behind it had served as his substitute for love. A rich solitude over any bleak partnership, that was the crux of Tim's choice. Now he would need to turn up a substitute for the Blues.

Could it really be his true-life sitcom, The Unk Knows Nothing Show? In tonight's episode, Unk shops and cooks! And be sure and tune in next week for an all-new one-hour special in which Unk goes plastic at The Pants Man, then drinks himself to bloody blue ruin! Whatever it looked like in fact, Donegal had never looked so good to Tim Bannon.

By now he was eager to see Charles again, and how bad were things when you craved a restorative dose of the white teeth, the gleaming black hair? But Tim was certain Charles could help him. Because Charles had joy. For all the wrong reasons, perhaps, and yet who needed reasons, right or wrong? What you needed was the joyfulness; you had it or you didn't, and Charlie had it, through the sheer dumb luck of personality.

"My new honey," he said, extending an envelope toward Tim and then retracting it. Teasing! Was Charlie in such transports he had lost track entirely of Tim's sexual preference, not to mention the fact that Tim was just coming back from a funeral?

"What? You're charging money to show them?"

"They *are* nudes."

"I *am* gay."

"Shit, there go the profits," said Charles, forking over the envelope. Most of the photographs were chaste Victorian portraits featuring the young lady's long blonde tresses. Only a few were nudes.

"I love this one," said Tim. Cassandra had covered her face with both hands in a lovely comic statement of reserve, given that the gesture left her entire torso exposed.

"Those are the breasts," Charles elucidated.

"I understood that."

It struck Tim that these photos were Charlie's way of explaining himself, excusing his behavior in dumping cindycrawford. With such compelling evidence as this in hand, even a gay man would get it.

"*The* breasts, I mean. Best of Boston, 1990."

"So then these must be the knees."

"Stick around, Tim, you may get to see her in the flesh."

This was a bizarre outburst of pride, yet it was also generosity. Charles was sufficiently solipsistic to believe he could lift Tim's spirits with these pictures, and in a way he was right. Tim did not stick around, though. He organized his work packet and stepped back into the heat and humidity.

The Fleet Bank clock was flashing 4 o'clock and 95 degrees, round numbers. Nearing Greenwich Park, Tim saw that Harriet, on a bench in the shade, had removed her fur coat. She had plenty more layers to safeguard her modesty, but Tim had never seen her without the coat. He gave her a quarter and pretended to admire the Miss Maine snapshot, as clearly this was a day for cheesecake. When he bumped into his neighbor Bill Mastronarde, Tim half expected him to flourish some shots of Connie.

"What have you been up to?" asked Bill, harmlessly.

"Good question," said Tim, not answering it. He had left a cardboard carton in the foyer, which his mailman had filled with unwanted mail order catalogues. These he transferred directly into the recycling bin. The telephone, ringing inside, was likely another commercial invasion, but Tim grabbed for it just in case.

"It's you, in person," said Joe Average. "You haven't been answering."

"Gee, I don't suppose you could guess why."

"I know, I know, and it's true. I may owe you an apology."

Here was the kinder, gentler Joe Average whom Tim had been hearing for weeks. Joe's latest messages were flat hopeless entreaties. They were pointless, really, for what was the point of a harassing phone call that neglected to harass. And now he was *apologizing*?

"I've done some reading. About the gay gene?"

"You have got to be kidding me."

"Not at all. This whole gay thing may be no different than a person having brown eyes. Or strong teeth."

"Joe, that's a very new theory. No one has even tried to prove it."

"It's incredibly honest of you to say that."

Whoa. The guy was so turned around he sounded like one of the clones; his voice blended with all the clone voices at Seth's service. Joe Average might yet prove to be one-of-us!

"I thought I could buy you a drink. Let bygones be bygones."

"Bad idea."

"I would tell you my real name."

"No! I don't want to know your real name."

"I don't mean now. I meant if we—"

"Why not now?" Tim fired back, blithely contradicting himself. The reflex of logic. He was chopping logic with Joe Average.

"Okay then, now. It's Ed. Just Ed."

"Just Ed. As in you have only one name, like Cher or Liberace?"

"No, no. As in it's not colorful. It's a Joe Average sort of name."

"Look, Ed. You sound a lot nicer than you did—"

"I am sorry about that, as I said."

"Okay, but we shouldn't get together. I can't help you. I've got these two kids to care for—"

"Yeah, right. You're a—"

"A homo, yes. But I really do have these children and I'm putting all my good work into them. If you see what I mean."

"I don't see, no."

"Never mind. You know what I do, when I want to feel better?"

"Don't patronize me, Tim."

"I talk with my therapist, that's what I do, and I come back feeling tons better."

"You bastard, you better cut this patronizing bullshit."

"And if therapy doesn't help?" said Tim, who had no therapist and had not spoken with one since freshman year, "there are some bars I can tell you about."

If Just Ed was in the closet, if this was his desperate attempt to squeeze out into the room, either Colours would work for him or it would scare him shitless. Let fate decide that. Tim simply wanted the calls to stop without any gunfire starting up. He wanted this call to end peacefully.

Meanwhile it had. Just Ed, on whom Tim was well advised to hang up (on whom he had hung up, a dozen times), had just hung up on *him*. Which took a moment to register.

The only new message was from Ben Fisher. A high school music teacher who looked like a high school student. Twenty-eight, though, or so he said. Played the cello. They had exchanged numbers at a party on West Springfield, talked about setting up a dinner thing. That was months ago and now here was Ben, shyly inquiring. In Ben's voice, Tim heard the sweetness he had found so appealing.

176

He could manage this—he did have coverage—but it was too early, hours until dinnertime, and the tricky phone tussle with Just Ed had spooked him. Ed could be anyone. He could be someone Tim knew, even someone with whom he had shared fluids, anonymously, in ancient times. For that matter, he could be Ben Fisher.

Tim did not believe any of it, he was simply spooked. Beating a retreat. For now he felt safer in New Hampshire. He knew what to do there, how to behave, perhaps in the limited yet comforting way you understand a job. His own world had gone temporarily out of focus.

He grabbed a cotton sweater and a light jacket (September was coming), replaced the cardboard carton in the foyer, and split. He made incredible time—or maybe it seemed that way because he was so zoned out in the transition. But back in Jaffrey well before the sunset, he was astonished to think he had left here just this morning. That it was still the same day.

To reclaim the kids, he had to absorb a bowl of Alice's leek and potato soup. Then it was time for *Jeopardy,* the game show which grimly enough had become part of Tim's normalcy thing and which Billy always dominated. The young were simply better at thinking backwards, the same way they had an edge with electronic gizmos. They were born to it and besides, their minds were still nimble.

Tim knew the answers (or the questions), he just couldn't transpose them quickly amid the bells and whistles. "February 29!" Alex Trebek shouted and you were supposed to shout back, instantly, "What day comes once every four years!?"

"February 30!" Tim shouted instead, helplessly.

"Unk had a long day," said Cindy, afterwards, by way of excusing Tim's dismal third place finish.

"Thanks, but the truth is your brother's brain works better backwards than it does forwards."

"Better than yours," said Billy.

"That's for sure. Anyway, here are your prizes. I brought you each a present."

"Neat-O," said Cindy, unwrapping a small wooden boat.

"They're a little oldfashioned," said Tim, who always felt on shaky ground offering gifts that had no power source.

"They're cool," said Billy. "Thanks, Unk."

"The sails are real canvas, correctly rigged and all. So they should actually go across a lake."

"Supercool. We launch them and follow in the canoe."

"But what if they go different ways?" asked Cindy.

"They won't, Simp. It'll be the same wind and current."

"If they do," said Tim, "we'll just have to think fast. But *forwards*."

"When can we try them, Unk?"

"Why not tomorrow?"

"Tomorrow we can't. We said we'd help Ms. Whitman set up her classroom."

"Good for you. So we'll try them on Saturday."

"Can't do that either. Saturday we have to go you-know-where."

This Tim had forgotten completely. They would be at Earl and Erica's house for what Billy was calling *Alien 2*. And Tim would be alone in Jill's house. No Jill, no Monty, but no kids either: a skewed stanza of the Mt. Monadnock Blues.

"Well, that should be fun," he said, purging irony, going for upbeat.

"Tons," said Billy, purging everything except irony.

"I love my boat," said Cindy. "It's really pretty."

Saturday afternoon, on his own, Tim hiked up Barrett Mountain and crossed a gap to New Ipswich Mountain. Just rambling under a cool bright sky. Apart from the absence of rain, it struck him that this was not so different from what he might be doing in Donegal. Part of what he might be doing, at any rate.

Sixty-five miles from Boston (which he could make out from the high ledges: the Pru, the Hancock, the gas tanks on Morrissey Boulevard) these peaks were surprisingly wild. The forest lay thick and unbroken below. Only from the summits could he discern villages (church steeples ascending through the crown of greenery) and one large farm. No visible roads, no cars.

That night he drove to the Souhegan River town of Wilton to see a Spanish film he'd never heard of. The movie had such wonderful faces, children's faces in particular, that it pleased him in spite of all their troubles. When it ended, he stood outside on a quiet hill, gazing at the moon and at the moonlike clockface on the theater's old brick tower. A cigarette break without the cigarette.

Then he went back in to watch the film again. Why rush back

to an empty house? And it worked for fifteen minutes, or as long as the popcorn lasted. After that, the story was entirely too recent and a bit thin. It was just the faces, really. Why watch it twice?

The answer was to take himself closer to bedtime, for there were limitations on a gay country squire with the Blues. Time would solve this, he told himself on the ride home, he would locate the outposts of gay life in the Monadnocks. Such outposts were inevitable, and the percentages were incontrovertible. This was one of the statistical Big Three, according to Peter Clippinger, who after all had a bloody Ph. D. in statistics.

If you flipped one thousand coins, five hundred would be heads and five hundred tails. Of any one thousand favorites at any racetrack in the world, three hundred and thirty-three would win. And if you met one thousand men, one hundred of them would be gay.

If not, someone was lying.

Around midnight, it began to rain. A new record for sunshine had been set, but now finally rain was pounding the roof and Tim woke to the rattling and blowing. He heard a drip somewhere inside the house, a leak. When dawn came, technically, it remained dark: water bucketed down from a sky as black as licorice.

Tim set a plastic tub beneath the drip, by the staircase, marvelling that it would be his responsibility (not Monty's, not some landlord's) to fix the roof. A radical concept. Tim had never owned a house.

He brought in the Sunday *Globe* (still delivered, still billed to Montgomery Hergesheimer) and made coffee. He read his way to nine o'clock, when the rain slackened. After that, a time-release capsule of changes, by the half-hour: a mist, a brightening haze, then the sun boring through. The road was like honed slate, a slick dark gray, and Jill's nasturtiums spilled over the rims of wooden tubs in cousinly reds and oranges.

Neighbors came out to work their gardens, but Tim wasn't ready for chatting or even friendly waving. He kept to the kitchen, hiding among the endless vapid sections of newsprint. Drinking more coffee. It was not that he yearned to be elsewhere. Donegal? Not really. He yearned to be nowhere, and to be no one in particular, a little while longer. There was the roof, however.

He pulled an extension ladder from the garage and climbed up to find the leak. Not that he knew what to look for. Would there be a symptom he could recognize, a gash or gaping hole in the asphalt? Tim had helped his father with roof repairs, but he never bothered to pay attention; he fetched things on command and handed them to Rex.

He should have paid attention. There was so much he should have learned from Rex, skills that now, as a householder, he would find invaluable. In the country, people still saw to their own houses; in the city, they watched a million fixit shows on TV and then called in workmen.

The good news was that he didn't fall off. The pitch was gentle and there was a comfortable enough friction underfoot. The bad news was that the roof looked fine. It looked like a roof. Tim considered a run to the hardware store, to ask intelligent questions, but the timing was iffy. The kids were due home soon.

On the ground below, all colors had been heightened by the rain and focussed by a spectacular clarity in the air. This air, with no aroma of its own, blended ambient gusts from the damp earth and steaming fields. If there were airtasters, equivalent to winetasters, they would pronounce upon a rare vintage indeed here in the Monadnocks. Caught between deep breaths and not such deep thoughts, Tim realized he had not spoken to a human being all day.

Maybe Billy knew about roofs. He really might. But when Billy arrived, he did not seem up to much. Tim was stunned by the change in him. Had vampires done this? Both of them were pale and puffy in the bright light, and so *small*. So silent. Of course Erica, who had brought them back, was still present. Between her opaque expression and their silence, Tim wondered if something truly awful had transpired at you-know-where. Had Earl shot, cooked, and eaten the little *ad litem*?

As he cast about for a pleasant remark, something mending, it occurred to Tim that he and Ric must look like bitterly divorced parents making the dread Sunday exchange. Ric was pale and puffy herself, so maybe it was just the soaking rain, the general sogginess of the morning. Maybe Tim looked every bit as puffy. But she seemed worse than that. Her large green eyes were moist, her shoulders sloped low. The children had literally run into the house.

"Did it go okay?" he said, gently.

"Not especially. No."

"What happened?"

"Nothing *happened*. They mostly ate. I mean, I bought five sacks of groceries and I think they ate it all. I'm not so sure they didn't eat the bags."

"They can definitely eat, those two."

"Like raccoons," said Erica, with a halting giggle. There was relief in spilling some of this out. "That little boy is *systematic*. He goes through the cupboards by category, you know. First he eats all the fruit, then he eats all the cereal—"

"You are allowed to tell him things."

"I know that, Tim. I didn't want to. I didn't mind him eating, I'm just telling you."

"Sorry. I appreciate your telling me. A lot."

Which he did. A friendly give-and-take with Erica? Unprecedented this quarter century. Still, Tim did come close to mocking her about the words she used. Systematic. Category. Those were four syllable words. Did Earl allow that many sylla-bles in his house?

But Earl was not the point. Ric was his sister and the point was they were connecting. She seemed almost glad to see him.

"So it was a normalcy thing. Kids, food, hanging around...."

"You might say that. Personally I had a real hard time with it. I found it very painful."

"You did?" New enough she was speaking to him. That she was speaking of emotion, *confiding* in him, was downright extreme. Erica experienced pain? (And *said* so?) But it was real, it carried no hint of manipulation.

"The little girl looks exactly like her, you know. *Exactly* like Jilly did. To me, anyway."

"I agree. And it can get to you."

"It's like seeing a ghost. She kept on hitting these ghostly notes, and I just felt so bad about everything."

Tim put out his arm and Erica leaned into him, snug against his shoulder. Molten lava flowing down Mt. Monadnock could not have stunned him more.

"Feel bad about what, though? You didn't do anything."

"I sure as shit didn't."

Erica pulled back to deal with her nose, but she didn't break away. Leaned back, leaned in again. For her the connection was literal, as though a live wire ran from her, through Tim, to Jill. She had been shaken by these hours with Jill's kids and Earl didn't get it, hadn't noticed. There was no room for sadness or reflection in his day-planner.

"All of it. Mama and Daddy. Jill. And you, you lousy—"

"Faggot."

"Creep. Lousy creep. You act like I don't count you as human, or something. Well guess what, Tim, you don't count me either. You don't. I'm just this dumb bunny to you."

"Come on," he said. It was the best he could muster, since Erica was right.

"Don't lie. If you won't I won't. I know we're both to blame, but it's Mama who suffered. And Jilly."

"Jilly didn't suffer, she just got hit by a car. Really, Ric, she was fine. She was one of the happiest people I know."

"Like that's not suffering."

Tim wanted the weight of her head again, the tickle of her long hair on his cheek, but the spell was broken. It was so simple to connect physically, so much harder to connect emotionally. Determined to push through barriers, he reached for her hand.

"Let me show you something," he said, steering her to where a grassy lane, farmwagon wide, snaked its way through sumac.

"What?"

"Just this."

"What about it, though?"

"Does it remind you of anything?"

"No, not really."

"Come on, you're not trying. Look at it."

"Tim, it's nice and all, but—"

"The path to the fort. Behind the Dreyers' barn. It's been transported across time and space."

"You really are messed up," she said, but with a softness; with affection.

"You don't see it?"

"A little, maybe. I mean, I forgot the silly fort to begin with. It was a lot more important to you."

"No way. It was all of ours."

"You thought. I never wanted to go hide in the woods and pretend we were starving to death. To me that was a sicko game."

"We had all different games there. Fun times. And I happen to know you and Sibby used to go there, later."

"I forgot that too," she grinned.

Back in the driveway, she leaned against her car. She seemed to require a leaning-post, of one sort or another. And she did seem reluctant to leave.

"You could hang out with us if you want," said Tim. "We might take the canoe someplace, but there's room for a fourth."

"That's okay."

Erica had made a firm decision not to cry until she found herself completely alone. From everyone's sight. But her brother was being so sweet it wasn't easy—to hold back her tears or to get going so she could release them. The most annoying part was that her nose kept running. She had a crying nose.

"I'd love it if you did stay a while."

"I'm fine, Timmy, don't worry about me. Sometimes a person can wake up a little, that's all."

"I hear you."

"It takes you and shakes you, as Earl would say."

"Noted philosopher that he is."

"You're hard on him too, you know. Earl's not what you think."

Tim scanned his mind for some way to squeeze out a drop of praise onto Earl, if only to maintain them conversationally. Failing, he settled for hugging her again, and patting the rump of her car as she climbed inside.

"Thanks, Tim," she said, though she could not say what for. Erica was intrigued by the contradiction: she had defended Earl, while she remained distinctly pissed off at him. Maybe it was in honor of that oily little preacher in Gideon Township. For better and for worse? That would be Earl.

Tim kept waving as she backed out, but Erica's hands and eyes were busy. She waved once, a hand flung out the window, as she negotiated the bend at the mailbox. Then she accelerated. She had gone a quarter of a mile down the road before she pulled onto a grass siding and finally let herself cry for her sister.

"So, how did it go over there?" said Tim, back in business. Billy and Cindy were in the kitchen, still eating. He had collected just three bags of groceries, so they were apt to make short work of it. Come to think, one bag contained nothing but paper goods.

"What do you mean?"

"Nothing special. Did you have an okay time?"

Cindy shrugged, her mezzo mezzo. Billy stared the slack-jawed teenage stare which translates, roughly, as "the grownup is perhaps insane?"

"Was our Ms. Taggart any nicer to you?"

This time Billy did the shrugging, while Cindy made her I-just-stepped-on-a-slug face. Tim kept needing another next sentence. Until he figured out what he needed was another next topic.

"So, what's the plan?"

"Can we try the boats?" said Cindy.

"Why not. We'll take them to Gilmore and race them."

"Like Pooh-Sticks!" said Cindy.

"No way, Simp. There's no bridge."

"Pooh-Sticks without the bridge. Open water Pooh-Sticks," said Tim, glad for this first small sign of life from his nephew. "And if someone should happen to win—"

"Someone has to win," said Billy, more engaged by the perceived inaccuracy than by the prize. He had no desire to be engaged by anything; had craved an escape, some time alone. Earl had behaved so strangely that Billy spent a lot of energy propping up the situation, patching over the blanks. Right now, he would welcome any blanks, maybe a whole blank week's worth.

"It could be a flatfooted tie," Tim pointed out. "Or both vessels could capsize."

What was it with Billy? Had he gone over to Earl, with his guns and tin cans and fishing poles? It could be age. Billy had aged in recent weeks, much more so than his sister. As her knight and protector, he stood staunch. But he was a child and she was a child, not long ago, where now he was something different—a tweener, between childhood and adolescence. So it could be confusion.

Whatever it was, Tim had sat around long enough. It was time for action and by God if they don't enlist you *draft* them. That was Rex Bannon's ringing pronunciamento on the Vietnam War. Naturally, Tim had disagreed; had hated his father's oversimplification. He even dared to argue the point (though never too far, with Rex) as the tide was already turning against the draft, and the war. "Hut hut," he said now, nevertheless, and with an almost Marinely timbre. "Let's gear it up for full dress canoe drill."

Secretly, he disagreed with Rex on everything in those years. Constantly he pondered how he could have been assigned to a father so unlike himself. He had to turn forty and lose a sister before he grasped the obvious, that kids never get to pick their parents, or their parentis. It was like lightning or tornadoes, a natural cataclysm. Authority Happens.

"Do I have to come?" Billy demurred.

Testing? If so, Tim was ready. "Indeed you do, Billy Boy Billy Boy. This outfit would be seriously undermanned without you."

"It's the real estate," said Karl that night. "It has to be. And Wal-Mart could be part of the picture."

"Wal-Mart the store?"

"They are looking at locations in the area."

"Here?"

"Here is one of the possibilities. Earl's buying up every buildable lot in sight of Cedar Street. He's playing Monopoly."

"Karl, he can't sell the house. Or, at least, he can't keep the money from a sale."

"Can't he? Isn't that a bit naïve?"

Undeniably, it was. Who knew all the moves a realtor-wheeler-dealer had (legal and otherwise) for shaping a fiscal reality? Certainly not Timothy Bannon. He reconsidered the glaze on Erica's face, her half-articulated distress. Had Ric glimpsed a future in which Earl dumped the kids on her and ran off with a younger version?

"Hell," he said, still Marinely. "Why don't I go over there and ask him about it, point blank?"

"Over where? To Earl's house?"

"Why not? I'll just shake the truth out of him."

Karl eyed Tim with considerable unspoken sarcasm. Recognizing the stirrings of a "Rex Attack," however, he played along—pretended Tim might really turn into Arnold Schwarzenegger.

"Don't do anything stupid," he said. "Talk to your lawyer first."

"What's stupid? Asking a few direct questions?"

"It would be stupid—and counterproductive at this point, I might add—to go and assault him verbally."

"Physically, I was thinking."

"Oh were you."

"What? What, Karl. You think I'm afraid of that sleazeball?"

So here it was, a fullblown Rex Attack. Karl drank some of his tea, to slow the pace. "No," he lied, "but any confrontation would be the exact opposite of helpful. Helpful would be to call your damn lawyer right away."

"It costs money to call my lawyer."

"If you don't call her, *I'll* send you a bill."

"Your bill I don't have to pay."

"I'll have your damn bicycle attached. God, Tim, you can be so stubborn."

With Karl gone, Tim decided to go through the actual bills stacked on Jill's desk. He paid the ones that needed paying. Paid for electricity, and propane, and one hundred gallons of *heating* oil. Was it September or *December* closing in on him now? And what must it cost to heat an entire house over the course of a New Hampshire winter?

He paid Jill and Monty's mortgage (which wiped out his checking account), then contemplated anew the leaky roof. What would that cost? His own credit card bill looked so scary that he closed the flap and went to make coffee.

He did call his lawyer, and outlined Karl's theory about Wal-Mart and the buildable lots Earl had accumulated. It was all a muddle to Tim, even more so in his retelling, yet he was somehow offended by her failure to be swayed. To find Earl guilty as charged, summarily.

"Maybe he's onto something, but it's not remotely provable— or illegal, for that matter. And you do see that Earl could as easi-ly assign the same motive to you."

"Jill assigned her *children* to me. That's *my* bloody motive."

"I understand that, Tim. All I'm telling you is that there's no legal connect between your friend's hypothesis and the case."

"But it's obvious. The law can't think? The law has no brain?"

"Don't go shooting the messenger," said Barnes, taken aback by his vitriol. "Why are you so angry?"

"I'm not angry," said Tim, straining to soften himself for con-sumption. Tim could not answer why, but he was angry, he did want to shoot the messengers—both of them. First Karl and now Barnes, a couple of liars after all. They were supposed to solve your problems, not make them worse.

He allowed his nerves might be on edge. The kids had moved out on him, leaving only their bodies, their "corporeal husks" behind. Wordless meals, wordless evenings. They spoke only during *Jeopardy*, spitting out their guesses. Someone *had* won the open water Pooh-Sticks that afternoon (the yellow boat, Cindy's) but neither of them cared, or asked, what the prize was.

"When you called," said Barnes, "I was hoping for news of the meeting in Taggart's office. It was yesterday, no?"

"Yesterday, yes."

Alien 3, this time a mere two hours of torture for Billy and Cindy, alone with Michele Taggart. But Tim had gleaned nothing about it, had nothing to report. He chose not to press them, and they chose not to volunteer a syllable. Really, they had been mum since *Alien 2*.

"So what was your sense of it? What did they say?"

"Say? The small wall of silence?"

"Still, huh. Those poor kids."

After dinner, Tim took Billy along to the A. & P. with an eye to bridging the silence. At the very least, they would be choosing flavors together. But Billy ripped the shopping list in half ("It's way more efficient, Unk") and took off like a wild turkey through the corn. He came back into view long enough to flip two packages of raisin bread in the cart, then raced after the frozen waffles.

By the time Tim cornered him briefly at the dairy case, he knew he had better be direct. "I'm really glad you came with me," he began, but Billy interrupted:

"You made me."

"Yeah, I wanted your company. Because you've been off in your own little world so much lately and I have been worried...."

Billy did not choose to fill in the blank Tim left him. Not even with a shrug.

"Well, so, how's it going? In your little world."

This time Billy looked up and seemed surprised to find Tim there. He laughed at the joke, but with his mouth closed. A snort. Tim had no next sentence until they were standing in the parking lot ten minutes later.

"You never answered my question. About how you're doing."

"Fine, Unk. I got three goals last night."

"That much I know. I was there—remember?"

"We won the league."

"And that's how it is in your world? We're Number One?"

"I know you came and watched, Unk. But it's not like you care."

"You little creep. I care *tons*."

"About soccer, I mean." Then, for Tim's sake, he appended: "At least you know the rules. Uncle Earl doesn't care, plus he's ignorant."

"I care about you, Billy. And so does your Aunt Erica."

It was only human to omit Earl (downright virtuous to include Ric) and wise to overlook the boy's rudeness. Although the word "ignorant," which lately had worked its way to the forefront of Billy's vocabulary, might just indicate some new trend in slang.

"I wanted Dad to know. It sounds dumb, but I really did."

"Come here, you little creep. Come."

Tim hugged him. Squashed him, really.

"I wanted them both to know, and there's no way they'll know anything about me ever again. I could win the Olympics, or anything, and there'll never be a way to tell them."

Tim guided them to the steep riverbank, which bordered the shopping center on one side. He craved the peaceful gurgle of the water, hoped its steady flow would soothe them. Above the mountain, the sky wore scarves of vivid color, fire and violet in woven strands.

"It's hard," said Tim, with the heat of the boy's tears burning right through his shirt. "It's a very hard part of the hardest thing in the world. But—"

But what? Tim paused, groping for some tool that could mitigate despair. The pause caught Billy's interest. He wanted to know What.

"When you're older—soon, actually, way before the Olympics—you're going to have a terrific girlfriend. And you'll want to tell *her* everything, the same way."

"Maybe I won't. Maybe I'll be gay, and have a boyfriend."

"Not you, kiddo. Trust me on this. It's not like magic, not something that happens to you all of a sudden."

"Maybe it's already happened. I'm related to you."

At least they were communicating. Although they had changed the subject. Or had they? What was the subject? Not soccer....

Despair. Despair was the subject.

"So are dozens of people, related to me and to you, buddy, and none of them are gay. Zero. It's your best gal you'll want to tell."

Tim stopped himself from mentioning Joyce Arsenault by name (or gender) despite her clear value as circumstantial evidence. To push that might be an invasion, a form of outing.

"I only wanted to tell Mom and Dad."

"So give it a shot. Who knows, maybe they can see us and hear us. Maybe they already know about the three goals, and about the three hundred totally wonderful things I've seen you do besides that."

Here Tim jammed, unable to speak more or swallow. He did want desperately to tell Jill about these two great kids of hers and he wanted her to know what a good job he was doing too, or at least how hard he was trying.

"What, Unk?"

"Nothing," Tim managed, pointing at his throat.

"You don't believe that stuff? About Heaven?"

"Do you?"

"I asked you first."

"I don't believe it, but I could be wrong. I hope I'm wrong."

"Can we go now? The waffles are getting soggy."

"Listen," said Tim, keeping an arm around Billy's shoulder. (And here was a lesson from Rex. Because Rex had never done it.)

"I'm listening," said Billy, which he was, so long as Tim kept moving toward the car.

"Just this. Whatever you accomplish in life—goals and grades and all the stuff they give prizes for—you have to be doing it for yourself."

Was this the What? If so, it was a complete dud. It was impossibly banal and came way too late in the conversation, but Tim forged ahead anyway, if only because his voice was working again.

"You want people to know, and you want them to care the way you care. And maybe they will. But you do a thing because it's what you love to do."

"Sure, Unk. That's cool."

A flat voice in the half-light of the A. & P. parking lot, uttering words which Tim took to be nothing more than a polite signal to shut up.

Tim was right about that. Billy feared if he made no verbal offering his uncle might keep up the pep talk all the way home. Or worse, stand around here while the waffles got soggier with every sentence.

In the car, Tim reached over to ruffle Billy's hair. Billy twisted away as if a snake had flicked at him. The ruffling of hair had been outlawed, weeks ago.

"Sorry," said Tim. "Old habits."

He pulled the headlights on and they rolled forward, silence restored and the twilight blooming around them like fog.

VI

INDIAN HATBAND

It rained again and the kids stayed upstairs reading. Which was fine, except they were still up there at dinner time. Pélé (whose life story Billy was reading) had entered the twilight of his career, though he had been in his prime at lunch.

In the face of so much more silence, Tim had begun to flail on the minute-by-minute decisions. Cindy loved Rice Krispies; now she would neither eat them nor name an alternative breakfast. Instinct told Tim not to let her starve, yet instinct also counseled against force-feeding. So he patted her head (still an option with Cindy) and left the kitchen, praying she would consume some Krispies behind his back.

"You can't assume they know what they want," said Olivia Goldsmith. "They are just now understanding they can't have what they want."

"But they've been with friends. They had a blast at the school."

"And that's good. Underneath it all, however, a new school year uncovers the extent of change for them."

"But why would they turn on *me*?"

Goldsmith was happy to issue rulings. She rarely played the sphinx. This time she did so, allowing a solid block of dead air before she spoke. "Do you see it?"

Tim saw it. Who else would they turn on? Who else did they trust that much?

"But don't assume they have turned on you—or that they know what they are doing."

"Of course not," said Tim, in utter confusion.

"And don't assume that they are a 'they,' an entity. Be sure you are seeing them each clearly, as individuals."

That afternoon, Tim spotted Al McManus charging his way. Al appeared uncharacteristically purposeful, hellbent in fact, and Tim's impulse was to flee. Flee Al's judgment, or his advice, for surely one or the other was coming.

Trapped in the open, he could only brace for the advice. He told himself to be gracious and pretend to listen—a lesson this time from Billy Hergie!

"I was Jill's age almost precisely," said Al, gravely, without preliminaries. "We were born in the same week. And the four of us were such close friends. But I know you saw us, Alice and myself, as a boring bourgeois couple who would be prejudiced against you."

It was a platform speech. Tim had no guess what the advice was going to be. "Al, I didn't."

"Well, the truth is we were prejudiced—in your favor. Because of everything Jill told us about you. She was so fond of you, Tim, and so admiring of your qualities. Concerned, though—"

"Al?"

"Give me a minute, I don't want to lose the thread. She was worried sick about AIDS, of course, but her main worry was the emotional side. All the ways you could be injured by society and how that shut you off from the possibility of love."

"Gays can't love?"

"Jill's words, not mine. She was afraid you could never settle down, never let yourself be comfortable. That you hid yourself in a small corner of society."

"I have friends. I have business partners. I travel."

"She felt you might have been—oh, not the President or any-thing ridiculous like that—but someone valuable to society."

"That's just my sis," said Tim, noting that Al had used the word 'society' three times and he had never heard Jill use it. "Believe me, Al, none of my teachers saw any such potential in me."

"My point. This incredible faith Jill had in you. She under-stood what a special person you are and because of her we knew it too."

"I appreciate the vote of confidence, and I'm ready for the But clause. Because that's next, right?"

"No. Just something for you to consider."

"Let me have it," said Tim, for Al's demeanor seemed to presage some mighty heavy advice.

"Don't you dare take this as criticism. It absolutely is not that. But Alice and I, and the twins I should add, since it was their idea, would be honored to have Bill and Cynthia in our household. If it helps. If it feels like a solution to this mess."

"You're kidding me, right?"

"No. Definitely not kidding."

"You mean adopt them."

"We never got into technicalities. Who knows about that sort of thing."

"Be the guardians. *In loco parentis.*"

"Honestly, Tim, we haven't put a title to it. They would be Bill and Cynthia and we'd be us and see how it all worked out. It's an alternative to you uprooting your entire life, or the kids getting tangled up with Earl Sanderson."

"So this would be a favor to me."

"Please don't be angry. If it's not an option, not a help, you can dismiss it out of hand."

"I really have to do that. I'm Jill's brother, I'm the guardian Jill wanted those kids to have. And even Erica is family."

"Fine. I understand completely."

"We're Billy and Cindy's family now. What's left of it."

"Not only do we know that, we know the children know it. Their loyalty and affection are very clear, and nothing will change that. But practically speaking—"

"They would feel rejected. Disowned. I wouldn't do that to them."

"That's a valid concern and we could ask a professional—without doubt we ought to ask a professional. As I say, everyone would have to want this."

"I don't want it."

"Fine. But let me finish my thought. We have the garage apartment. It's small but comfortable. In-law quarters. And there's a balcony off the bedroom—"

"You want to stick them over the *garage?*"

"Not them, you."

"Oh, I see. Me and the in-laws."

Tim's laugh was bitter, an Oilcan Harry sneer. Al had anticipated a polite refusal, not this demonic cartoon. He had never glimpsed Tim at his snippiest, with feathers ruffled, and it took an effort to keep his composure and plough ahead.

"No one has used it in two years. Alice's folks live in Idaho and mine are pushing eighty. They don't visit anymore."

"So the idea is I hang around the garage while you raise the children....Which somehow keeps me from being uprooted?"

"I'm making a botch of this, Tim. The apartment would be yours so you could come and go easily. Every weekend, every other weekend, three weeks in October. Whatever worked for you, in terms of going on with your own life."

"I honestly don't believe things are that bad."

"Neither do I. If anyone said things are bad, I disagree with him. Look at it another way. We've got these two kids, we're stuck with them for the foreseeable future. That's what we'll be doing. So it would be no great sacrifice—"

"I don't mind the sacrifice."

"Fine. But it can be a long winter up here."

"I like to ski."

In truth, Tim hated to ski and struggled against hating friends who did ski. He struggled now against hating Al McManus with his outlandish Unk-in-a-bunk scheme, but at least he understood why he was so angry. He was angry because everyone was attacking him. He was doing his best, doing just fine, and they were all coming after him with sticks and brooms, like the spooked villagers chasing the Frankenstein monster.

"I hear you," said Al. "Just so you know that for us it would not be a sacrifice. It would make our lives easier. That's the selfish part, because Hugh and Henry are easier whenever your two are in the mix. There has always been this charmed connection—"

"Al?"

"I'll stop now. And I'm sorry—"

"I'm sorry too. It's a hell of a gesture, don't get me wrong. Let's just say thanks-but-no-thanks and leave it at that."

"Fair enough, as long as you don't punish us."

"Of course not."

"We only want to help, in any way you find useful. An errand, the car pool, whatever. Don't punish us for offering more."

"No. And don't think I'm not grateful for all you have done."

"Prove it," said Al. "By coming to dinner tonight."

"Tonight?"

"To prove there are no hard feelings," said Al, perversely tightening the noose. He was perfectly aware that he was the one meting out punishment; that Tim would as soon spit at him.

"But it's after five o'clock."

"That's right, and you aren't cooking. But Alice is."

"What are you having?" said Tim, rallying into a more sociable pose. "That's what Billy would ask."

Tuning it down, down. Yet why did he need to keep convincing the world he wasn't angry? Wasn't anger sometimes the correct response? Instead Tim surrendered in a blaze of phony bonhomie. Agreed to eat fried chicken, agreed to keep biting his tongue.

He was so agitated afterward, however, that sleep was an impossibility. Tim was a gifted sleeper. Everyone else complained of bad nights, but when Tim went to bed he went to sleep. Except tonight. Tonight he found himself caught in that exhausting conundrum whereby the more desperately you crave sleep, the less likely sleep becomes. His thoughts ricocheted around a universe of distress, beginning with the kids. The two mutes.

Their sleeping, at least, Tim had taken for granted. But why had he? What if they tossed and muttered in the dark? What if they argued with God every night, unleashing their sadness at the stars? He had been so careful not to invade their space, or compromise their privacy. If he went to their rooms at two a.m. would he find Billy wide awake with jaws clenched or Cindy weeping softly, pawing at her ancient scrap of blanket?

Al. He went back over the conversation with Al, rewriting it. He had labored to remain civil despite feeling undermined, betrayed. Now he let Al have it, forming whole paragraphs in the dark, acidly refuting all Al's points. Letting anger be okay.

Then it was Earl's turn, for really Al McManus was just a well-meaning guy whose wife wished she had more children. Why be pissed at him when Earl Sanderson was the true villain? Earl had ignored Jill's wishes, manipulated Anne, confused Billy—and all for the love of money. To make money off Jill's death! Tim ought to have gone straight there and pounded Earl into dust. Yes, physically. Should have held him to account, just as Tim's father had done with Joss Lyman. Was there any doubt what Rex would have done when he learned that Earl was in this for the money?

No one liked Joss Lyman, but no one ever intervened in his drunken sprees. In Carolina, in 1958, you minded your own business, especially when it came to family. Until Rex had to make an exception. There were people who believed it concerned a loan, since Lyman never paid back the fifty dollars Rex gave him when Clara was sick and they couldn't afford the hospital. Anyone who knew Rex understood he never expected to see that money again, that it wasn't a loan, just charity—same as when he intervened.

Lyman's sins usually stayed within his walls. You never saw

it, but Clara Lyman somehow walked into a lot of doors. This one time, though, she was running through the yard as they chanced by in the pickup: Tim, Jill, and Rex. They saw her trip in the debris (tires and frames and rolled fence) then claw her way toward the road. Saw Lyman twist her arm until her face came around and smash her with his fist closed. It made a sound Tim had never forgotten, like an axe splitting bone.

He had never seen Rex move so fast. Rex shouted, but Lyman ignored him. He tried to pin the man's arms, but Lyman shoved free and stood snarling at Rex about private property and goddamned Communists. Tim guessed it was the Communists that did it, for Rex promptly coldcocked him. Laid him out like a sack of meal, right there in the man's front yard.

When Lyman came awake, Rex apologized. Said he was sorry to hit him, he was only trying to keep him out of jail. It was a crime to lay hands on your wife, didn't Joss know that? Didn't he understand if he ever did it again, Rex would have to call in the sheriff?

"You said that part so he wouldn't. Right, Daddy?"

"That's right, Jilly. But he will anyway."

"Maybe not, Pa. You really whomped him one."

"I lost my temper, Timmy, I truly did. When he said about private property, I thought he meant poor Clara Whipple—like she was in white slavery to him. I reckon he meant I was in his yard, is all."

So it wasn't the Communists. But this was by far the fullest explanation Tim (eight at the time) ever heard from his father, the strictest accounting. Rex did what he did with such clarity of motive that words rarely attached to his actions.

"She should have stayed Clara Whipple," he said to them with a sheepish grin. "That's where the problem began. Never marry a Lyman."

Rex was on rare uncertain ground, his voice still troubled, when he told Anne what had happened. It stayed with him for weeks, surfacing in hints that Tim could hear clearly. Tim himself had no doubt his father had behaved nobly. It was shocking to see Mr. Lyman get exactly what he deserved, yet it was grand. It was like the frontier justice doled out every Saturday at the matinée western.

Thirty-two years later, the lesson was intact: when someone

truly earned a punch in the nose, a real man went and punched him. But Tim was not a real man, not his father's son. He was a coward, who had never hit anyone in his life.

Or not yet. Sliced through by this sharp memory, his eyes raw with exhaustion, Tim began to plan (or fantasize) an assault. He would coldcock Earl Sanderson and he would scatter a few dollar bills on Earl as he lay on the ground rubbing his busted jaw. "You want money? Here's some money for you." It sounded so right, this new resolve, and it soothed him. It let him drift into a brief light sleep, too quickly jostled by a dream. A dream so quick and vivid he might have slept simply in order to dream it...

At the COURT HOUSE in Keene, Tim was imploring the judge. He shoved papers forward, spoke forcefully, made his case. The judge, leafing through a newspaper, showed no interest. Then Earl was lodging an objection ("Enough of this gobbledy-gook") and the judge was amused. He and Earl laughed together, a ratcheting metallic laughter that drove Tim from the room.

As he left, Earl heckled him ("Homo homo homo") and Tim whirled, screeching like a toucan, trying to lash out. His arms were pinned. "Timmy Timmy Timmy," mocked Earl, and finally Tim broke free and began whacking at Earl's knees with a canoe paddle. He woke hot and frantic, flailing in the bedsheets.

And he lay there, the Timmy Timmy Timmy echoing inside his head. A crow was cawing on the road. The children were downstairs crashing plates in the kitchen. He reached for the phone.

"A question. When you ran down Earl's scheme for me—hoarding land, Wal-Mart—what did you expect me to do about it?"

"Do? I didn't expect you to do anything." (Except maybe be grateful. But no, Karl certainly did not expect that.)

"You didn't think I'd be angry?" demanded Tim, clearly angry now.

"Sure, Tiger, absolutely. Royally pissed."

"Pissed enough to go after him?"

"Not this again. Not the Rex."

Tim begged for the chance to explain himself—which Karl, stunned, could hardly resist. Tim *never* explained himself. But then the explanation was so silly. Confirmed: a full-blown Rex Attack.

"Bust his chops, Timothy? You are in fear for your mortal soul because you failed to 'bust Earl's chops'?"

"I'm a wimp, Karl. A coward."

"You just have this huge Rex hangup. It's way too obvious."

"This has nothing to do with my father."

"It has everything to do with him."

"You think that."

"Yes I do. Listen, my poor dear boy. We are gay, in America. Which does not grant us easy perspective from which to assess our manhood, of all things."

"How does anyone prove his manhood?"

"*Why* does anyone prove it, is what I always say. Timmy, you've been under a terrific strain."

"I am so incredibly tired, Karl. I haven't been sleeping well."

"You?"

The children were still at the kitchen table. Billy (head down, the oval of brown hair presented) was reading the box scores. He glanced up for a nanosecond—"Hey, Unk"—when Tim said good morning. Cindy was reading *Jessica Ballou, Balloonist* which, as far as Tim could tell, she had read six or seven times by now.

She greeted him so blandly she might have been one of those windup dolls: you pull a string and it squeaks out set phrases in a waning soprano, Have a nice day.

They were doing just enough to place themselves beyond criticism. Then, abruptly, they were stuffing knapsacks with apples and granola bars, and mumbling a plan for the day that sounded safe and approvable. Tim, who had not had his coffee yet, could only give approval and watch them go. They weren't even talking to each other, just pedaling their bicycles like automatons.

Who *were* these two short people? It rattled Tim to lose track of them, to lose the threads of union that made running a household (even this one, with himself at the helm) possible. He was the cook and the maid, reduced to feeding them and cleaning the house, though he had not cleaned their rooms in a month. Had not laundered their sheets. He went upstairs now to gather the bedding, but really he went to snoop for clues.

Billy's room, like its occupant of late, had little to say about his identity. Or no: it said what it always said, in cards and magazines and posters. It said Larry Bird and Diego Maradona. The boy was terrific, yet all he could offer future archaeologists was sports paraphernalia, plus a few candy wrappers under his desk.

Cindy's room was more eloquent. It was shockingly direct and Tim had no excuse for missing the message it delivered—nor had he the slightest doubt that the tightlipped *ad litem* had heard it loud and clear. The room was a small airless shrine. Cindy had locked the windows, drawn the curtains, and dotted the perimeter with candles. None of them had been lit, thank God, though even from within his caisson of obliviousness Tim might have noticed that.

There were photographs of Jill and Monty everywhere. As teenagers, in college, ice skating, marrying. On the nightstand was a framed enlargement of Jill hugging Cindy that looked recent, possibly taken the last day of school, in June. The school entrance and the sign were visible behind their sundrenched heads.

Alongside the photo lay Cindy's copy of a book Monty had made for her with the title *Cautionary Poems*. He made one for each of them; Tim recalled that Billy's copy sported the famous "cowlick picture" with the ever-tilting tuft of hair. Where had that tuft gone, and when? Everyone assumed it was permanent, that it would be there when Dr. William Hergesheimer, aged sixty, performed complex brain surgery with the cowlick poking up through his green hospital cap.

On each page of *Cautionary Poems* Monty had drawn an animal and written two short lines of verse about it. *Don't get in line/ behind that porcupine. Don't lock the skunk/ in your steamer trunk.* The sketches, the poems, even the binding had all been done by Monty. *Better not wake/ that poison snake.*

Cindy had been clinging to history, to these happy fragments of her past. Tim read the inscription ("To my baby girl with LOVE from Daddy") and looked at the picture of Cindy at three and a half, with a two-tooth hole in her smile, the fair hair much curlier. It was a devastating sight. His tears came hot and steady, his body rocked on the child's bed. The tears were general, for everyone (not least for himself), though first of all for Cindy. Her room, her shrine. Her grief concentrated here like an intense local storm.

He fled the house. Vaulted the low stonewall to go through woods to the main road. There he began to run, with no destination in mind, nothing in his head beyond the echo of Monty's rhymes. *Don't swim in the dark/ so close to the shark.* Running in the bright air slowed his tears, though the sadness had bored into his muscles like a cramp. He shut his eyes and inhaled aromas: freshmown fieldgrass, cold kettle water from the nearby pond, tarry heat building on the road.

Life gave you those green fields, and lakes, and laughter. It gave you love. Then, sooner or later, it took everything away. It gave you youth (and hair!) only to blow it away like stray paper. And yet loss—whatever you lost—was your best evidence of blessings for you could only lose what you had and *having* was irrefutably a temporary condition. Was this consoling, though, or just a way of framing the bad news?

It did seem tears could be cathartic, because Tim was cleansed of anger, released from any urge to demonstrate his manhood. All that was gone the way a trailer is gone after a cyclone—*gone* gone—and his concern had come back around, quite purified, to the children. He was himself again—just Unk—and he was there to do what he could for them. Though first he would have to find them.

He went straight to Alice. Earlier, feeling awkward and resentful, Tim had avoided her. With his anger as mysterious now as it had been vivid then, he wanted to bring Alice in on the case. She would know where Billy and Cindy had gone, plus he could thank her (belatedly yet sincerely) for her largehearted gesture. Thank both McManuses, and let them know he had given their proposal careful consideration. He had not given it one moment's consideration, of course, but surely that was beside the point. The point was to find the kids.

Alice was not at her house, however. Too restless to wait around, Tim made a circuit of likely spots: the schoolyard, the riverwalk, soccer field, convenience store. Apart from Hugh and Henry, he had no idea where their pals lived. The kids were safe, Tim told himself, no reason to suppose they weren't safe. Possibly they were *with* Alice. But there was nothing he could do at the moment and because he could not do nothing, he started making calls.

"I wanted your opinion," he said to Attorney Dee Barnes. "There's a new offer on the table."

"No one's called me."

"This didn't come from Earl and Erica, it's the neighbors up here, the McManuses. Should I give you the quick and simple version?"

The quick and simple version was the only version there was:

Al and Alice would take the kids. And there was the garage apartment, with Unk in a bunk.

"We could sell it," said Barnes.

"What does that mean?"

"Enneguess will like it. You do understand this is still in his hands. You and Erica can't make it happen simply by agreeing. But I'm sure he'll like this."

"Why will he?" said Tim, with reflexive prickliness.

"It gives him a way to compromise. Judges like to do that. And it's good. With you so strongly in the picture, and Erica right close by? The kids could do worse. Presuming they go for it."

"The kids don't know about it."

"But the Sandersons are agreeable?"

"They don't know about it, either. And I haven't made a decision, I was just letting you know."

"You do remember we're due in court on Monday?"

Barnes could be curt. She was his lawyer, not his friend, and she worked without a secretary. Fair enough for her to end a conversation abruptly. But Karl Trickett was every bit as impatient with him. "I'm in court, Tim. Why didn't you tell me this yesterday, when you were maundering on about your manhood?"

"Are you really in court, or is that what lawyers say to get themselves off the telephone?"

"I am standing inside an actual bricks-and-mortar courthouse. Though I admit I'm downstairs buying Lifesavers at the precise moment."

"Then you can spare a minute to go over the pros and cons."

"What cons? Do the deal, Timmy. You could not hope for better than those two people."

"They're nice people, Karl, but they're not family."

"There you have it. They are nice people and Earl is family. *Quod erat demonstrandum. Reductio ad absurdum.*"

"*Agricola agricolae,*" said Tim in response.

Maybe Ellie would be nicer to him. She had called last night to chat with Cindy—and Cindy had chatted! A couple of times, Tim heard Cindy's best laugh, sort of a hum inside a gurgle. (Heard it for the first time in over a week.) Then she had breezed past him en route to her secret cave of sadness.

Ellie was perfectly nice to him, she listened patiently, but her response seemed oversimplified. "Great," she said.

"What's so great about it?"

"Wasn't your big thing that you had no alternative? Well so here's an alternative and a pretty good one, I'd say."

"Is it?"

"Yes. Good for the kids and good for you, don't forget. You could come home. We need you here."

"You noticed I was gone."

"Just a little. You know how insufferable Charles can get when he has two women. He thinks it proves something—which it does, of course. Plus he has this new *scent*—"

"Two women? What about Cassandra? Two weeks ago he was head over heels in love."

"Cassandra is the fair, but Donna is the dark."

"I don't believe you. Does he have photos of Donna too?"

"*Photos*?"

"Never mind," said Tim. He could see Ellie draw back, as if the pictures might prove even more obscene than the new scent.

"Listen," said Ellie, pushing her way past a fresh and startling insight that Tim and Charles were not so different, that *stability* scared them both silly. "Tell Billy and Cindy. Ask them what they think about it."

"I knew you would say that."

"Because it's so sensible?"

"No, because it's what you always say."

"It's what you always seem to forget."

"Ell, I've got to get off," he said, as he spotted Alice's van at the mailboxes. He rushed out.

The twins were with her, Billy and Cindy were not. Alice said she hadn't seen them in two days. The Hugh (or the twin Tim suspected of being Hugh) hazarded a guess: "They might be at the graveyard."

"The graveyard?"

"At the tennis courts, Mom. On the hill."

"Why would they be there, honey?"

Hugh shrugged. "Maybe they aren't. They go there sometimes is all."

"Okay, that's good to know. It might help."

Minutes later, Tim was driving back down the bumpy dirt lane that led to the soccer field and the town tennis courts. He had never noticed the cemetery, which spread over a plateau above the courts, obscured by a fence that ran along the ledge. It seemed unlikely the kids could have dragged their bicycles up the steep embankment, but Tim scrambled up the dirt cut in the hillside, stepped through a portal in the fence, and saw them. Score one for Hugh.

"Why are you here, Unk?" said Billy, more puzzled than rude.

"Why are *you* here, is the question. I've been looking for you all over town."

"We were coming home by six."

"And we ate lots of carrots," said Cindy. She was relieved to see her uncle, having feared the person they heard coming might be a gravedigger, or a policeman.

"So this is a place you like to hang out," said Tim.

It was sheltered and peaceful here, the way it was intended. There was a clear prospect across a palette of greens to Monadnock—always Monadnock. You saw it from a hundred angles, in a dozen different towns. Wild crabapple trees, their miniature fruit hung like ornaments, marked the forest edge.

"You can look, if you want," said Billy, after emerging from a quick huddle with his sister.

"I would like that."

"It's not a real stone," said Cindy, as she tugged him along by the hand. "It's only wooden. Billy wants to get a real stone."

"I want them to really be here, too."

"Close to home," said Tim.

Billy nodded. Though the grim set to his face mostly reflected Billy's quarrel with God, Tim gathered that he and Anne had incurred some blame for the Carolina burial.

"They were made into ashes," he reminded, gently. He had a thought, though, a way around that might prove helpful.

"We know."

They appeared to know everything. And certainly they had done an impressive job. The short plank, roughsawn and weathered gray, blended in with the old slate markers. The orange chrysanthemums (planted as purchased, rootbound in plastic pots) were alive and bright. In an amateur stab at memorial calligraphy, one of them had inscribed accurate dates for Jill and Monty: birth and death.

"How did you manage this? You didn't even have the shovel."

205

"We took the old one, with the cracked handle."

"You did a beautiful job. And this is a beautiful place."

"Do you really like it, Unk?"

"I love it, and I love you. You guys are way too great for words. And you know what? Maybe we really can bring them here someday."

"After Grandma dies? She's old."

"You don't have to be old," said Billy, pointedly.

"Are you going to die, Unk? From AIDS?"

"I don't have AIDS."

"You don't?"

"No, sweetheart."

These two were up to some tough talking. And they knew more at their young ages than Tim had known, or been told, at sixteen. They studied AIDS and sex education, sat in ampitheatres watching condoms being waved about, scribbled notes on the warning signs of genital herpes. In Tim's health class, there were spelling bees (he won one, with the word esophagus) and lectures on the proper care of the teeth and gums.

"I never even catch cold," he said.

"Me either," said Billy.

"Christmas you did," said Cindy. "You sneezed in the stuffing."

"Anyone can sneeze. You can sneeze from a flower, Simp."

"So we're all healthy," said Tim. "And your grandmother may be old, but she's a tough old bird."

"I'm a tough young bird."

"I'll say you are," said Tim, poking her belly until she gave back a giggle. "But we don't want to rush your Grandma into old age. So I saved some of the ashes."

Giving birth to this idea minutes earlier, Tim had felt inspired. (Karl wasn't the only one with ideas!) The falseness, and the difficulty attached to it, seemed mere details. Now as he released it into the open, he could survey the boundless swamp he had entered. "Where are they?" asked Billy, and instantly the layers began to build around Tim's white lie.

"A friend has them," he said. "I hired him to make a special box."

"What's his name?"

"Peter," said Tim quickly—the slightest hesitation would ring false—yet not quite randomly. He did have four friends named Peter. Before they could press for a surname, he plunged ahead: "I told him we need it soon. Before the first frost."

"Can we call him, when we get home?"

"Sure. Though maybe tomorrow would be better, when he's back in his workshop."

His workshop, no less, like one of Santa's elves! This offering, this well-intended lie would grow like a grapevine until Tim could make it true by excavating the Berline ashes. A crime, no doubt, even if his family did own both the ground and the ashes.

If this was a time for impossible topics, from AIDS to ashes, maybe it was as good a time as any for Unk-in-a-bunk too. If he was going to ask them, he had to ask them soon.

"There's something else we should talk about," he said.

"We know what it is."

"You do not. You'd have to be a mindreader."

"Uh uh, just a private eye. They want us to come there and live. Mac and Mrs. Mac. We heard them."

"You little sneaks."

"You can't help hearing from Henry's closet."

"Oh, right. When you hide in the closet, quiet as a mouse, and *eavesdrop*."

"Quiet as four mice," said Cindy.

"The twins do it all the time. It's their crow's nest."

"Anyway, you're way ahead of me, as usual. And I don't even know the other part of this—whether you'd rather be stuck with me or with your Aunt Erica."

"Get real, Unk. We'd much rather be stuck with you."

"We like being stuck with you," said Cindy.

"Well I like being stuck with you, too. The thing is, I'm just me..." (Unlike Just Ed, Tim did not intend a self-deprecation nor did the children hear one. They understood him to mean quite precisely that he was something other than a parent.)..."whereas the Macs..."

They understood and, moreover, had been wrestling with the problem for days. It was clear to Billy they had to bail Tim out and he had been able to make it clear to Cindy; that was the easy part. The hard part would be doing it. Living in someone else's house, with someone else's ways. But they had to act excited about it, had to be convincing, or The Alien could send them to Earl and Erica.

"I can dosss it," Cindy had said, because Billy kept needing her to say everything three times. *"I just don't want to leave my room, or listen to Hugh and Henry argue all day, or bake a million brownies with sappy Mrs. Mac—"*

"I thought you said you could do it."

"I can. But can't I even say the truth to you?*"*

"Don't cry, Simp. I'm really sorry."

"...whereas the Macs," Tim was saying, "are real parents. They know how to be real parents."

"Is that where you want us to go?" asked Billy, maintaining discipline fiercely; not ripping into his uncle's incredibly dumb theory. As if Mr. Mac or anyone else was ever going to be their "real" parent.

"Only if you do. You two generally seem to know what you want."

"Mr. Mac said you could have the apartment."

"He said that to me too."

"It's pretty cool," said Billy, who all spring had tried to extract a promise from Monty to make him a clubhouse over their own garage.

"Did Mr. Mac say we could get our own dog?"

"He didn't mention a dog, sweetheart. We didn't go into a lot of details. He just wanted us to know they'd be happy to have you there, if you liked the idea."

"He said you would be there on weekends."

"That would be up to us. If you guys got sick of me—"

"No, Unk."

"Or if I got sick of you—"

"Of him. Not of *me*."

"Weekends would be good, Unk," said Billy. "But maybe sometimes we could come to Boston. Without the twins."

"That's the thing. We get to make up the rules."

"Or school vacation. We could come for the whole week sometimes." Billy was hammering out terms, and this was an aspect that appealed to him, keeping a foothold in the big city. Boston was fine by him. "Maybe we could see the Celtics at the Garden."

"Whatever we wanted. School vacation? Hey, we could decide to tour Kansas and Nebraska. All up to us."

"Why Kansas?"

"I just mean we can go anyplace we choose to go—take trips together. We've never done that."

"We have so."

"Travel trips, though. To Paris, or London."

"You mean it?"

"Why not? Camp White Sneaker on London Bridge!"

"It's good by us," said Billy.

"London Bridge? Or this plan?"

"Both."

Was it a plan? Billy seemed to think so, and the way they all were talking it seemed a wonderful opening-up in their lives. But Tim did notice that no one was talking about Al and Alice. They were concocting a dream world, pretending the McManuses would not exist, or have a say. They would, though. That was why it was a question, not a plan.

"You don't sound so sure."

"No, it's good. It'll be pretty weird if some other kids move into our house. But maybe we'll like them."

"Probably you will. Cynthia, what do you want?"

"I want you to call your friend."

"Karl? Or do you mean Ellie."

"The friend who's making the box. Peter."

"Oh, Peter. But what about the Macs? We need your vote on that, one way or the other. You can say no, if you don't like it."

"We like it, Unk. I would have my own room."

"Me too," said Billy, "if I go to the basement."

"The basement? You don't want to do that."

"Guess again, Unk. It's really cool down there. There's a pool table and a TV."

"What about windows? Would you have a window?"

"I don't know. I mean, it's a basement."

"There's two windows," said Cindy. "They're little, but they work. Remember? They always plug the Christmas lights in through there."

Erica stood in the doorframe eyeing Tim's approach quizzically, mistrustful, as though he might prove armed and dangerous. "Am I expecting you?" she said.

"I came on an impulse."

"We're not always home, you know."

"Hey, I'm not always impulsive," said Tim, though in truth he was famously impulsive. His evening activities aside, Tim was a man who once spent three days freezing his ass in Reykjavik simply because a free courier trip turned up.

"Well, anyway, Earl's not here."

"Of course not, he's out buying up real estate."

"Honestly, I don't know where the hell he is. But I'm going to Montreal in a half an hour."

"What do you mean?"

"I don't *mean* anything. It's a trip, with a friend. A girl friend, if that's what you're looking so fretful about. She'll be here any second."

"If you're really going, there is something important we need to discuss. To decide."

"I am really going, Tim. That is a fact."

"Jill's neighbors, Al and Alice. You know them?"

"Not particularly."

"With the twin boys."

"If you say so."

"They were best friends with Jill and Monty. Their kids are best friends with Billy and Cindy."

"Can we do this inside? I'm not done packing."

"Sure, Ric."

"I'd offer you some coffee, but Jody is going to show up on high holy fire to hit the road."

"No coffee," he said, trailing her through a kitchen where even the instant coffee might have been a difficult proposition. The sink was overflowing pots and dishes, the gold-fleck formica was littered with beer cans and empty Chinese food cartons.

"There was a little party last night," explained Erica as they trooped through to the bedroom. Tim was startled to see they slept on a waterbed. When was that, 1975? He watched Ric trying to fold a slippery red dress. Silk. She could have just put it in her pocket.

"Al and Alice made an offer. Which would impact you and Earl."

"Nothing impacts Earl."

"You had a fight. You're pissed at him."

"No. No big deal if I was, though."

"Anyway, they think they can make things easier on everyone—mostly the kids—by, I don't know, taking them in."

"Taking them in how?"

"It's a bad phrase. Makes it sound like charity. Not adopt them, exactly, but care for them at their house."

"Alice and Al." Erica reiterated the names like a joke, a whoopie pie of words. "You know these people."

"A little, yeah. The kids, of course, know them very well."

"Myself I don't know them from the Marvelettes."

"I know why you guys want the kids, by the way. I did figure that part out, finally."

"Glad to hear someone has."

"Seriously. I found out about the Wal-Mart."

Erica stopped fiddling with the zipper on her suitcase and stared. For this one second she could believe her brother completely insane. Not the usual, crazy as in flaky, but crazy as in straitjackets and shock therapy.

"What has effing Wal-Mart got to do with the price of green apples?" she said.

"Come on, he must have told you."

"If you mean Earl, I can tell *you* he hates Wal-Mart worse than the Shanghai Flu. Thinks it's the biggest house of crap ever assembled. Earl wouldn't shop there if he had to stand naked on a stage carving the Christmas turkey."

"It's not about the shopping."

"Down South, in Bushel City? He bought a pair of pants that snagged him in the crotch and left his backside flapping in the breeze. That was it for Earl and Wal-Mart."

"I guess he wants his money back," said Tim, trying to steer her. But Erica wouldn't steer.

"Oh he got his money back, don't worry about that."

Hoisting the suitcase, she marched from the bedroom. Fearful she might keep going straight on to Canada, Tim pursued her to the kitchen. There, he was tempted to pitch in, start washing pots; conversely tempted to send polaroids of the squalid mess to the little *ad litem*. With time collapsing on him, though, he stuck with the question at hand.

"This custody business gets decided Monday, Ric. You go to Montreal for the weekend, you come back, it's Monday. See the problem?"

"It's just too new. How can I tell you anything about this when

I'm hearing it for the first time?"

"It's new to me, too. It's not like I've been keeping secrets."

"Talk to Earl."

"I thought you didn't know where he was."

"I know he's not in Timbuktoo. He will be sleeping in this house tonight. He had better be."

"You can't blow this off, Ric. We need to get it sorted out."

"Isn't that what that smug little judge is for? And the sweetheart in the powder-blue pants suit?"

They both heard a new commotion outside: car wheels grinding gravel, car doors slamming, dogs barking. It sounded like pandemonium with a cast of thousands, but it was just Earl and a tall woman (her hair dyed brick red) patting a golden retriever.

"Well look who's here," said Earl. "If it isn't The Defendant."

"Tim, this is Jody," said Erica. "And vice-versa."

"Hi, Jody. I like your dog. She's a real beauty."

As Earl stroked the dog's forehead, Tim was gratified to see that behind the pompadour, The Plaintiff had his own saucer of baldness. This was a critical time (he should bear down, bear down) but Tim's one thought was to maybe shave his head. Why not turn it into a virtue, the smooth look, like Michael Jordan?

"He," said Earl. "He's a he."

"And he is a beauty, but he's not mine," said Jody.

"This is Hammett, named after Earl's favorite writer. The guy who wrote *The Big Sleep*."

"No, babe, Hammett wrote *The Maltese Falcon*. *Big Sleep* is by Raymundo Chandler. Someday we'll name a dog for him too."

There was some question whether the smooth look worked on a white man's head. Then again, it did not always work on a black man, either. A few of those guys looked like passengers on a flying saucer, cartoon characters from the planet Ebony.

"Ready for pushback, old lady?" said Jody.

"She'll need to kiss me goodbye, Red, then she's all yours. Right this way, babe."

While they were sorting through comings and goings (exchanging reminders, shifting keys), Tim resolved on letting Billy make the call. Maybe he and Billy would both shave their heads, in a gesture of White Sneaker solidarity.

Erica hugged Earl, Earl hugged Jody, Jody hugged Hammett. No one hugged Tim, though Erica did remember he was there.

212

"See you soon," she said, waving to him from a distance of three feet.

"Have a nice trip," he said, then gave way briefly to the travel agent in him. "You might check out the Bras D'ors on St. Catherine Street. Best wine list in the city."

"Wine list," said Jody, laughing. To her it was a punchline.

"Thanks for the tip, but I'm sure Jody has our every breath planned out."

Tim and Earl stood side by side waving and not only did Tim feel zero urge to attack, to coldcock Earl, he felt not a ripple of anything like hostility. There stood poor Hammett (whom Earl would blow away next summer, would he not?) and Tim saw no need to bring in the A.S.P.C.A. He had grown too accustomed to these Sandersons. Possibly he had been too long in New Hampshire, the "Live free or die" state.

"Those two will be lucky to hit Montreal before midnight," he said conversationally.

"You have never driven with Big Red. They could be there before you finish your first beer."

"Beer?"

Tim found himself sitting on the deck with Earl, summarizing once more the McManus offer, and sipping a can of Coors Lite, a beverage he normally would not allow anywhere near his tongue. This one tasted pretty good, though. Nice and cold. To Earl, the stuff went down so fast it need not have a taste.

"You're saying these folks believe they can handle the job. Al, and his wife."

"Are you willing to consider it?"

"Hell, son, I have *been* considering it for at least ten seconds by now. Show me a burning house and I call the fire department, not convene a meeting to discuss it. The plan has obvious promise."

"What about Wal-Mart?"

Earl gave Tim a blank, questioning look, then took down an eight-ounce swallow. Crushed the first can and snapped open another.

"The land grab. I heard they are building a store near Jill's house."

"Did you now? That is one slick operator, my brother-in-law—just a tadpole slow. Friendly Wal-Fart is going to build in

Rindge, as it happens. But that's all right."

"I'm serious, Earl. The house would be gone. Sold. The money would go in trust for Billy and Cindy."

"Whatever. Giddings will know about all that shit."

"Giddings, your liar."

"Exactimo. Your liar can talk to my liar, as they say. Let them work out what to call it. Trust fund, escrow, scholarship, old age. Beats shit out of us—right, Hammett?"

"You really don't care?"

"What it's *called*?"

"About the kids. The house. The money."

"What is it with you, Timmy? I fight you and you don't like it, then I agree to agree and you still don't like it. What's the story."

"I'm just amazed you can let go so easily."

"Like I say, there are tough ones and there are easy ones. Critical part is knowing the difference."

"You were dug in. To the death."

"I have nothing against this Al, and his boys. Sounds like an okay gig to me—like it could *work*, you know."

"Dug in against *me*."

"That is so. Hell, Timmy, you're a nice enough guy, but still. You're a homo, and I'm a homophobe. Isn't that the word?"

"You simpleminded asshole."

"That's the spirit, I know you hate me too. Though, truth be told, I almost like you. Question my sensibilities on the matter. Can't relax the military vigilance with a youngster's life at stake."

"You asshole," Tim repeated, emboldened, luxuriating in this new aggressive vulgarity. "I should bust both your knees with a two-by-four."

"And this would be by way of thanking me for my hospitality? Or for confessing that I like you?"

"You don't believe for one minute that I'd molest those kids. Even you can't be that dumb."

"Easy now, Timbo, let's don't take a joke too far. I never said molest. You wouldn't molest, willing to bet on you there. But there's an example to be set. I can't allow my wife's own blood to be raised among Sodomites, can I?"

"You are perfectly serious."

"Hell yes. I'm not speaking in philosophical detail regarding chapter and verse, but yes, I am telling you the gospel truth."

"As seen by Earl Sanderson."

"Earl Sanderson is who you asked, son."

Now Earl pulled two more cans of beer from the cooler and slid one across the table to Tim. Then he went inside and came back with a pistol, a big stripshooter with a bandolier of cone-tipped bullets set like penny candy on a backing.

"Show-and-Tell hour. Something I'd like to share with you."

"If it's quick," said Tim, not entirely confident Earl was not about to fill him full of holes.

"Quicker than wind. Quickness of it being the whole damned purpose, as you will see. That plus the raw ingenuity."

"Your own, I take it."

"It is my invention—the Sanderson .357 Magnum Chainsaw. Step this way for your free demonstration."

Earl raised the gun and started blasting away in the direction of the woods, shots that rippled like firecrackers. Then he blew a wisp of smoke off the tip of the barrel and grinned what he liked to call his Southern-fool grin. If he was potting squirrels, Tim had not spotted any of them, aloft or on the ground. Yet Earl was wearing a look of triumph, or at least goodnatured smugness.

It soon emerged that he was shooting a maple tree. One substantial limb, twenty feet up, was nearly torn loose. "This is the key—no ladder required," said Earl, as he casually squeezed off a last round which severed the tissue of bark hinging the limb. Shunting its way down through lower branches, it landed hard, then reverberated with a heavy rustle of leaves.

"Once she's down, of course, you bring in more conventional equipment to finish the job proper."

"I'm impressed. By your ingenuity and your accuracy."

"They say wood warms you twice. Me, it only warms once. Plus I never cared for heights."

"I never cared for noise, myself. Or waste. What was that, twenty dollars' worth of ammunition?"

"Buck-fifty, and think what it saves on the back. Lower back? But here's the crux of it, Timbo. You are a hypocrite. Nobel Prize quality hypocrite. You're so damn sure I'm a howling cheese, maybe one jump up from the amoeba? In *taste*. In *breeding*."

"Where is this coming from?"

"It's just some truth," said Earl, stepping outside the Earl persona. He was shooting absolutely straight with Tim now. "You hate people who disapprove of you, of who you are, but you don't mind disapproving of who they are. Who I am, por ejemplo. What's harmless fun to me is ignorance and waste to you, and no two ways about it."

"Is that what this little demo was about?" said Tim, not as forcefully as he intended. The gun had not scared him, but he was shaken by this new intellectually dangerous Earl.

"Outing you. I am outing you as a hypocrite—hard kernel of truth, Timmy. Are you man enough to admit it?"

Tim and Al were standing in the very spot they had stood when Al came forward with his proposal. Their four shoes might even be filling the same imprints in the grass. But the mood was substantially altered.

"Where did you say Alice's parent live?"

"Idaho. Someone has to, I always tell them. Not that it isn't the most gorgeous place on earth."

"And they come east infrequently."

"Never. Which is pretty damned infrequent."

"I would have to pay some kind of rent."

"Nah."

"Something nominal, at least. To help out."

"Alice will kill you if you try that. Seriously, the place is just sitting there, crying out to be used."

"It crossed my mind to look for a place up this way. Something small and cheap, maybe on a pond."

"You wouldn't be getting back together with Karl, by any chance?"

"Why would you think that?"

"Well, the house hunting. And you look right for each other. Jill always said you were right."

"I keep trying to tell you, Jilly liked to overlook my many shortcomings."

"She told us you've never lived with anyone else."

"That's one of my many shortcomings. I can't handle the feeling I'm being invaded."

"Except with Karl."

"Even with him. All my fault. Karl is perfect; I am not nearly."

"He seems awfully sweet."

216

"He's the best. But he was always *there*."

"Isn't that the point, Tim?"

"I'd come home and there he'd be, every damn night. It got to be a terrible weight, just knowing he'd be somewhere in that apartment. I remember walking in one night and being sure the place was empty. It felt so empty and quiet and I felt a rush of relief—honestly, it was a thrill. Then I found him reading in the bathroom."

Al raised an eyebrow.

"See? I'm way weirder than you thought."

"No, I take your point. Marriage is not for everyone."

"No point, actually. Unless the point is that I've figured out the best I can do for Jill's kids is to be their Uncle Tim. I believe that's what they want me to be. But I can't say I'm completely comfortable with this arrangement."

"I'm pretty sure it will work out. We'll make a nice family, the seven of us."

Al was in earnest. He and Alice agreed that including Tim gave them a way of keeping a piece of Jill in their lives, not merely of keeping faith with her. Al was comfortable with the arrangement. He even looked forward, perhaps too optimistically, to further revelations of Tim's hidden facets.

And Tim's discomfort was limited for a reason that felt mildly shameful to him. His many advisors had been so quick to approve the "arrangement" that Tim simply let go of any protest or hesitation. He did not decide, he let others decide for him. But then he realized he had pulled a fast one.

Shameful, perhaps, yet quite acceptable in light of the very real possibility he could lose the kids flat out on Monday. And it was accidental, if that was an excuse; it was not premeditated. Nevertheless, he had outmaneuvered Earl, had arranged him right out of the equation. The court as well: the judge, the liars, even The Alien. The kids were his.

Yes, Alice would make the lunches—at least for now. Tim would be the one in charge. There was no way the Macs would try to usurp his authority. The decision to rent out Jill's house rather than sell it, for example, had been his entirely. He had done the math, he had made the call. And the realtor, who sounded so bouncy on the telephone, might keep an eye out for his cottage.

He would indeed be around on weekends. He could also talk

to the kids every night if he wanted, show up on a Wednesday in November for the big game against ConVal, maybe move north within the year. Why not? His ties to Billy and Cindy were real, as he had argued from the start. Argued correctly! Relationships trump contracts.

Though he had his contract too. If Tim felt a trickle of guilt run through him (Al so sincere with his family of seven) he also felt a flood of justification. It was the correct outcome that he be in charge of those children. Were it otherwise, he would owe real guilt and not to Al McManus. Jill had drafted the only contract that mattered and Tim would live up to its terms.

"There is one potential deal-breaker," he said now, without a trace of the ambivalence churning inside him. He had put on the happyface, was talking the happytalk. "The kids will need a dog. It's their only non-negotiable demand."

"Alice already thought of it. No one is about to replace their parents, but we could take a shot at replacing Gus."

"And you don't even have to replace me."

"No. Here you are."

"So it's agreed. A dog."

"Make and color to be specified. And Tim? If it makes you feel any better, we'll let you buy the Alpo."

Finally it was September. The day was summer-warm and windless, yet with altered light, pale and soft on the old bricks. On Route 124, alongside the Gridley River water meadows, the red maples had already gone to yellow.

Waiting on the COURT HOUSE steps, Tim experienced a strange nostalgia for the day he had come here nervously girded for battle with The System. Nostalgia too for the subsequent days of summer vacation in the pristine hills. Winter was a different proposition, Al was right about that, but winter did not worry him.

Indeed, he and Billy had already discussed going up Mt. Monadnock on New Year's Eve—maybe this year, maybe next year when Cindy was older—as a band of hardy locals did each winter. New Year's was always a downer, the blues in spades. Tim would start out psyched and end up depressed. By the big par-tee; by himself in costume; by growing old.

Better something new on New Year's and Monadnock would be new to them. They saw it constantly—it was a veritable polestar—but because it was rocky and a thousand feet higher than the other peaks in the area, they had deferred hiking it. Now it was on Camp White Sneaker's short list.

So much would be new, and Tim aimed to discover it day by day, to unwrap it week by week, like gifts. This was the luxury the Macs afforded. They could see to the normalcy thing, while Tim sorted out the future. This morning he had circled October 14 on his calendar; he would be there for the Parent-Teacher Pizza Night.

Something in Tim had changed over the past months, a deep chemical change that lodged the children at the core of his consciousness. They occupied his heart not just in the old way, but in what must be a parental way: when they stumbled, you fell. Yes he would be there for them, but he would be there for his own sake just as much.

Maybe this was inevitable, with Jill and Monty gone. And maybe Jill knew it would happen when it needed to. Her faith in him. But just as Dee Barnes had brought Jill with her to the courthouse the last time, Tim was the one who brought her today.

The judge looked ten years younger. He possessed the clarity of eye, the light bouncing stride of a man who either has just finished a perfect cup of coffee, a perfect bowel movement, or both. He welcomed the "parties" to his chambers, where he sat them around an oval conference table. "If Attorney Barnes needs to perambulate," he announced, "there is a fair amount of space over by the windows." Lighter, leaner, downright merry was the judge.

Tim was the one who gravitated to the windows. These deliberations required very little of him, and he found it distasteful dealing with the state over family matters. He gazed down at a green and white awning, two café tables under Campari umbrellas. A young woman wheeling a stroller stopped to read the menu. When Michele Taggart testified that she had seen "no dramatically disqualifying factors in either household," Tim turned and for a bemused conspiratorial instant locked eyes with Earl. What households was *she* looking at?

Taggart was quickly dismissed (her observations irrelevant now, the judge hearing her report so she would not feel unappreciated?) and the discussion narrowed to a virtual tête-a-tête between Enneguess and Barnes. Tim tried to monitor their every word (joint custodians, primary custodian, the liquid assets, the real estate), then decided Earl was right: let the liars decide what to *call* it.

Besides, Enneguess and Barnes huddled close as though these recondite matters concerned only the two of them. In the end, even Enneguess gave way and merely nodded approval as Barnes, with quiet charisma and inexorable good sense, simply dictated whole paragraphs of an agreement to Mr. Giddings. Giddings transcribed at a furious pace. "Most expensive secretary in the U.S. of A.," said Earl, who was paying him.

They went downstairs as a group, stepped out into the sweet autumn sunlight as a group. Then, as the judge pointed himself toward his frugal smoke-free luncheon at home, Tim who had not spoken a word in two hours, stopped him. Detained him—literally at first, by the sleeve. "Your Honor? Excuse me, sir?"

Mr. Giddings let his mouth fall open. Ric was frowning her what-shit-is-this? frown. Attorney Dee Barnes placed a hand lightly on Tim's forearm as if to tell him, Better not, whatever this is.

"Mr. Bannon?" said Enneguess.

"I am going to spend the rest of my life wondering and you are the only one who can tell me. So I thought I'd ask."

"Ask," said Enneguess.

"What did you decide? What would have happened here if the McManuses hadn't stepped in?"

Enneguess stroked his chin. From close by, in the silence, Tim could hear the sandpaper rasp of his stubble.

"Isn't that like folding your cards at the poker table and then asking for a peek at the winning hand?"

"Is it? I don't play poker. I guess I was hoping it wasn't a secret. Is it a secret?"

"It might very well be, Mr. Bannon, but the truth is I don't know. That's what we were gathering to determine. There was to be a process, reports and arguments to hear."

"You are saying you didn't know."

Inside Enneguess' blithe denial Tim heard a more strident, expansive statement: we are not bumpkins here. On the wall of the judge's chambers, Tim had noticed his diplomas, Dartmouth College and Harvard Law.

"The name of that game," said Mr. Giddings, "is Indian Hatband. It's a form of poker where you see everyone's hand except your own. Hell of a game for bluffers."

"Mr. Giddings," said Enneguess, "I'll just remind you that I am not dealt a hand in this particular game. Now again, good day to all and good luck to the children. Attorney Barnes, I hope we will someday see you grace our chambers again."

"I will welcome the opportunity, your Honor."

Tim had to gag a bit as the charade played out. Why do away with waistcoats and periwigs if they were all so eager to prattle and prance about? Barnes he could pardon. She was advocating for him, after all, not for herself. Moreover, he needed a friend at this very moment and Barnes was the only candidate. At her car, he dared to put an arm around her shoulder. Impulsively, of course.

Had she flinched? Had she ever got past her disapproval (no, say it, her *disgust)* at his proclivities? Bypassing this issue, doggedly affable, he told her, "Don't worry, it's purely avuncular."

"You aren't converting?"

"No, but I'm glad that our impartial judge converted for you."

"Don't be ridiculous."

"He lusted in his heart, I saw him. But you can read him better than I can. Was that an honest answer he gave me?"

"No. I'm sure he had made his decision."

"And?"

"That I can't tell you, but he must have decided. He had seen the players, heard the arguments, read the reports."

What was "Dee" short for? Not DeeDee, hopefully! Tim had a classmate at Chapel Hill who was actually named DeeDee. But what were the possibilities? Delia. Deirdre. Delilah. How could he not have debriefed her on this?

"You know," he said, "maybe it wouldn't have mattered so much. Maybe it would have been okay either way."

"Whoa now. Do I hear you saying Earl wouldn't have shot the children after all?"

"You don't have to make fun of me. I just meant that I might be as fucked up as he is. I probably am as fucked up."

"Don't do that, Tim. I hate guilt, and I *really* hate phony guilt. If we want to stay friends."

"Are you allowed to be my friend? Do you want to?"

Barnes smiled indulgently. She had not expected such an

eager or literal interpretation of her throwaway remark. Remain on friendly terms, was more what she had in mind. Not that she ever fell out with clients.

"Because if you do want to, you can be the first one invited to my party."

"And the first to politely decline. Thank you, Tim, but I also hate parties. And Leon hates them even more."

"Just drop in, then. A twenty minute cameo. You'll get a boatload of new customers out of it."

"I'm not looking to drum up business," she said, cheerfully.

Barnes felt sorry for Tim. He had won, in a way, yet she saw him as a man who could not win. Which might be unfair. What man could win? What constituted "winning" in life? Still, she worried about a perfectly decent person who seemed to need trouble more than peace.

"I thought we'd go down to the diner," he said, as she unlocked her car. "You don't want a cheeseburger? My treat."

"I'm not hungry, believe it or not."

"How about a gallon of black coffee? To go?"

"I'm all set, Tim." The engine was running now.

"Great, then. So thanks for everything and I'll see you at the party. I'll hand deliver your official invitation."

She reached out to give his arm a quick squeeze, then pulled away from the curb.

"A *cameo*," he called after her. "Five minutes. And you can leave boring old Leon at home."

Tim was not surprised when Barnes sent her regrets, blaming the husband Leon, who may or may not have existed. What did surprise him was having no word from Just Ed. Tim had recorded a memo for Ed, giving the particulars and requesting an R.S.V.P. "You are flat out nuts," said Karl, but instinct informed Tim this was the correct thing to do. Or the appealing thing.

Just Ed did not R.S.V.P., or attend, or ever call again. In time he would fade to become no more than a story Tim could tell to fresh acquaintances at bars and clubs. It was such a good story that he never embellished it, never "added a piece onto it" as his friend Mary McDermott used to say. Sometimes he regretted not having a better ending, although the open-endedness had some appeal. After all, Just Ed might yet call (or start shooting from a rooftop) any next tomorrow to come. Danger in the latent stage.

The party itself was sedate, until Pete Weissberg produced his infamous Very Worst of Disco tape. This music, though universally despised, managed to surface at every party. Tim saw it coming and slipped outside with Karl to taste the night air.

"I'm pretty sure this is the first party I've been to since your barbecue in Jaffrey. You are becoming quite the host, Timmy."

"You hosted that one with me."

"I was in the neighborhood."

"You have been right there for me through all this mess, Karl. Don't think I haven't noticed. And I know you've had your little friend to worry about the whole time."

"Do I believe my ears? Am I really hearing jealousy from Timothy R. Bannon?"

"I am not jealous."

"But you are, and I love it. It's certainly preferable to your lousy gratitude."

"The charge is denied. And look who's coming. I think we both know who's jealous now."

Jay Collingsworth joined them at the back gate, angling between them as though determined to prove Tim's assertion. "I trust I'm not interrupting anything too important."

"Hey, what's important?" said Tim.

"Your place is so charming. I'm amazed you pay only four hundred."

"Shhhh, don't wake the landlord."

"All right, a very quiet toast, then: to your ambitious new adventure, Tim. May it prosper."

Ambitious? Watching Billy and Cindy grow up; helping them do so? Tim's real ambition (accurately stated by the BeeGees, of all people) was staying alive. If he stayed alive for ten years, he would see the kids through to college.

"Thank you, Jay, and don't be too shocked if you find yourself drafted into the adventure from time to time."

"Honored. But I gather you are off on a short trip first?"

"Before I settle into the grind. The Spittle of Glenshee is calling out to me."

"Ravenglass!" said Karl, raising his glass again.

"I'm sure it will be every bit as wet as Ravenglass."

"Soaked and shivering! Tim's idea of bliss."

"Hey, it's the least I'm owed. After that I'll be settling down bigtime."

"Everyone else is. Do you remember Mo D'Angelis?"

"Sure I do. Hunky T, Artie used to call him. The Hunky Tradesman. He was with Norm Boucher, among others."

"Right. And he also chased women."

"Seriously? That I never knew."

"Anyway, the moral of the story is that times have changed. It's the 90's now and sex is safe. Even Mo D. has settled down—way down, as in married. Monosexual and monogamous."

"That guy? He was supposed to be a wild man."

"Not anymore. He walks the dog, burps the baby."

"Just like you, Tim," said Jay, wedging back into the conversation.

"Just like me."

Victor Perry appeared, wearing a grimace of apology. He had answered Tim's phone. "Sorry. I was practically sitting on it when it rang." Tim excused himself and went to take it on the bedroom extension. Just Ed calling to R.S.V.P.? (Or Cindy, her first night sleeping at the McManuses....) But the call was from his mother, seeking a progress report.

"It's too soon for progress, Mom, but I think they're fine."

"Who was that answering the telephone?"

"A friend. I have a few friends here, visiting."

"Is Ellie Stern there?"

"Yes she is, actually. I'll tell you all about it tomorrow, Mom. I'll call after your breakfast."

By the time Tim returned to the living room, everyone was moving toward the door. Exodus. It was as though the bell had rung, math class was over and history would begin somewhere down a long polished corridor. Call me, said Ellie. I'll call you, said Karl. A rounding-off.

Tim trailed his guests down the block to Columbus Ave., where they dispersed. The avenue was parked up solid, even the fire lane in the middle, and he watched the Peters thread their way across to Concord Square. A Buick ragtop streamed past, underlit in lavender neon cool, riding a booming radio surf.

Then he spotted a figure in front of Jae's—just some guy standing underneath the restaurant sign. Eight million stories in the naked city, he smiled, and then amended it to three million for provincial little Beantown. A lot of stories, either way. But what if the guy was Ed? Just Ed, lacking the final push that would take him over to Tim's party. Sad, lurky, anonymous Ed.

The man stomped out his cigarette and turned into Concord Square. If he stopped to look back, Tim decided, that would constitute proof. But it was impossible to tell. The darkness thickened as the street curved away, and the form receded until it was just a skating shadow which quickly merged with the shimmering gray-black night.

VII

GRAVY

Tim did not make his way to the Spittle of Glenshee that week, or to Semipalatinsk. He went home.

Flew into Charlotte, rented a Ford Ludicra one shirt size larger than himself, and meandered south through the familiar farm and lumber towns. He rolled into Berline right on schedule, three o'clock of a bright dusty afternoon.

His mother was restless and wanted to walk around the village, which suited him after six hours of sitting. Anne liked to walk the flat area behind Railroad Street, where the lower, older structures were clustered—a neighborhood oddly unchanged over half a century. The feed store, the moribund trainshed (now a farmer's market on Saturdays), the corn mill with faded red paint last renewed in 1969.

Nothing here stopped the sun, from any angle. It spread over the unpaved lots, spilled down roughwood fire escapes. At this hour, it lay like a carpet all the way out to the switchyard.

"It's not a garage," Tim was explaining. "It's pretty much the size of my apartment in Boston."

"I'm not concerned about the garage, Timmy, I'm concerned about the children."

"Don't be. I know them, Mom. They are going to be okay."

"Oh Lord, Timmy. Those children have no mother, no father."

"They will be loved, though. And they're a lot older than you think."

"Younger than *you* think," she said, stopping to watch two squirrels winding their way up a live oak, noting that the Spanish moss was sturdy enough to take their weight. Days like today, when she felt her energy and the weather was fine, Anne toyed with the idea of bringing her grandchildren to Berline. There were too many days of the other kind, though, and the world had changed too much.

"What I'm concerned about," said Tim, "is you, here, alone."

"Timmy, I've been alone for six years. Or is it seven?"

"I know that, Mom. But, you know: *more* alone."

How could Tim reassure his mother about the future when the future meant death? A year from now Tim could see himself with the children full time; increasingly that was his working scenario. But death was a possible scenario too. A year from now, he and Anne might both be dead.

"I have no end of tears for Jilly. No end. But I find I don't mind about you. In a way, I'm relieved to have an explanation. I was so afraid you were one of those unreliable selfish men."

"Oh I am."

"Don't you tell me more than I asked to know. I truly do not mind, Timmy. It is your life, after all."

"Mom, you're a liberal."

"That's what your daddy used to say. Sometimes, Anne, I believe you are going *lib*eral on me."

"Daddy was a liberal too, in some ways."

"He didn't hate the blacks, if that's what you mean. That was about it, though, for liberalism. Truthfully he was not a political man at all, just a practical man who minded his own."

"Erica is the only rock hard reactionary in the family."

"Rock hard? She's just a branch in the wind, that girl. Always was."

"We're getting better, Ric and I. I think we're friends."

"That's a good thing. Maybe in time you can graduate to being sister and brother."

"Maybe. You know, politics doesn't matter much to me, either. Not as such. It's not like I have a big political agenda."

"That's good too. No one ever got happy having a political agenda."

"Though there are always battles that need to be fought."

"No doubt there are. But why are *we* fighting about it?"

"We're not, we're just walking and talking. Do you want to drive out to the cemetery? Walk some more out there?"

"I was there this morning. I'm not exactly a stranger to the place."

They went anyway. Tim did not go to see Jill's marker, or to scope out the crime he intended to commit. (Would he really be a graverobber, like Burke and Hare? But that he would find out in the days ahead.) It was his father's marker he wanted to see today.

Rex had engraved it himself, the year he was sick. His latest and last hobby, tinkering with stone. And nothing could be farther from politics than the inscription he chose, from Ecclesiastes, a time to be born and a time to die. Judge Enneguess would have approved. Insofar as Rex Bannon was concerned, your time to die was whenever you did so. Until then you went about your business. A practical man, to be sure.

An oldfashioned man, Tim thought, with some pride, as they came back over the dense springy grass. It was silly to ponder Rex overmuch, obsess about him, as though there were truths about yourself to unlock simply because a man was your father. He was an oldfashioned man and you were gay in the 90's. He was a silent man and you liked to joke and banter. Tim might have more in common with Blind Teddy Copeland, if both their lives hinged on persecution and on the blues.

But that was a false positive. In truth, Ted Copeland's life hinged more on certain heavyset women (among them his wife Thelma), on his children and grandchildren, his friends and good-natured enemies like Ben Creek who had once cut him with a knife. It hinged on big noon dinners and naps in the open air; on farmwork, for which he had a genuine talent, and music, which for Ted happened to be the blues.

"I only hope you can be happy," Anne had said, back at the switchyard. "That's all I ever did hope, so why change now?"

Happy? What about Anne, strolling with her queer son from the premature resting place of her daughter and beloved husband? Anne lived alone and had no work to absorb her. She had been assigned to live in grief for the duration, yet she did seem, in some ungraspable way, a happy person. Her life also hinged on other matters: on sunshine warming her porch, the ritual arrival of the morning newspaper, old friends, bridge games and Bingo, Oprah Winfrey. The list was fairly long and the Lord, Tim understood, did move in mysterious ways.

Tim, who viewed his own life as meaningless and in a way hopeless, took stock of himself next. I am half bald, one-eighth gray, very likely HIV Positive, and I haven't even got a dog. I am going nowhere fast. Or not even fast, just nowhere.

Except New Hampshire. And I could get a dog—how hard is it to get a dog? The kids could take care of him when I needed to be in Boston, he could be great pals with their dog (name them Melville and Hawthorne maybe) and when they went away to college I'd take over. I'd have the dogs instead of the kids, so I would still be somebody's uncle.

Tim and Anne moved in silence, leaning arm in arm. The burial ground smelled of baked earth and windfall peaches, seasoned not so nicely by the sour sulfurous afflatus of the pulp mill, ten miles west. There was no happy ending for Tim here or anywhere else ("It's not like that," as Dee Barnes was fond of saying) yet he felt distinctly optimistic, inexplicably excited. You could be happy without happiness, apparently. Wasn't that the true meaning of the blues?

Anything beyond breathing was gravy.